PLEASURE AT HOME

BETH YARNALL

PLEASURE AT HOME

Happy Reading!

LUSH
Beth Yarnall

Copyright © 2014 by Elizabeth A. Yarnall

All rights reserved under the Pan-American and International Copyright Conventions.

The reproduction, distribution, or transmission of this book in whole or part, by any means, without the express written permission of the author is unlawful piracy and theft of the author's intellectual property.

This is a work of fiction. Names, places, characters, and events are either the product of the author's imagination or are used fictitiously. Any resemblance to actual events, locales, or persons, living or dead, is entirely coincidental.

Any trademarks, service marks, product names, or named features are the property of their respective owners and are used only for reference.

Digital ISBN: 978-1-940811-97-0
Print ISBN: 978-1-940811-96-3

Cover Designer: Mayhem Cover Creations

BOOKS BY BETH YARNALL

Pleasure at Home
Rush, Book 1
Lush, Book 2

The Misadventures of Maggie Mae
Wake Up, Maggie
You're Mine, Maggie
Find Me, Maggie

Azalea March Mysteries
Dyed and Gone

Recovered Innocence
Vindicate
Atone
Reclaim

God of Redemption Series
Far From Honest (2017)
Far From Innocent (2017)
Far From Safe (2018)

Stand Alone Novels
A Deep and Dark December

Crafting Unputdownable Fiction Series
Making Description Work Hard For You
Going Deep Into Deep Point of View

DEDICATION

For the survivors of domestic violence—the ones who got out—and for those still looking for a way out.

And as always, to my husband, Mr. Y, for buying into and supporting every single one of my crazy Lucy and Ethel schemes...including the one where I thought I could write a book.

Lucy Monroe stood outside the thick wooden door with the gleaming brass nameplate, preparing to beg someone she couldn't stand for something she didn't want. Tugging at her slightly too-tight blouse, she hoped she hadn't overdone the perfume in an attempt to mask the stale stench of desperation. And desperate she was or else she wouldn't be standing outside of Cal Seller's office door.

Tossing back her hair, she rubbed her lips together and took a deep breath. She raised her hand to knock, pulling the gesture at the last moment before she rapped on the chest of the man who suddenly opened it.

"Well, hello, Lucy." Cal set his hand on the doorframe, blocking her entrance with six feet of lanky, overconfident cowboy. If he was surprised to see her, he didn't show it. His gaze traveled over her leisurely, not stopping to admire anything in particular as though he'd seen the view a thousand times before. Her body reacted as if he'd stroked her, aroused despite her burning hatred for him.

When he'd looked his fill, he stepped back, motioning her into the room. "Come on in."

"Er, ah, thank you." Chin high, she strolled into the room like she had a right to be there and hadn't told him to shove the job she was here to get back where the sun don't shine. As though she hadn't rubbed her new marriage and pregnancy in his face with the giddy glee of a teenager who'd snagged the star quarterback and wanted her cheating ex-boyfriend to know it. *Oh, how the mighty have fallen*, she thought. And fallen hard.

"Have a seat." Cal waited for her to be seated before sliding into the high-backed, leather chair at his desk. Behind him the Dallas skyline gleamed in the heat of mid-day. He reclined back, regarding her with those same cool blue eyes that used to rake her over as if he could see through her clothes. "What can I do for you?"

He'd asked her that same question before under entirely different circumstances. Naked and panting circumstances. Teasing and pleasing circumstances. Right here on top of his desk, her legs hooked over his shoulders... She cleared her throat and those memories from her brain, struggling to keep in mind the real reason she'd come here today. Her daughter, Poppy.

"You're going to need a new host for *Pleasure at Home*. At least temporarily. I can help." There. That didn't sound desperate, it sounded helpful. She was doing him a favor really. And if that favor turned into a permanent job for her, then so much the better. Cal loved win-win situations. Especially if he was the one doing all the winning.

"You're looking for a job?"

She was looking for more than that. What she needed was a miracle, a way to hold on to what little she had left. "My daughter will be eight months old next week."

He inclined his head in acknowledgment. Of course he knew that, nothing passed Cal's notice.

"I thought it was a good time to venture out and explore my options." Which were exactly zero. Unless she counted working retail with its long hours and measly pay. And how would she protect Poppy if she was never home?

"So you ventured my direction."

"I figured with Mi going out on maternity leave in a few months I could fill in for her. It's not like I'd need to be trained. I cohosted the show with Mi for two years before...before I left."

"Yes. I remember."

This wasn't going well. She could tell by the way the right corner of his lips had tugged up along with his eyebrow as soon as she'd opened her mouth about resuming her old job. She used to call it his *oh really* look. That mocking, *I'm in the driver's seat* tilt of his lips and brow set off all the warning bells inside her. He was plotting something. Something dangerous for her.

She stupidly plowed ahead anyway, too needy to walk away from what might be her last chance. Her only chance. "Yes, well, I thought I could start right away. Mi and I could cohost like we used to until she leaves, and then I could host alone until she comes back." And hopefully she could parlay that temporary into permanent.

"What happened to your... How did you put it? Ah, yes. Your husband's aversion to his wife prostituting herself by selling sex toys on TV."

"That was an unfortunate choice of words on my part. I apologize."

"Unfortunate. Yes. But still a problem for you, unless something's changed?"

The bastard. He knew. And now he was tormenting her by trying to make her confess what an idiot she'd been, how her life had crashed and burned. She thought about her daughter, and all her prideful anger drained away, leaving her more desperate than before. She'd do anything to protect Poppy. Anything.

She picked at the skin beside her thumbnail, knowing

she had to tell him in order to get him to give her back her old job. An extremely well-paying job. A job she needed more than her next breath. "I'm not married."

"I thought you didn't believe in divorce."

"I'm not divorced."

"An annulment?"

"No." Damn him. "It turned out my marriage wasn't legal."

"Not legal? It seemed perfectly legal from where I sat in the church."

She'd invited him out of spite. She imagined he had attended out of pride. Their relationship—so passionate and exciting—had ended in barbs and jabs meant to wound. Now that too was coming back to bite her in the ass. *Keep your cool. Don't let him see you sweat. He thrives on the weaknesses of others. Don't be weak.*

"I thought so too," she said, sounding more confident than she felt. "Unfortunately he was already married when he married me."

"I see."

"So there's no conflict. I can start right away, or whenever you need me."

"But I don't."

"Don't what?"

"Need you."

She bolted up out of her chair, toppling it backward. "You son of a bitch! You let me sit here and spill my guts to you, knowing all the time that you weren't going to hire me back?"

"Sit down."

The door behind her opened. A willowy brunette with the body Lucy used to have poked her head in the door. "Is everything all right in here, sir?" She cast Lucy a look like she'd be happy to have her escorted out.

"Everything's fine, honey," Cal answered.

Thank God this wasn't *the* Honey Cal had employed back when Lucy had worked for him, but she was made from the same mold. Cal called all of his assistants *Honey*, and they all looked like they'd been ordered from the *Playmate of the Month* catalog. Rumor was that Cal's *Honeys* did more than run reports...a lot more. Unfortunately Lucy knew all too well the rumors were based in fact.

Cal's *Honey* gave him a look that could melt ice in a snowstorm. "You let me know if you need anything, sir. Anything at all."

"Thank you. I will." Cal waited for *Honey*—or Felicia McAdams as the nameplate on her desk read—to close the door before turning his attention back to Lucy. "Please, sit down."

She folded her arms across her chest. "Why? So you can humiliate me some more?"

"You need a job, and as it happens I might have one for you."

"But you just said you didn't."

"I said I don't need you to fill in for Mi. Her sister-in-law will start cohosting with her today and then take over while she's on leave."

"So what's the job then?"

"Sit down and I'll tell you."

Cal waited with the patience he used to close multimillion-dollar deals for Lucy to right her chair and sit her pretty little ass back down. Truth was he knew why she was here and what she was going to ask before he'd even opened the door to find her standing on the other side. His gut twisted, thinking how desperate she must be knocking at his door. It was his fault she was in the straits she was in. He'd kept tabs on her, but apparently not close enough.

She'd shown up sooner than he'd expected, but as it

turned out she'd come at a time when he'd just gotten his ass handed to him and was feeling a bit beaten up. Funny that sparring with Lucy had him rebounding with the energy of a champ. She always brought out the best in him. And the worst.

Lucy sat at the edge of the chair and crossed her arms and legs. "Well?" she demanded.

Now this was going to take some finesse. He'd been chewing over this predicament for some time and then he'd opened the door to Lucy and the solution had very nearly tumbled right into his chest.

"It's a bit high profile," he began.

She squared her shoulders and lifted her chin. "I've been on TV. That's the tiniest bit high profile."

Damn, but he'd missed her spirit. And her smart-assed mouth, and the way she tossed her blonde hair when she expected to get her way. He'd missed a whole lot of things about her, including the way his body reacted to her.

"The hours are fairly flexible," he continued. "You have a reliable babysitter who can work days and evenings?"

"I do."

"Good. Good. And you don't mind dressing up?"

She narrowed her eyes at him. "What kind of *dressing up* are we talking about?"

Now she had him remembering the time she'd worn that pretty little cowgirl outfit and had ridden him bareback…backwards. It fit with what she thought of him, he supposed. Pervert, bastard…what else had she called him? Ah, yes. A lowlife, two-timing son of a bitch with a dick for brains.

Maybe she was right. He certainly hadn't been able to accurately access the head he *should* be using ever since she'd strolled into the room and stroked him with the scent of her perfume.

He leaned back in his chair, stacked his boots on his

desk, and clasped his hands in his lap. The blue of her eyes was barely visible now. She'd narrowed them into slits that told him his window for possibly winning her over with his idea was quickly closing.

"Not that kind of dressing up." He'd keep this to business if it killed him. "Cocktail dresses, ball gowns that sort of thing."

She tilted forward in her chair a little and uncrossed her arms to stack them on her knee. He hadn't gotten to where he was now without being able to read an opponent's body language to know when things were starting to swing his direction.

"Would they be provided?" she asked. "Or would I have to come up with the money to rent them out of my salary?"

"They would be provided. You'd have an expense account for whatever you'd need."

"And what exactly would my duties be?" She was interested. Good.

"Charity events, dinner parties, corporate functions, hostessing, that sort of thing."

"Sounds more like something you'd need a wife for than a corporate employee."

"That's exactly what I need. A wife."

She put up a hand palm out. "Hold up. You're asking me to marry you?"

"Yes. For at least a year...maybe a little longer."

She exploded off her chair, propped her hands on her hips, and leaned over the desk at him. "What kind of dim-witted dumbass do you take me for?"

"No kind."

She turned and snatched up her purse. "I don't know what kind of joke this is supposed to be, but I'm not going to be any part of it."

She started for the door, but he was faster, getting

there ahead of her to block her exit.

"Just hear me out."

"No. Hell no."

"You need a job. I need a wife. I'm in negotiations to buy a company that could turn Sellers Investments into a multinational corporation. But my board is packed with a bunch of traditionalists. They've been after me to clean up my reputation and won't agree to the purchase unless I make some significant changes."

"They don't want their company headed up by a man-whore? I'm shocked. I also don't see how paying a woman to marry you—especially one who can hardly stand the sight of you—is going to improve your reputation. And isn't that prostitution anyway?" She jabbed him in the chest with her sharp, pointy fingernail. "If you think I'm low enough that I'd prostitute myself to you, then you're an even bigger dickhead than I thought."

Well, shit. This all had sounded so much better in his head. "No. Never that, darlin'."

This was supposed to be a deal where he'd help her get back on her feet. The fact that it also helped him was a distant third. Ridin' second was the hope that maybe they would end up in bed together, but now she'd gone and made it all feel so unseemly.

"Really? Because paying a woman to sleep with you *is* prostitution. Look it up."

"I wouldn't be paying you to sleep with me. I'd be paying you to be my wife. The sleeping-with-me part would be optional."

She blinked slowly up at him. "Optional." At least she'd retracted that nail.

"I need a wife. You need a job. This is a sound business agreement."

"And what makes you think I'd want to sleep with you, optional or not?"

His gaze dropped to her mouth. He wanted to answer her with a kiss that would make her remember just how damn good they'd been together. How goddamned hot they'd been for each other. And maybe get her to look at him like she used to and not how she was looking at him now. He was damn sick and tired of being the asshole who'd broken her heart by being the careless, unthinking bastard he was.

"I'll give you a twenty percent raise over your original salary. You and your daughter would come live at my house—for appearances—all expenses paid."

"Oh, like a frat house bed-and-breakfast. Yes, that's exactly the environment I want my daughter raised in while her mother prostitutes herself for a twenty percent salary bump."

"Stop using that word. That's not what this is about and you know it."

"All I know is that you haven't changed one damn bit."

She tried to go around him, but he sidestepped and she slammed into his chest. He gripped her by the arms to keep her from stumbling. Before he knew what he meant to do, he was kissing her the way he'd wanted to from the moment she'd appeared in his doorway.

His body recognized hers immediately, reacting instantly to the feel of her curves pressed up against him. She resisted at first and then it was as if her body recalled his as well, and she came at him like a bull out of a shoot, going from zero to all over him in thirty seconds or less. Goddamned if he burned hotter and brighter with her than with anyone else he'd ever been with.

He gripped her ass, bringing her fully against his growing erection. The lushness of her, the sounds she made, that thing she did with her tongue...fucking Christ. How had he gone a day without her, let alone nearly a year and a half? He turned them, pressing her between his body and the door.

They'd been in this position before. He'd taken her rough and fast, hardly thinking at all about what was on the other side of the door. He hadn't even taken the time to pull her panties down. He'd just shoved them aside and thrust deep, needing to be inside her more than he'd needed his next breath. That need was building now, threatening to break his infamous control.

He eased back and looked down at her. Her full lips were swollen from his kisses, her eyelids heavy with desire. Her breaths came in short pants that told him she was as turned on as he was.

"I *have* changed," he told her, whispering the words, wanting her to feel his sincerity. "This between us hasn't. And it never will." He stepped away from her, trying to show her the change he'd just bragged about. "But it will *always* be optional."

She wiped the back of her hand over her mouth, considering him—he hoped in a new light. "You're the craziest son of a bitch I've ever met, you know that?"

"Maybe. Maybe I'm just a businessman who enjoys a well-negotiated business deal."

"Is that what you call bending your *honey* over your desk—negotiating a business deal?"

"No. That's what I call a mistake. Because that's what it was."

"Call it what you like, but I don't think you'll ever really change, no matter how many deals you *negotiate*." She fumbled for the knob behind her and opened the door.

He didn't stop her. He'd done all he could to convince her. "Consider my offer, darlin'." But he knew she wouldn't. He'd screwed everything up by kissing her. She didn't do well with pressure. Like an unbroken filly, you had to come at her from the side, sweet-talking and reassuring with a lump of sugar in your palm. But damn if the ride wasn't worth all the effort.

Lucy bolted out of Cal's office like her tail was on fire when it was her whole body that was ablaze. She wasn't sure which was making her hotter—anger or arousal. With Cal it was always so hard to separate the two.

She marched past Felicia's desk, down the long hall to reception, and out to the elevators. *Consider his offer.* What she was considering was getting her daddy's Smith & Wesson and filling Cal's lying, cheating ass full of lead. Changed. Right.

She jabbed at the elevator button. The only thing that had changed was a new little trick with his teeth he'd learned from someone *somewhere* that had her grinding against him like a sex-starved bitch in heat. *He'd* picked up new tricks in the past seventeen months whereas the only thing she'd picked up was an extra fifteen pounds of post-baby weight that wouldn't come off.

Goddammit. She was actually tempted by his offer. She'd seriously considered it even as she'd accused him of trying to turn her into a whore. His whore. The truth was she needed the money. She needed a job with flexible hours so she could spend time with Poppy. But most of all she needed the security of living in Cal's house so she could protect her daughter.

But she wouldn't do it. She hadn't stooped so low that she'd sell herself to Cal Sellers like one of his prized heifers. No way in hell.

TWO

Lucy pulled up to her mother's house in Arlington, outside of Dallas. Spring was asserting itself early, scorching a path across North Texas that heated up the earth like a big ole electric blanket you couldn't turn off.

She was late picking up her daughter. She'd had to work an extra half hour to make up the time she'd taken to go all the way to downtown Dallas to Cal's office on what had turned out to be a fool's errand.

A car she didn't recognize sat in the driveway. Maybe one of her mother's friends was here for a visit. She angled out of the driver's seat and came up the drive instead of the walk so she could check out the car. Nothing on the seats or dash gave away anything other than it being a rental. She didn't like this one bit. A prickling at her nape had her quickening her steps. All she could think of was getting to Poppy and making sure her daughter was okay.

She opened the door—not bothering to knock—and went right on in. Her mother came up off the couch, no doubt with a reprimand on the tip of her tongue, but Lucy didn't give her a chance to spew it.

"Where's Poppy?"

"That's not the way—"

"*Where's my daughter?*" Panic crawled all over her. "Where is Poppy?"

"Right here."

Lucy turned to see Kevin Walker, the no-good, rotten, polygamist bastard she'd thought she'd married, holding *her* daughter.

The last time she'd seen him he'd been standing over her, screaming obscenities, while she tried not to move or do anything to provoke him further. His anger was a near-tangible thing that whipped out and lashed at her, turning her handsome husband into an out-of-control monster who terrified her.

Kevin smiled as though he had every right in the world to be there. He didn't. She had a restraining order out on him for God's sake. He wasn't supposed to go within five hundred feet of her home or work, but it looked like he'd found a way around that—her mother.

"What are you doing here?" she demanded, trying to keep her voice even and not scream like she wanted to so she didn't scare Poppy. "You don't have visitation rights."

"Well." Her mother, Nadine, stepped forward. "I thought it would be good for Poppy to spend some time with her daddy. A girl needs her daddy."

A girl didn't need a lying, cheating, scary-assed bastard of a daddy. Lucy would know. Her own daddy had been just like Kevin.

"What Poppy needs," Lucy said, walking over and prying her daughter away from Kevin, "is for Kevin to follow the rules the court set out. There's a reason he's not allowed to be around us, *Mother*."

Poppy started to fuss, putting her fist in her mouth. She must've sensed the tension in the air. Lucy held Poppy to her and nearly gagged when she smelled Kevin's after-shave on her baby.

"I have a right to see my child," Kevin had the nerve to

declare. "Prepare to be served. I'm taking Poppy back to Utah to live with me."

What in the hell had she ever seen in him? He'd been charming and she'd been hurting and then before she knew it she was standing at the front of the church next to a man she hardly knew. She'd gotten a good taste of the real him a few short hours after they'd been married. He'd accused her of looking at Cal like she should've been looking at him, and he'd hit her. He knew how to do it, striking where the bruises wouldn't show.

He sure had been convincing about where the blame lay—with her. It was *her* fault he got so angry. *Her* fault she wasn't the kind of wife he expected her to be. *Her* fault she got hurt. And she believed him. She'd burned every bridge she had by quitting her job and distancing herself from her friends, too ashamed to let them know what her life had become.

"The hell you are," Lucy shot back. "I have the police reports and photos that will keep you from ever getting your hands on her."

"Lucy, watch your language," her mother admonished, her pale, watery eyes pleading. "Have some respect for your husband."

Nadine had been a beauty once. Lucy used to love looking at pictures of her mother before she'd married her father. Living with Larry had chewed Nadine up from the inside out. Covering for him and pretending nothing was wrong had worn away her softness, leaving behind a woman on the edge of brittle. The invisible nicks and scars from years of abuse had whittled her down to the point where Lucy hardly recognized her mother as the person in those old photos.

I could've been her. I almost was her.

"I have your mother's blessing and a new lawyer who's a shark. You don't stand a chance against me."

Lucy looked at her mother and knew what Kevin said was true. Nadine had been harping on Lucy to get back together with Kevin so that Poppy could have a real family, not a broken one. Her mother had always been the keep-the-family-together type. No matter how many times Nadine's husband, Larry, had come home drunk reeking of perfume and alcohol, Nadine always put him to bed as if he was the long-lost king come home.

Now Kevin had charmed Nadine just the way Larry had. She didn't see past the good looks and good manners to the soul of the man who'd nearly put her own daughter in the hospital more than once. It had taken Lucy too long to realize that by marrying Kevin she'd repeated her mother's history. That wasn't what she wanted for *her* daughter or for herself.

"I will fight you with everything I have in me," Lucy swore. "You are not taking my daughter anywhere, and you are certainly not leaving the state with her."

Kevin's eyes went cold, and his hands balled into fists the way they always did right before he struck her. Lucy standing up to him was new, and she could tell he didn't like it. If her mother wasn't in the room, Lucy would be on the floor.

Poppy was sobbing now. Lucy patted her back and tried to soothe her, but her own insides were a tangled mass. She believed Kevin. He *would* take her daughter by any means, and he would make Lucy pay for her insolence.

"She's my daughter too," Kevin said. "You're gone all day working. Nadine is a terrific grandma, but Poppy needs a mother. She needs to be cared for in her own home, not shuttled back and forth between caregivers. My wife—"

"And which wife would that be, hmm? Wife number one or two? Maybe it's wife number three."

"She doesn't mean that, Kevin." Nadine had the nerve to back him and not her own daughter. And then she took it further, making Lucy the bad guy here. "He's your husband. I know you've gone through some rough times—"

"Rough times? He has three wives. And he beat me, mother. *Beat me.*"

Nadine worried her hands, glancing from Kevin to Lucy and back again. "Lucy, please. Listen to him. I know the two of you could work things out if you'd just be a little more understanding."

"I've cleared my legal troubles. I know I wasn't always the best husband to you, Lucy, but I love you, and I want to make it work with you. Maybe go to counseling. I want us to be a family again. I'll do anything to get you back, Lucy. Anything."

"You see," Nadine continued. "He loves you."

Lucy knew he meant it too. He would do anything to get her back, including turning her mother against her and taking her daughter from her. She'd never be free of him, free from his threats. He would keep chasing her like he'd chased her from room to room of their house, hitting and screaming at her. It would never stop.

"No." Lucy gripped her daughter tighter. It wasn't going to work this time. He wasn't going to sweet-talk her into forgiving him as she'd done too many times before. "Get out." She pointed at the door. "Get out right now!"

She'd hidden the worst from her mother, from everyone. And then she'd gotten her and her daughter out of that hellhole. She was never going back, and she sure as hell was never going to let her daughter be raised in a home like the one she grew up in.

"This is my house, and I say who stays and who goes," Nadine said.

"Fine." Lucy shook, her face hot, her heart racing. "I'll leave." She grabbed Poppy's diaper bag from the chair and headed for the door.

"This isn't the last of it," Kevin threatened. "I will be back for Poppy and for you. I want my family with me, and I always get what I want, Lucy. Remember that."

Lucy ran down the front steps as though Kevin would reach out and rip Poppy from her arms. She believed him. He'd do anything to get what he wanted.

She bundled Poppy into her car seat and then took off down the street without buckling her own belt. It wasn't until she got to the light and checked her rearview mirror that she put her seat belt on. She almost expected to find Kevin in his car behind her. It had been more than six months since she'd seen him, and he terrified her more now than when she'd been with him. She knew what it would be like to go back. How small her and Poppy's world would be.

There was no way she was ever going to let her daughter grow up the way she had. Walking in on her father screwing the next-door neighbor on their dining room table and the beating she'd gotten from him not to tell. It wouldn't have mattered if she'd told her mother or not. Nadine wouldn't have believed her and would've punished her for lying. Lucy was always the one who paid to keep their family together.

Until the night when Lucy was fourteen and Larry had been killed in a car accident that was entirely his fault. Two other people died that night because Larry got drunk and decided to drive to see his girlfriend in Garland. After that it was just Lucy and her mother, who never really got over the loss of the husband she adored.

That was when Lucy started spending afternoons with her maternal grandma, Poppy, who she adored so much she'd named her daughter after her. Baby Poppy even had strawberry-blonde hair like her namesake.

At a light, Lucy glanced back at her daughter in her

car seat. She'd fallen asleep with her finger in her mouth and tears still clinging to her eyelashes. The sight just about broke Lucy's heart. She'd done her best to care for her precious baby and support them financially. Her best wasn't good enough. She was faced with losing their apartment because she couldn't afford the raise in rent next month, and she couldn't afford to move. Kevin was back threatening to take Poppy away, and now she'd lost the only babysitter she could afford on her salary—her mother.

As if sensing Lucy was nearly to her breaking point, both the check-engine light and gas light came on at the same time. She dropped her head on the steering wheel and burst into tears.

෴

Cal poured himself a whiskey neat, propped his bare feet on his desk in his home office, and turned on the TV to the business report. He turned the volume up to drown out the rain beating against the windows. This was the way he wound down most of his days. He hadn't been the hell-raiser the local papers accused him of being for several years now, but that didn't mean he'd lost the title. Once pigeonholed, the press seemed to look for ways to make it stick. Especially when you were as successful and rich as Cal was.

Oh, he'd more than earned his reputation—had the tattoo on his ass to prove it—but he wasn't that guy anymore. There'd been a time when he'd thought up ways to get in the newspaper or on TV. When his business had been as young as he was. But he knew better now, made better choices, and had grown his business empire into something he could be proud of.

The *Pleasure at Home* shopping show for adult toys

had started out as a lark, a way to snub his nose at conventional business. He owned the TV station, why not put whatever he wanted on it? Over the years it had grown into a very steady, very lucrative source of income. And that was how he'd met Lucy. He couldn't help grinning at the memory even now. The first time he'd seen her she was tail up in an exceptionally short skirt, trying to find something under the couch on the set for *Pleasure at Home*. Rounded hips, rounded ass, and long legs that ended in stilettos. She'd popped up, flipping back her long blonde hair, holding a vibrating bullet that had slipped out of one of the products.

Pink cheeked with a wide smile, she'd stolen his breath like a mule kick to the chest. And then she'd spoken, asking him if he'd enjoyed the view. She'd called him cowboy with a wink and adjusted her skirt, and he didn't think he'd ever seen a woman more beautiful in his life.

After that he'd set about trying to woo her, breaking his number-one rule—he didn't date, mess with, or sleep with his employees. Ever. But as soon as he'd laid eyes on Lucy he'd wanted to do every single one of those things with her, personal rule be damned.

It had taken nearly two years and a lot of effort, but he'd eventually won her over. The next couple of months had been the most interesting, frustrating, and exciting of his entire life. Then he'd gone and screwed everything up. He'd tried to tell her he was sorry, that it was a stupid, careless mistake, but Lucy would have nothing to do with his explanations or with him after that.

He only had himself to blame. After years of cultivating a debauched reputation and allowing the rumors about him to go unanswered, he'd paid the price and lost Lucy. When she'd stumbled into his office today, he couldn't help but feel like maybe this was the redemption he'd earned by trying to reinvent himself ever since she'd walked out.

He swirled the last swallow of whiskey around in his glass and then downed it in one burning gulp. If she wasn't going to take him up on his offer, he'd have to find another way back into her life.

The doorbell rang, startling him out of his thoughts. Whoever it was had bypassed his front gate. Very few of his friends had the gate code and the kind of relationship with him that they could come over unannounced. Must be his good friend Lucas Vega, dropping by with a report on Lucy's ex. Lucas's security firm was the only one he trusted with this kind of job. It had to be bad news for him to show up at—Jesus—nearly ten o'clock at night in the pouring rain.

Cal turned on the porch light and opened the door to a sight he'd never thought he'd see again—Lucy, here, at his home. She was soaked, her hair and clothes plastered to her. How long had she been standing there? Her eyes were red-rimmed and swollen as if she'd been crying. Her car idled in the drive behind her. Whatever she'd come for, she wasn't staying.

She lifted her chin and flipped the wet strands of her hair back over one shoulder. Damn if she wasn't beautiful, standing there dripping on his porch, defeated yet defiant.

"All right," she said, lip quivering. "I'll marry you."

Lucy turned and started back down the steps away from him. This was wrong. This was all wrong.

"Lucy, wait."

She wouldn't wait, she kept on going, and so he followed her barefoot out into the rain.

"Hold up." He got to her just as she reached for the handle of her car door and gripped her arm to keep her from opening it. "What's wrong? What happened?"

She jerked out of his grasp and spun around to face him. "I said I'd marry you. What more do you want?"

"I want to know what's got you so upset."

"Does it really matter?"

"Hell yes, it matters."

"There wasn't anything in your offer that said we had to confide in each other. I agreed to your terms. You're going to get what you want—a wife—isn't that enough?"

He reached for her again. She flinched as though he'd hit her. *What the hell?* He put his palms up to show he wouldn't try to touch her. She crossed her arms over her chest and glared at him, clearly embarrassed at her overreaction.

Something or someone had her spooked, and he'd bet it had to do with her son-of-a-bitch ex. He took half a step back and gentled his tone. "Come inside and dry off. Let's talk about this."

She looked for a moment like she might agree, glancing up at the house and then back at him. "It's late, and I already said all I came to say."

"Where would you like to do it?"

"Do what?"

"Get married. And when? We need to set a date."

"Does it matter? This is all your deal." She paused, looking away and then back. "Soon. I think it should be soon."

"Okay. We can do it as soon as you like. Why don't you come inside, and we can work it out?"

"Poppy's supposed to be asleep. It's past her bedtime."

"I'd like to meet her. Show her where she'll be living."

"She's only eight months old. She's not going to be impressed by how lavish your house is."

He cracked a half smile. She was starting to sound more like the Lucy he knew.

"Well, I don't know. She might think the new media room is kinda cool."

"And you think she's gonna care how big your screen is?"

"Maybe. I've been told it's quite impressive."

Her laugh rumbled through him, deep throated and so damn sexy. "All right. I guess we can come in for a little while."

"Hang on. Stay right there." He jogged up the front steps and grabbed an umbrella from the stand just inside the front door. Returning, he was relieved to find she hadn't moved.

He popped open the umbrella. "For Poppy," he explained. "So she doesn't get wet."

She eyed him as though she was trying to decide if he was for real or not. Again he wondered what the hell had happened with her since he'd seen her earlier that day. Whatever it was had driven her to him, and for that he couldn't help but feel grateful. At the same time it pissed him off. Someone had messed with her.

He held the umbrella over her as she unhooked the baby from her seat. She wrapped her in a blanket and reached for a big bag, which he took from her. He walked up the steps with her, protecting them from the rain. Motioning her into the house, he followed her inside. He dealt with the umbrella and closed the door to find her examining him like there was something wrong with him, but she couldn't make out what it was.

"Go on in to the living room. I'll grab some towels and be right back."

He waited until she started that direction to run upstairs. She looked so lost he wasn't sure if she'd stay or bolt. He made it back downstairs in record time, out of breath and glad to find her standing in the middle of the room as though she wasn't sure what to do with herself.

He set the towels on the coffee table. "Here you go." He held his arms out. "I'll hold her while you dry off."

"Do you even know how to hold a baby?"

"Of course I do. I even know how to change a diaper."

"Don't tell me you've got a secret baby holed up somewhere."

"Hell no. My parents are foster parents, and they frequently get babies to care for. I know my way around babies as well as you do I'd imagine."

He could tell she didn't believe him, but she handed him the baby anyway, watching all the while to make sure he didn't drop her. He easily repositioned Poppy so she wasn't pressed against his wet shirt. He moved the edge of the blanket back and got his first look at her. She resembled Lucy so much it blew him away. Except for the red hair. Where had that come from?

"Her hair is red," he blurted out.

"Just like my grandma's. Are you sure you're okay there?"

"We're fine." He stood there staring down at Poppy who stared right back. And then she smiled at him, and damned if she wasn't the most perfect baby he'd ever seen. "She likes me better than you do."

Lucy glanced up from rubbing the water out of her hair to find Cal and Poppy grinning at each other. He looked so strange and yet so right, standing there soaking wet, holding her baby, that it made her chest pinch. If things had gone differently between them, Poppy might have had him for a father instead of Kevin. She blotted at the sudden tears that sprang to her eyes, disguising the gesture as checking for mascara smudges.

"Well, hello there, sweet pea. You're as pretty as your momma, aren't you?" Cal's low, honeyed voice made Poppy giggle. He was devastating to ladies of any age.

"You'll flirt with any female."

"Nah, just the good-looking ones."

And that right there had her worrying she'd made a mistake in coming here and agreeing to marry Cal. He'd earned his bad-boy reputation honestly. She'd been hurt by him before. She couldn't bear the thought of him hurting Poppy as well if she got too attached to him. What was she thinking, bringing a new person into her daughter's life who not only wouldn't go the distance, but could potentially disappoint her? This was going to be a disaster.

But what choice did she have?

She must have traipsed back and forth in the rain between Cal's front door and her car about eighty times, mumbling to herself like a crazy person, before she'd gotten up the nerve to knock. Once she had it was like someone had popped an invisible balloon inside of her filled with tension and apprehension. Maybe this wouldn't be the disaster she expected it to be. Maybe they could keep everything businesslike and cordial and in a year's time she'd be on her way with enough money socked away that she could move her and Poppy as far away from Kevin as possible.

She dried herself off as best she could, all the while keeping a sharp eye on Cal. He was good with Poppy, so natural. He hadn't talked much about his family when they were together. But then they hadn't done much more than screw each other's brains out every chance they got. Talking had pretty much been limited to *your place or mine?*

When she was sure she was as dry as she was going to get, she walked over to the sofa where Cal sat with her daughter. He seemed completely oblivious to how his wet clothes would ruin the leather. But then he could just buy himself a new one the way other people replaced holey socks.

Lucy held her hands out. "I can take her now."

"We're fine. Want a drink?"

"I want my daughter." She still wasn't over Kevin's threat, she realized. It was as though Kevin hung in the air above her, waiting to snatch Poppy away the moment she turned her back.

"Sure." Cal gave Poppy over, eyeing Lucy like she was the one who might disappear. "Want a drink, something to warm you up?"

"That would be nice. Thanks."

Cal rose and went over to the bar in the corner. He moved with the grace and power of a predator. Long and lean, his body never ceased to draw her attention and every other woman's in the room. She'd been so proud to be with him, thinking herself something special. Now she was going to be his wife.

"Why me?" she asked, sitting down and adjusting Poppy in her lap.

He turned with two tumblers half full of amber liquid in each hand. He offered her the one with ice. She couldn't help but be surprised that he remembered how she liked her drink.

He sat next to her on the sofa. "I'm assuming you're asking me why I asked you to marry me."

"I wouldn't put it like that. You didn't really ask me. It was more of an offer like you'd put on a house or a car. But yeah, why me and not, well, *anyone* else?"

"Oh, shit." He set his glass on the table with a thunk. "Hold on. Don't move. I'll be right back."

She followed him out of the room with her gaze. He was acting so strangely tonight. But then this whole thing was strange, from the way he'd made his proposal to the way she'd accepted.

He came back into the room and headed straight for her, and then he did the most astonishing thing—he dropped to one knee in front of her. He took the glass from her and clasped her hand between both of his.

"What are you doing?" She couldn't help the panic in her voice. And she really wished she had three hands so she could knock back that drink.

"Lucy Monroe, would you do me the honor of becoming my wife?"

"What are you doing? Get up."

"Not till you give me an answer."

"I already said I'd marry you. This isn't necessary."

"Yes, it is. Now are you going to give me an answer or not?" He actually looked kind of nervous.

"This isn't real. None of this is real. What are you trying to do here?" Get her hopes up? Make her feel as though this was the beginning of a real engagement that would become a real marriage? This was insane. *He* was insane.

"It's as real as this." He reached into his pocket and pulled out a small, signature blue box, and her heart rate doubled. Then he lifted the lid, and she thought her heart might stop altogether. The most beautiful cushion cut diamond surrounded by sapphires winked up at her.

"I don't understand." She flipped the box lid closed, unable to stand how incredibly perfect the ring was. "This doesn't make any sense. Why are you doing this?"

"We need a story to tell people. How you came over and we were sitting here having a quiet night in during a rainstorm and then I proposed and you accepted. Only you haven't done your part yet." He opened the box again. "If you don't like the ring, we can exchange it."

Poppy made a grab for the ring, which Lucy blocked just in time.

"Well, Poppy seems to like it. Don't you, sweet pea?" He tweaked Poppy's nose, making her giggle. "Are you going to make me stay down here until my legs go numb?" he asked Lucy.

Lucy stared at the ring, which was so dang beautiful it made her eyes water.

"Oh, damn, darlin'. Don't cry. You hate it. I get it." He snapped the lid closed. "We'll get you another one."

"No, you big dumb cowboy. I love it, but I can't accept it."

"Why not?"

"I can't answer your question until you answer mine. Why me?"

"I trust you."

Well, it wasn't poetry or flowers, but it was something he never gave idly. And he'd answered quick enough that she believed him. She supposed it was enough. It wasn't like she expected him to profess his undying love for her. She never would've believed it anyway.

She slowly stuck her left hand out. "Then yes, I will marry you."

He reopened the box and took the ring out. Poppy made another swipe for it, but he slipped it on Lucy's finger before the baby could get a hold of it. It fit perfectly, and her eyes started filling up all over again.

"God, darlin', you're killing me with those tears." He swiped the tear that escaped down her cheek with the pad of his thumb, following it with a kiss. "It won't be so bad, I promise. You might actually like being married to me."

She sniffed, waving his words away. "No, it's not that. I just can't believe what we're going to do. It's crazy."

"It is. It's completely insane."

"While we're talking about crazy, improbable things, do you think it would be okay if Poppy and I move in here before the wedding? My lease is up at the end of the month, and it doesn't really make sense for me to pay the extra expense of a month-to-month lease. You know, if we're going to be married soon."

She held her breath. This was too much to ask. It was a complete betrayal of his trust not telling him the real reason she needed a new place to live. But the fact was, she was too ashamed to tell him how bad things were for her. She'd lost the only babysitter she could afford, which meant she couldn't go to work tomorrow. And she couldn't look for a new job without someone to watch Poppy. Not to mention she'd be homeless at the end of the month.

"That's next week," he said, still on bended knee.

"Yes, I know." She shook her head. "It's okay. Never mind. I'll make it work."

"No. It's fine. You can move in whenever you like."

She let out a heavy, relieved breath. "Thank you. That's very generous of you."

"Now I have a question for you." He grabbed his drink and stood up. "Why did *you* agree to marry *me*?"

FOUR

Ah, yes. He would ask that. Nothing was ever easy or taken at face value with Cal. He always looked at cause and effect. He hadn't gotten to where he was in business without examining things from every angle before coming to a decision or making a commitment. She supposed she should've been relieved he took the same care in his personal life, however impersonal this marriage really was.

He'd opened his home to her in her most desperate time. Whatever he was getting out of this marriage, she was getting far more. It wouldn't be fair not to let him know exactly what he was getting himself into. She only hoped he wouldn't back out once he learned just how screwed up her life was and how much of it she was bringing to his doorstep.

"Well," she began. "I need the money. If I could find a job with the same pay, hours, and perks, I'd take it."

He swallowed a rather large amount of his drink. "No doubt."

"I recently lost my babysitter, so I'll have to look for a new one right away. Which brings up another question—when will I start getting paid?"

"Don't worry about it."

"Well, see, I kind of need to. Without someone to watch Poppy, I can't go in to work tomorrow." She hated how reedy and needy her voice sounded.

He refilled his drink and then hers. She hadn't realized she'd drained the glass.

"Darlin', I'd really appreciate it if you'd get to the part where you answer my question. Why did you agree to marry me?"

She looked down at Poppy, who had fallen asleep with her little fist in her mouth. She'd do anything for her baby. Anything. She gulped back more liquid courage and forged on.

"I'm getting to that."

"Is it all about the money?"

"No."

"Then what's it about? Cuz I've got to tell you, darlin', you look like a woman running from trouble. I think as your husband-to-be I should get a heads up, don't you?"

She went for another swallow only to find her glass empty. He offered her another refill, which she accepted. Admitting to Cal how completely stupid she'd been about everything and throwing herself at his mercy had to be one of the lowest moments of her life. A couple more sips and she might be able to get it all out. As long as she didn't look at him. *Just look at Poppy.*

She drained the glass once more, but this time instead of refilling it, he pried it from her hand and set it on the table.

"My mother would watch Poppy for me while I went to work," she began. "It wasn't the best situation, but she was the only babysitter I could afford. It's hard to turn down free, you know?" She glanced up at him to find him watching her with that Cal intensity that both thrilled and unnerved her.

"What happened with your mother?"

"I was late picking Poppy up. I had to make up the time at work that it took to go into Dallas."

The time it took her to come to his office and ask for her old job back, Cal realized. There was more going on here than losing a babysitter. He believed her that it wasn't all about money. If it took all night, he'd get to the bottom of it.

"When I got to her house," she continued, "there was a car I didn't recognize in the driveway. It was Kevin's."

So this was about her son-of-a-bitch ex. Great.

"He wasn't supposed to be there. But Mother let him in to see Poppy. He doesn't have visitation. To my mother, a family is a unit no matter what. She took his side against me. If I leave Poppy with her, she's going to let Kevin see her."

"Why doesn't he have visitation? Because of his arrest for bigamy?"

"That's partly why. Also he's threatened to take Poppy back to Utah with him. I'm afraid he'll make good on that threat, and if he does, I might never get to see my daughter again."

Something wasn't jiving here. But her fear that her ex would take her baby was very real. She was terrified. It was that terror—way more than the need for money and the flexible-hours bullshit—that had driven her to accept his offer. The disappointment he felt over that revelation surprised him. He knew she hadn't agreed because she loved him or even wanted him. He was literally her last and only resort. But *son of a bitch.* A part of him had hoped she might care for him at least a little.

"That's one of the reasons I asked about moving in early," she admitted. "The gates and security. I promise we'll stay out of your way. You'll hardly know we're here. Poppy's a very good baby. We'll clean up—"

He put a hand up to stop her. "You're not a guest here,

Lucy. You're going to be my wife. This is going to be your home as much as mine."

"Okay. I just don't want you to think I'll take advantage."

"Stop acting like I'll kick you and Poppy to the curb for the slightest infraction. As long as you wear my ring, you have a place here." He wanted to add that as long as she wore his ring she had a place in his life *and* his heart, but he didn't think she could handle much more pressure than she was already under.

His instinct told him there was more to the story, something to do with the ex. Maybe the feelers he put out earlier that day would pay off and he'd get a look at the whole picture and know exactly what he was up against.

She shifted Poppy to the couch next to her and adjusted the blanket around her. She was a devoted mother to her daughter. It had occurred to him more than once that Poppy could be his. He and Lucy had certainly been careless more than a time or two. If things had gone differently between them...

She glanced down at the ring on her finger. He'd spent nearly the entire afternoon looking for the right ring, betting against the odds that she'd agree to marry him. Maybe it wasn't fashionable to have colored stones in an engagement ring, but the sapphires reminded him of her eyes. She said she liked it, but she kept staring at it oddly, like it didn't quite fit her.

"Thank you," she said, eyes still on the ring. "I promise I'll do my best to uphold our bargain and be the kind of wife you need me to be."

He grabbed the bottle of whiskey and splashed more into each of their glasses. She was acting like a wounded puppy, and it pissed him off. He wanted the Lucy who went toe-to-toe with him and gave as good as she got. So maybe he'd have to draw that Lucy out.

"What kind of wife do you think I need?" he asked.

"Well," she started and then took a sip. "You said you needed a hostess, someone to hold dinner parties?"

"That's right."

"I'm a fairly good cook, but I think it would probably be best if we had the dinners catered."

"And what about the charity balls? You do know how to dance, don't you?"

"I...ah...know how to sway..."

She finished off her drink, so he refilled her glass. He wondered if she'd realized it yet that she was too drunk to drive home.

"Do you know anything about corporate wives?" he asked

"I'm not sure if I've met very many."

"And your wardrobe. We're going to have to make some changes. That blouse you're wearing, besides being cut too low—" but not low enough for his taste, "—is too small. I can see half your bra."

She glanced down at her chest, then her head popped up. The fire was back in her eyes just as he intended. "You cannot see half my bra. It gapes a little, but it's not obscene."

"Darlin', from where I'm sitting, my eyes have practically gotten to second base with you. And your skirt—"

"What about my skirt?"

"It's tight enough for when we're at home. Personally the office sex kitten look does a lot for me, but it sends the wrong message to every other man who is *not* your soon-to-be husband."

"Look, I know I've put on some weight—"

"Yeah, and you put it in all the right places. That's what counts." He ran his gaze over her the way he'd been wanting to ever since he'd seen her again this afternoon.

She flushed under his gaze. "You're making me want to add an addendum to the option we discussed in my office."

Her gorgeous mouth dropped open for a second and then she rebounded. "You're a pig." She didn't sound half as pissed off as she would've been if she wasn't so intoxicated.

"I can't help it. I'm a male pig. And you, darlin', are very female."

"I have a question about that option." She downed the last of her whiskey and pushed her glass at him for more. He obliged. "How open to options is it?"

"What do you mean?"

"I mean just how many option clauses do you have open?" She was slurring her words now.

"Just the one, darlin'. Just the one."

She tried to point at him, but she couldn't quite focus enough to nail him down with it. "I mean, there's not like a brunette option or a redhead option or even another blonde-headed-ded-ded option, is there? Cuz, I know you. You're a man who likes his options. So if we're gonna get married, I'm gonna have to insist you cut..." she made a slicing motion with her hand and tipped over slightly then recovered, "...all your other options. You get me, cowboy?"

"I get you, darlin'. Yours is the only option for me. But I'm going to want the same assurances from you."

"Psshh." She waved him away. "Between my giant ass and Poppy, there aren't any men who would even give me a second look let alone options." She rolled her eyes, weaving a little, and then finished off her glass.

He took it from her before she could ask for another.

"I seriously doubt that. But just so we're clear on all our options, why don't we write them down." He wanted her to remember this conversation tomorrow.

"Oh! Like a contract. Good idea. And we should have it notarized so there's no weaseling out of it."

He was halfway to grabbing a sheet of paper when her words stopped him. "You want to make our agreement formal?"

"Well, yeah. Sure. Why not? You like binding contracts, don't you?" She giggled. "I know for sure you like binding." She waggled her eyebrows at him.

"You want to put binding in our binding contract?"

She slapped her knee, wide-eyed. "We totally should!"

He sat back down next to her with a pad of paper and a pen and started writing. "So binding is option number one. What's option number two?"

"No, no. Scratch that out. Number one should be the option that says neither one of us doesn't get any other options. Or we're the other's only option. No other optioning. Or something like that. Otherwise I'm not havin' any kind of options with you." She shook her finger at him, then held up three fingers. "Two can be binding. Oh! And we should make three or is it four...I can't remember...but it should definitely be that thing you do with your teeth and your tongue right here." She made a sweeping gesture that encompassed her whole body.

He started writing, jotting down all of the *options* she wanted, adding a few of his own with her permission. When they were done, they had a five-page list of some of the most inventive sexual activities ever compiled.

"Okay. Okay," she said. "I've got one more. This is the last one. I promise."

Somehow when he wasn't looking she'd gotten ahold of the whiskey bottle and refilled her glass...two...no, maybe three times.

"And what would that be?" He really couldn't believe it. She'd outdone anything his imagination could come up with by yards. He couldn't wait to see what she came up with next.

"We need a..." she hiccupped, "...an optional option."

"An optional option. What exactly is that?"

"It's an option that says that all of the options are completely optional." She waved her hands around. "Optionally speaking of course."

"That goes without saying."

She snorted. "Right. That's what *I* thought. Didn't turn out that way." She tapped the page with her finger. "Write it down. I want it in writing this time. Op-tion-al."

He stared at her for a moment, not quite believing what she'd inadvertently told him. What in the hell had her marriage to that asshole been like? Had he forced her to have sex with him? How bad had things gotten for her?

He cleared his throat, which had become inexplicably clogged. "How about: Everything in this option agreement is absolutely and completely optional, and either party can pull their option at any time during any option?"

"Oohhh. That's good."

He wrote it down. "Now what?"

"Now we sign. Wait! No. We need a notoriety to make it all officially official."

"You mean a notary."

"Right." She squinted up at him. "Isn't that what I said?"

"Close enough. Let me make a phone call."

Twenty minutes later they had a signed and notarized option agreement thanks to Cal's business connections. It was going to cost him a couple of hundred dollars extra for the late-night service, but if it made Lucy feel secure in marrying him, then it was money well spent.

He was still trying to wrap his head around what Lucy had let slip. What had she been through in the past seventeen months? Whatever it was had nearly broken her spirit. He was going to have to be extra gentle, extra careful to gain back her trust and make her feel secure again.

He returned from showing the notary out to find Lucy passed out on the couch next to Poppy. He stood in the doorway a moment, watching them, hardly able to believe they were here. His gaze tracked to his ring on Lucy's finger. Twenty-four hours ago if someone had told him that they'd be engaged, he would've laughed in their face. But here she was broken and alone and now his, finally his.

As he bent down and kissed Poppy's then Lucy's cheeks, he swore that they would never again want for anything. As long as he was in their lives, they would never be insecure and afraid.

FIVE

Lucy woke up with the worst hangover she'd ever had in her life. Or else she was dead and the pain in her head was punishment for all the bad things she'd done. She risked opening her eyes to a dark room she didn't recognize.

Where was she? *Where was Poppy?*

She climbed out of bed faster than she should have, swaying so badly she had to grab the bedpost to keep from falling over. She found the door after three tries—who in the world had two closets in their bedroom?—and stumbled out into the hall. Wait. She knew this house.

Cal's.

Locating the staircase, she made her way downstairs. Last night came back to her in drips and dribbles with each step. Oh my God. Had they really made a sexual option agreement? And had it notarized? No. That couldn't be right. What exactly had she agreed to?

Noises from the kitchen drew her that direction. She stopped in the doorway, gaping at the unexpected vision that greeted her. A shirtless Cal had Poppy down to her diaper, tied to a chair with a towel, and he was feeding her applesauce. It had to be the strangest, sexiest, and most confusing sight she'd ever seen.

He'd always had a great body, but now... She resisted the urge to fan herself. Holy cow. He must work out every day to get a body like that. Not an ounce of anything except hard, chiseled muscle on him. Da-yam.

It took her a moment to find her voice. "What are you doing?"

Cal looked up at her and grinned. "Breakfast. How are you feeling?" He spooned some applesauce into Poppy's mouth, then held out a bowl of Cheerios for Poppy to feed herself.

"You let me drink too much."

"I cut you off. You snuck more." He turned, running his gaze over her. "There's coffee if you can handle it."

"Ugh. Maybe." She watched as he wiped Poppy's face and hands with a washcloth. "How do you know how to do all this baby stuff?"

"Told you. My parents foster children. Even now when I visit, I'm drafted into diaper duty."

She made her way over to the coffeepot and poured a cup. "Wow. Cal Sellers, the internationally known business mogul, changes diapers and feeds babies. Who would've guessed?"

"I'm a man of many talents, aren't I, Poppy?"

Poppy squealed as he lifted her out of the chair and stood up. Lucy nearly lost her breath. Cal looked so good, so right holding her daughter that she had to bite the inside of her lip to keep from bursting into tears. Kevin had only ever held Poppy if he had to. He'd never fed her or changed a diaper in his life. And here was this man who'd broken her heart—but not nearly as devastatingly as Kevin had—caring for her baby as if she was his own. She'd made many mistakes in her life, but choosing Kevin to help raise her child had to be the biggest, most irreversible mistake she would ever make.

Cal wiggled his nose against Poppy's, making her

giggle. Poppy slapped her chubby hands on Cal's cheeks, trying to get him do it again. He did, and Poppy put her head back and laughed harder than Lucy had ever seen her laugh. Cal blew a raspberry on her belly, and she laughed harder. Cal's answering chuckle did funny things to Lucy's insides. Or else it was the coffee mixed with the leftover whiskey in her belly.

"I can take her now," she blurted out.

"What? Nah, we're fine. Go take a shower. I don't have to leave for another half hour." He didn't even look at her. All of his attention was on Poppy.

"About last night…"

Both Cal and Poppy turned to glance at her. "What about it?" he asked.

"I'm not really sure what happened after this." She held up her hand with the engagement ring.

"Besides you getting drunk?"

"Yeah. Besides that."

"And passing out."

"Besides that too. Was there a notary involved?"

"You were rather insistent on that, darlin'. What else could I do but oblige you?"

"Where is it?"

"The option agreement? In the living room."

Why did he seem so totally unconcerned about it? And what exactly did it say?

She set her coffee down, then picked it back up and took it into the living room with her. She had a feeling she was going to need the fortitude it would provide.

Cal followed with Poppy. Lucy found a small stack of pages with Cal's neat block lettering on the coffee table where he'd said it would be. She dropped down on the sofa and leafed through it. It was worse than she thought. Swallowing her panic on a bitter sip of black coffee, she turned to Cal, who was trying to pry Poppy's fingers from his chest hair.

"This, uh, agreement." She held it up. "What exactly does it mean? I'm not, like, bound to any of it or anything, am I? Cuz I'm not exactly sure how number twenty-three would work."

He came over, took the papers from her, and flipped through them. "Me either," he said. "But you insisted I write it down."

"But it's not legal, is it?"

"If you're asking if I'll force you to do any of the naughty things your dirty mind thought up—read the last option." He handed her the agreement back.

She found the last page and read it, then let out the breath she'd been holding. "Oh, thank God."

"We were just joking around." But he didn't sound like he thought it was much of a joke.

"A joke. Right."

"I made a couple of phone calls this morning. The movers are going to pack up your things day after tomorrow and bring them here. Also, I hired you a nanny. Her name's Sam."

"I don't want a nanny. I can take care of Poppy just fine."

"I know you can, darlin', but I thought you might need some help while you get things settled. The nanny can be here with you while you do that. That way you can get to know her and hopefully like her."

"I don't even get to meet her first? How do you know she's any good? She could be one of those nannies who beat the children they care for."

He gave her a *get real* look. "You really think I wouldn't hire the absolute best?"

"Maybe your best is different than my best."

"Let's go get you dressed, Poppy." He turned to leave the room.

"Cal."

He stopped and glanced back at her.

"I can't leave her with a stranger," Lucy said. "She's just a baby."

"You wouldn't be, darlin'. Sam's going to be here to help you, like I said. If you don't approve of her, we'll find someone else. But trust me on this, you're going to approve." He started out of the room again, then turned back. "By the way, how did you like the room you stayed in last night?"

"What?" Her mind was still stuck on nannies and moving.

"The bedroom. It's the largest one besides mine. If you don't like it, you can pick a different one, but that would mean we'd have to move Poppy's room too."

"What do you mean Poppy's room? I didn't know she had one."

"The one between yours and mine." He said it like she should've already known.

She rubbed at her pounding forehead. This time yesterday she was nearly homeless and jobless. Twenty-four hours later she was engaged, moving into a mansion, and getting a nanny. Oh, yes. And she'd signed some kind of optional sex contract with her fiancé that may or may not be binding in a court of law.

"Everything's going to be fine, darlin'. Isn't it, Poppy?"

She watched as Cal left the room with her daughter as though they started their day like this every day. She must have upset some kind of space-time continuum when she'd walked into Cal's office yesterday. Nothing since then had been the same. It was all off kilter and out of whack. But other than the ridiculous option agreement, she couldn't think of one single thing she'd change.

And that worried her most of all.

Three days later, Cal sat in his office overlooking the Dallas skyline, contemplating the changes his life had gone through in the past few days. Lucy and Poppy had moved in. Cal and Lucy's engagement had been announced and was big society news. He found himself racing Lucy to get to Poppy when she cried first thing in the morning. He usually won.

Lucy approved of Sam the nanny, who turned out to be a manny. Cal had trusted Lucas to find the perfect nanny/bodyguard for Poppy. He'd grilled Lucas about Sam's qualifications up one side and down the other, but it had never occurred to him to ask if Sam was a man or a woman. He'd assumed. And now there was another man in his house, spending all day alone with Lucy.

Cal hadn't so much as kissed Lucy since that peck on the cheek when she'd cried as he put his ring on her finger. He began to wonder if they'd ever get past option number one in the option agreement. Not that he was complaining. Much. Whatever Lucy had been through was because of him. He was going to have to tread lightly to re-earn her trust.

At least he'd gotten her to set a date for the wedding—a week from Saturday. There wasn't much time to plan. All he really needed was Lucy, a license, and a preacher, but he wanted her to have the wedding she'd always wanted. So he'd hired a wedding planner who was showing Lucy table linens and centerpieces at this very moment. He was supposed to meet them later to look at venues.

Right now he was waiting for his good friend Lucas, who he'd asked to check into some things for him concerning Lucy's ex. Lucas had started his own security company a couple of years ago. He'd met his now-wife Mi when Cal had hired him to be her bodyguard. Lucy and Mi had been hosts of *Pleasure at Home* and good friends until Lucy quit to marry that asshole. The show had done quite well with Mi as host, but in a few months she'd be going out on maternity leave.

Cal wondered if Lucy had confided in Mi about her ex and how much of that had Mi divulged to Lucas. Lucy had been circumspect at best about her ex and downright evasive at worst.

There was a knock at the door, then Lucas opened it and came in, closing it behind him. "Hey."

Cal stood and shook hands with his friend. "Can I offer you anything?"

"I'm good."

"Have a seat." He waited for Lucas to settle in a chair and then tried to act cool as he asked the most important question he might ever ask. "What have you learned about Kevin Walker?"

Lucas shifted in his chair. Not a good sign. Nothing ruffled the six-foot-six, two-hundred-and-seventy-pound former Navy SEAL. Lucas opened the file he'd brought with him. "As you know he was arrested for bigamy eight months ago."

Cal knew it because it was him who had discovered Kevin Walker's other wives. Lucy had been his third wife. Walker had missed Poppy's birth because he was sitting in a jail cell.

"What's happening with those charges?"

"He was released on bond and fled the state. They suspect he might be living with one of his wives in Utah. If convicted, he could get anywhere from two to ten years in jail and a hefty fine." Lucas smirked. "The D.A. would really like to know his whereabouts."

"If I find out, I'll be sure to be a good citizen and let him know."

"Did you know that Lucy has a protective order against him?"

"No. She said that he didn't have any visitation rights, but she didn't say why."

Lucas grunted. "Restraining orders are typically given to victims of violence."

"What are you saying?"

Lucas pulled a stack of photos out of the file and laid them on the desk in front of Cal. At first he wasn't quite sure of what he was looking at, and then it came at him like a bullet, punching a hole into his chest and knocking him back into his seat. He flipped through the photos, the sick knot in his belly growing. They'd been taken at different times he realized. How could this be? What kind of sick bastard did this to a woman? He swallowed the bile rising up the back of his throat.

"How many times?" he managed to ask.

"Seven are documented here," Lucas said quietly. "There are notes on several more. There was one brief hospitalization. For a burn."

"Why isn't this asshole in jail?"

"First conviction carries a small fine. There are charges pending on a second case that could include jail time and a bigger fine. It's messed up, but the penalty for having more than one legal wife is heftier than beating your wife nearly unconscious."

"Jesus fucking Christ. He better hope I never set eyes on him."

"He better hope neither of us does."

Cal handed the photos back to Lucas. "Find him."

"Already on it. The lead about the rental car was a good one. He rented it under an alias that we can track if he uses it again."

"I wanted to talk to you about the security at my house. It's not adequate enough."

Lucas handed him a second folder. "My proposal. Besides the nanny, what other security personnel would you like to add?"

"Yeah, and thank you for that. That's just what I wanted, another man around my fiancée."

"He's British Special Forces with a certificate from a highly exclusive English nanny school. I'd trust him to guard my own kid."

Cal gave his friend a dirty look. "Yeah, I'll believe it when you hire him to hang around Mi all day. He sings and plays guitar like a fucking rock star. Plus he's got an accent. I can't get a word in between all of the praise Lucy heaps on this guy."

Lucas had the balls to laugh at his predicament. "Yeah, but does a rock star know over a hundred ways to kill with his bare hands? He's the best I've got. What's better than a ninja nanny?"

"I'm not sure that helps."

"He's been married nearly ten years. Besides that, he's a professional. My guys don't fuck around, or they don't have a job."

"That helps. Got any gardener ninjas or cooking ninjas? Maybe a hot-maid ninja? I could use some of those."

Lucas rose. "I'll see what I can do." He headed for the door.

"One more thing."

Lucas turned back. "Yeah?"

Cal came around the desk. "Will you stand up with me at my wedding?"

"Yeah, man." Lucas held out his hand, and Cal shook it. "I'd be glad to."

Cal clapped him on the back. "That means you're in charge of the bachelor party. Make it good. And by good I mean poker and booze."

"I thought for a minute you were going to say strippers."

"Only if you've got a ninja stripper on your payroll."

"I'll look around for one."

Cal showed his friend out, then went back to barely noticing the view outside his window. Lucy filled his thoughts. Those photos... Goddamn. He'd never get those images out of his head, the cuts, the bruises, the bite marks, and other damage he couldn't tell how it had been caused. He scrubbed his hands over his face. She'd lived through hell and had somehow gotten away. She'd run to him when she had no one else.

He would do anything for her, but the thing she needed from him most was to be safe. In that, he wouldn't let her down.

SIX

Lucy stared at her reflection in the dressing-room mirror, hardly recognizing herself. The hairstylist had rolled and twisted her hair into a half-up, half-tumbling-down style that was both chaste and scandalous. The makeup artist had done something to her skin that made it glow and had even managed to cover her scar so that both of her shoulders appeared smooth and flawless. The last thing she wanted today was a reminder of the damage her last marriage had done to both her body and heart. Kevin had been drunk when he'd burned her or else he'd never have left so permanent a mark.

Her silk wedding dress was also a contradiction with a strapless, sweetheart neckline, flowered belt, and A-line skirt. It left some parts exposed and others chastely covered. She felt...beautiful. For the first time in seventeen long months she wasn't worried about repercussions for a skirt that was too short or for makeup that was too garish.

She hoped Cal liked the way she looked.

"Here." Mi handed her the pearl earrings she'd given Lucy as a wedding gift. They perfectly matched the string of pearls Cal had gotten Lucy as his gift.

"Are you sure you want to marry him?" Mi asked. "You

have other options, you know."

No. She didn't. She didn't have any options, but she wasn't about to confess this to Mi after keeping what Kevin had done to her a secret for so long. The shame of it was always there, always hovering over her. Speaking of it was more than she could face because if she said the words, the enormity of everything she'd been through would come crashing down over her.

"I know this is going to sound a little crazy," Lucy said. "But I want to marry him."

She did, she realized. The doubts were there, hovering in the background, ghosts from her previous marriage. She mentally flicked them away. Cal wasn't Kevin. She knew this. She was doing the right thing for both her and Poppy.

"That does sound crazy. Are you very sure? You and Poppy deserve the best."

"And you don't think Cal is the best?"

"I don't think Cal has a full grasp on what's happening here. He's about to become a husband and a father all on the same day. This isn't a merger or acquisition, this is a family."

"I know you don't like him—"

"With good reason. He cheated on you. With his secretary. It would be laughable if it wasn't so tragic. Are you sure you can trust him? Are you sure you want to?"

"Honestly? No. But this isn't what it was before. We're not involved that way. I'm walking into this with wider eyes. Every time I start to soften towards him, the image of him bending his honey over his desk pops up, and my heart hardens all over again. Besides, you and Lucas have enough changes to deal with without taking in a homeless friend and her daughter." Lucy rubbed her friend's gently swollen belly. "Are you going to tell me what you're having, or are you and Lucas keeping it a secret?"

"It's a boy."

Lucy threw her hands up and hugged her friend. "I'm so thrilled for you. For both of you. But my Lord is that going to be a big baby. Lucas is such a big guy."

"Ugh. Don't remind me. And whatever you do, don't remind Lucas. He's freaking out about it."

The wedding planner popped her head in the door. "Five minutes!" Then she popped back out again.

"Okay, this is it," Lucy said. "How do I look?"

Tears appeared in Mi's eyes. "Really beautiful. He's a lucky man, even if he doesn't know it."

"Don't cry. You'll make me cry and my mascara will run."

Mi dabbed at her eyes. "Let's go get you hitched."

಄

Lucy carried her daughter unescorted up the aisle to Cal. He stood so tall and straight in his black tuxedo under the wisteria-draped gazebo. Lucas stood to his left and Mi and the minister to his right. The way Cal stared at Lucy nearly stopped her in her tracks, then made her want to run up the aisle toward him. Her cheeks heated under his gaze. She almost forgot this wasn't a real marriage. She needed to remember this was a business arrangement and nothing more.

And she could do that...when she wasn't looking at him. If she glanced at Mi or the minister or stared just past Cal's shoulder, she could remember that none of this was real. It was all for show. But then her gaze would be drawn to his and she'd be sucked into its tractor beam, imagining that this was the wedding she'd always wanted to the man she'd dreamed of with their future stretched out before them.

But it wasn't.

She repeated after the minister. Listened while Cal pledged his life and love to her. Held out her hand for Cal to place the thin platinum band on her finger. Put her ring on Cal's finger. Said "I do." Heard Cal say it too. And then he lifted her veil. She stared up at him, and the panic hit her sideways. She struggled to keep her feet planted and not run back down the aisle. He leaned toward her, and she closed her eyes, going to that empty place in her head where no one and nothing could touch her.

He kissed her briefly and that was it. It was over, and he was holding her hand, leading her back down the aisle. She'd done it. She was married. All that was left was the party, and then she'd be alone with Cal. Her husband.

Accepting the well wishes of the guests was easy. She'd pasted on enough fake smiles as one of the faces of *Pleasure at Home* that it came automatically. Sam had taken Poppy, so she could carry out her duties as Mrs. Cal Sellers. Cal stood at her side, frequently touching her—on the small of her back, across her shoulders, around her waist—branding her as his.

She tried not to think about tonight even as their guests reminded her with good-natured winks and elbows to the side. Would Cal expect there to be a true wedding night, especially after creating the option agreement? Everything he'd said and done told her he wouldn't, but he was a man. A man who went through women the way most went through socks.

She suddenly felt self-conscious, tugging at the top of her dress. What had she been thinking, wearing something so revealing? Even if the dress had made her feel more beautiful than she'd felt in months, maybe years.

The last guest passed through the receiving line, leaving Lucy alone with Cal.

"How about some champagne?" he asked.

Alcohol. "I'd love some."

He took her hand and led her toward the head table set up at the front of the room. On the way, he snagged two flutes of champagne and handed one to her. She had to concentrate on not downing the entire glass at once. It had occurred to her more than once that if this wedding had taken place seventeen months ago, she would've been the happiest bride who ever wore Vera Wang. But now she stood beside her handsome husband surrounded by mostly strangers and wished that the earth would open up and swallow her whole. Or else that she could drown herself and her memories of her previous marriage in enough champagne that she'd be too sick to think about what came next.

Cal watched Lucy out of the corner of his eye. She was so pale her blue eyes were nearly black. And she gulped the hundred-dollar-a-bottle champagne like it was air and she was under water…drowning. When she drained it, he handed her a glass of water. She was not getting drunk tonight. She was going to be completely sober for their first night as husband and wife. To ensure that, he excused himself and gave a whispered order to the head waiter that his wife was to only be given alcohol-free beverages.

When he returned, Lucy gave him her stage smile, her gaze passing over him as though he was part of the scenery. He'd had just about enough of Lucy trying to endure what should've been a fun evening.

"You know what I think?" he asked.

"Hmm?"

"I think we need to test out your swaying skills."

"What?"

He held out his hand to her. "May I have this dance?"

She stared at it as if it would strike her, then slowly

placed her hand in his. He drew her up and out onto the crowded dance floor. Holding her close, but not as close as he'd like, he danced with his wife for the first time. After a few moments her shoulders relaxed.

"Have I told you how beautiful you look?" he whispered in her ear.

She shook her head.

"You are. Absolutely stunning. I don't think there's a set of eyes that hasn't been on you since you came up the aisle."

"Oh, I don't think—"

"It's true. You're beautiful, darlin'. More beautiful than I deserve, that's for sure."

"Don't be ridiculous."

"Thank you for marrying me."

She looked up at him, surprised. "That was our deal."

"Yeah, but that doesn't mean I'm not grateful." She didn't respond so he pressed on. "I think we're going to get along very well." Still nothing. "You know if we swayed like this every day, we might end up trying some of those options."

"Wouldn't you like that."

"I'm pretty sure you'd like it too. If memory serves, you especially liked number six. The first time we tried it you made this sound that reminded me of—"

She slapped his chest. "Ssh! Keep your voice down."

"That's exactly what I said the first time we tried it. We were in the bathroom at that bistro downtown that you were crazy about—"

"Cal Sellers, if you say another word…"

"You'll what? Do number sixty-four to me? Cuz I might be into some of that with you, darlin'."

"Have you memorized the entire agreement?" She sounded scandalized and kind of turned on too.

"Just my favorite numbers. Tell me about some of

yours. What are your favorites?"

"This isn't exactly—"

"This is our wedding, darlin'. And we're slow dancing to our favorite song—"

"This isn't my favorite song."

"It wasn't mine either until about two minutes ago when you started rubbing your body against mine and calling it 'dancing'. Feels more like foreplay than dancing to me."

"Cal!"

"Tell me your top ten favorite options on the option agreement and I'll stop."

"No."

"Top eight."

"No."

"Five and I'll throw in a glass of champagne."

"Two glasses and a promise that you won't smash the cake in my face."

"You have a deal, darlin'."

"Number two." A pale pink blush crept up her chest to her neck, making him want to lick its path.

"The binding option. Good choice. Me or you?"

"You."

"Also an excellent choice. Which others?"

"Seventeen."

"*Really?* Now I wouldn't've expected that from a woman dressed in virginal white, but who am I to argue?"

"Forty-nine, but I think one of those beds with the head and feet that go up and down would be essential in making it successful."

"I agree." Did she even realize how lovely she was, blushing like a nun watching a porno flick? Or how much he wanted to do every option she'd put into their agreement with her...for her?

"Sixty-three."

He clenched his teeth from groaning out loud. Sixty-three had been one of the few suggestions he'd offered. "I can't argue with you. One more."

She was quiet for a long moment, her tongue sweeping once, twice across her bottom lip. This was the one. The one she really wanted to try. He could tell by the way her gaze darted away and the fact that she'd left it for last. That was his Lucy, always thinking of herself last.

"Thirty."

He did groan then. "Jesus God almighty, darlin', are you trying to make me embarrass myself right here in front of our friends and family?"

"You'd consider thirty?"

"Consider it? I've been dreaming of it practically all my adult life." He was so looking up number thirty when they got back to the house. Whatever it was, he was going to figure out a way to do it better than anyone had ever done it before. She'd be talking about it to her friends for years to come as the end all be all of sexual fantasies fulfilled.

When they got that far. If they ever got that far. First he had to get her to stop looking at him like he'd turn on her at any moment.

"You've never done number thirty?"

"No. And please tell me you have, darlin', so you can teach it to me and I won't feel so inept."

"No. I haven't."

"Then I guess we'll have to learn it together. Someday," he added, so she wouldn't think he had any plans for them other than this moment. "That's five options, and I now owe you a glass of champagne. Shall we?" He held out his elbow for her to take and led her off the dance floor.

The rest of the night went by in a blur of obligatory socializing and wedding traditions. They danced twice more, but neither compared to their first dance as man and wife. Cal couldn't wait to get Lucy out of there and all to himself. He'd booked the honeymoon suite at the Ritz-Carlton for their wedding night. He'd also arranged for Sam to take Poppy.

One night. He'd get one night to show her what marriage to him would really be like. One night.

SEVEN

Her wedding night.

Lucy followed her new husband into the suite at the Ritz-Carlton, dread heavy in her belly. The honeymoon suite. He must be expecting her to fulfill her duties as his wife. He'd said everything between them would be optional. He'd even signed a notarized agreement to that effect. But she knew from experience that men didn't always mean what they said when it came to sex. And they didn't always take no for an answer.

Cal had booked this suite. In this fancy hotel. On their wedding night. If that didn't have unspoken expectations all over it, she didn't know what did.

"Are you hungry?" he asked. "I don't know about you, but all I've eaten tonight is that piece of cake you fed me."

Her stomach rumbled as if on cue. "I'm starving."

He found the room service menu and started leafing through it. "I could eat one of everything. What sounds good to you?"

"A cheeseburger. With fries."

"You got it. Why don't you get changed while I order? Your bags should already be in your room."

Her room. That meant they weren't... He wasn't expecting... She wasn't sure if she was grateful or disappointed. It was a confusing set of emotions that knocked together inside her like stress-ball clackers.

"Which one's mine?" she asked.

"The master. Whichever that one is. Hi," he said into the phone. "I'd like to order some food."

Lucy wandered off toward a set of double doors that had to be the master bedroom. It was and the bed was huge. And was that...? She rushed forward. A Jacuzzi right in the middle of the bedroom with a view of the Dallas skyline. How romantic. Except this wasn't a romance.

"I'm looking forward to that," Cal said from over her shoulder, making her jump and squeak. "Sorry, darlin'. Didn't mean to startle you."

"No, that's okay. It's just that this carpet is so plush it totally absorbed your steps." And now she sounded like an idiot.

"I told Hazel to pack you a bathing suit." He pointed at the Jacuzzi. "Right there is where I plan to have a drink and soak with my wife after dinner."

He gazed at her like she really was his wife and he had all kinds of husbandly plans. She peered inside the Jacuzzi. It looked like heaven. Lots of jets and places to put your feet up. She risked a glance up at Cal, but he'd already turned away and was walking out the door. What in the...?

Hot, cold, hot, cold. Right when she thought she had him and this—whatever it was between them—sorted out, he'd throw her a curve and do the exact opposite of what she expected. He flirted with her like he used to, only it was just words, no action. He'd kissed her exactly twice since she'd walked into his office almost two weeks ago. The one time in his office and then again when the minister had told him that he could now kiss his bride. Three times if she counted the peck on the cheek he'd given her when they got engaged. He'd progressed to hand holding and an arm around her shoulders or a hand at the small of her back in the past week or so but no further.

It was almost as though they were virginal high schoolers with their first crush. She half-expected him to ask her to prom. Well, she guessed their wedding was sort of prom like. She was in a big dress and they'd danced... And now they were in this suite that was made for romance.

What was he up to? Because with Cal there was always a plan.

She followed him into the living area and then across the hall and into another bedroom. He was already starting to strip. His jacket was strewn on the end of the bed and he was working on his tie.

"Hey, darlin'. Need help with the zipper on your dress?"

She did, but that wasn't why she'd come in.

"Spin around," he told her. When she didn't comply, he took her shoulders and turned her himself. "It's got one of those hook thingies. Hang on. These always stump me."

He shoved his hand into the back of her dress, probably farther than was necessary to unhook a simple hook-and-eye closure. It took him a long damn time to work it. All the while he stroked her skin and moved her closer and closer to him. She was pretty sure she was too close now for him to have any kind of angle at all to work the hook. She slid back another half step and came right up against him. Then she heard the rasp of the zipper and felt a rush of cool air on her skin. He brought the zipper all the way down past her waist.

His touch was featherlight on her exposed skin, scattering goose bumps. Her chest heaved with the effort to breathe, and she was caught between wanting him to rip her dress away and fear that he actually might do it and leave her with a choice to make.

Then his fingers were gone. "There you go." He gave her a perfunctory pat on the shoulder. "Go get changed into something comfortable. I have plans for us after we eat." He disappeared into the adjoining bathroom and closed the door. A second later she heard the shower.

She shivered, more turned on than she'd been in a long time, and actually contemplated following him into the bathroom. Instead she fled to the safety of her room.

ఆ&so

Cal put a hand on the tiled wall and jerked faster on his dick. He hadn't masturbated this much since he was fifteen and had accidentally come across a nudie magazine in his father's garage. He thought of Lucy and the way her breasts had nearly tumbled out of the top of her dress when he'd unzipped it. He imagined gripping the front and ripping it down to her waist and then lifting the back of her dress and pounding into her from behind.

He came with a jerk and a long, low groan. It wasn't enough. Goddammit, he wanted her. He wanted her in a way he hadn't wanted anything or anyone ever. She was his wife but not *his*. He was going to have to earn her back, earn her trust, earn her love. He'd do it if it killed him and he grew calluses from jerking off nearly every hour of every day. She'd be his and they could do option number thirty a hundred times a day until they passed out from exhaustion.

He shut the water off and grabbed a towel. He knew she expected him to make a move on her. It was their wedding night. What else did newly married couples do except fuck like they'd never get to fuck again. And goddammit he was hard all over again. He looked down at himself and laughed. This would be part of his penance—

having a perpetual hard-on. He'd survived worse, he supposed...but not much. Being around Lucy and unable able to touch her, make her sigh and scream his name was a crueler punishment than any he could've ever come up with.

He dressed in loose sweats and a T-shirt. Just about the least sexy thing he could come up with. This was about Lucy and helping her feel safe and secure. It was about trust and commitment, two words he hadn't ever given much thought to before he'd seen the photos of Lucy and the way her eyes went blank when she thought he was going to make a move on her.

He wanted to punch something so badly. That son-of-a-bitch ex of hers had taken the most precious, most vital woman Cal had ever met and made her a shell filled with fear and shame. Cal would bring her back. She was already starting to come back to him in tiny increments. He'd go slow with her if it killed him. And it just might.

There was a knock on the door. Cal went out into the living area. The double doors to Lucy's bedroom were closed, but he could hear the water of a shower running. He opened the door to room service and signed the check as they set everything up. Lucy wouldn't be expecting what he had planned for them.

He poured himself a glass of wine and stood at the window overlooking the city, waiting for his wife. His wife. The moment he'd slipped his ring on her finger and pledged himself to her, he'd known he could never go back. He could never look at another woman and not compare her to Lucy.

He heard the door behind him open, but he didn't turn.

"Oh," she exclaimed. "Dinner. I'm starving."

He turned then and nearly wished he hadn't. She was wearing a robe, her hair wrapped in a towel on top of her head. Her skin was scrubbed pink and clean. The scent of whatever soap or shampoo she'd used coasted toward him, stroking him like a lover. She wore nothing beneath the robe, and it nearly brought him to his knees. God couldn't be this cruel to him. Surely he hadn't been that wicked.

She sashayed toward the table and plopped herself down. The rest of his wine disappeared in two desperate gulps.

"Wait," he said as she reached for one of the lids. "We're going to play a game."

She tilted her head to the side. "With food?"

"Sure. Why not make dinner fun?"

She looked like she might argue and then she withdrew her hand, relenting to him. "Okay. What are the rules?"

"The rules are we're both blindfolded."

"Why?"

"No utensils," he continued without answering. "I feed you, you feed me, and we have to guess what we're eating."

"But you ordered everything. You already know what's here."

"No. Actually I don't. I asked the kitchen to prepare a variety of finger foods, but I didn't specify what they would be. We'll both be surprised."

"Can't we just eat? I'm starving."

"You'll eat what I feed you. It'll be fun. Now close your eyes. Please."

"You first."

"Okay." He sat next to her at the table and rolled two napkins. He handed one to her. "Put this around my eyes and then put this other one around yours." He waited as she tied the napkin around his head, cutting off all sight. After a few moments he asked, "Is your blindfold on?"

"Yes."

"Okay. You go first. Lift a lid and then feed me what's

underneath."

He waited, listening as she fumbled over the metal covers, and then he heard one hit the floor.

"I didn't know what to do with it," she explained.

He grinned. She was getting into this game. "We'll pick it up later. Don't worry about it."

Her hand hit him mid chest and then climbed slowly toward his throat and chin. She put her palm on his cheek, and her thumb swept across his lips. He opened his mouth, and she pushed something rough coated into it. He moved it around and then bit into it.

"Chicken nuggets," he guessed.

"I have no idea. I can't see anything."

"Okay. My turn."

He felt around on the table until his hand hit one of the plates, then he moved his hand to the next one, then the next and lifted the cover. Whatever it was, it was kind of slimy. Shrimp maybe?

Reaching across with his other hand, he found her knee and grazed the outside of her thigh, over her hip and arm, across her shoulder to her neck, and up her throat to her lips, which were parted in apprehension or expectation, he wasn't sure. Sliding his thumb along the seam, he parted them farther and slipped the bite into her mouth.

He kept his hand on her jaw as she chewed then swallowed.

"Mmm, shrimp. My turn."

He wished he could see her and her reactions. The soft sighs and throaty moans she made when he fed her something she liked drove him nuts. They were the same sounds she made during sex. Three bites later, he ripped his blindfold off to find Lucy watching him.

"You cheated," he declared.

She laughed, tipping her head back. "I just took my

blindfold off. I swear. And shut up. You cheated too."

"I can't help it. I'm starving." He placed both his hands on her knees and leaned in. "Feed me."

She stared at him for a moment and then reached out without seeing where her hand landed and grabbed something. "Here." She pressed a mini quiche into his mouth, filling it, and watched as he chewed and swallowed.

"My turn." He picked up a strawberry that was almost too large for her and slipped it partway through her lips. "Bite."

He bit into the other half of the strawberry and their lips touched briefly before he pulled away.

Lucy couldn't believe what they were doing. This had to be the most erotic thing she'd ever done. They took turns feeding each other until she was so full she thought she'd burst.

"That was fun, but I can't eat another bite," she told him. "Is there any more wine left?"

He lifted the bottle and poured the last bit into her glass, then tipped it upside down in the bucket. Settling back into his chair, he took a sip of his wine. A comfortable silence settled over them as they gazed out at the view of the Dallas skyline.

He was the first to break it. "Can I ask you a question?"

"Sure."

"What do you want to do?"

"Tonight?"

"No, with yourself. Have you ever thought about going back to school and finishing your degree?"

She couldn't believe he remembered her talking about doing just that when they'd been together the first time. Quitting school was one of the things she regretted most in her life besides her marriage to Kevin. Since then she'd hardly been able to think past next week let alone a year or more from now. "I used to."

"You could do it. Go back to school I mean. You've got Sam to watch over Poppy now and no job. The corporate things I'd need you for would mainly occur in the evenings. You have days free to take classes if you want to."

"I guess I hadn't thought it would be an option, so I haven't given it any consideration."

"What kinds of classes would you take? What are you interested in?"

"You ask really tough questions."

He shrugged a shoulder. "Not that tough. What did you want to be when you grew up?"

"Well, when I was four, I wanted to be a ballerina. You've seen my dancing skills, so that would've been a bust. Then when I was twelve I was crazy about horses, but I don't think you could make a living at that. I went through a series of occupations—veterinarian, singer of a rock band, interior designer, firefighter—"

"Firefighter?"

"I was dating a guy who had just started at the academy so..." She shrugged. "I did look into nursing a couple of months ago, but I didn't have the funds for school, so that was out."

"You have the funds now."

"No, you have the funds."

"Lucy, we're married. What's mine is yours."

"That's a fair trade for me, but not for you. Besides nursing school would take longer than our marriage would last, and then what?"

He looked down at his hands folded in his lap. "Yup. One year. That was the deal."

"I think I'm ready for the Jacuzzi now." She stood up and adjusted her robe.

He grabbed the belt of her robe. "This year can be anything we want it to be. Anything at all." He tugged, making her move toward him. "Sign up for that school if that's what you want, darlin'. If you like, you can think of it as my parting gift to you. I won't be the reason you don't follow your dreams. I won't hold you down or hold you back. Ever."

"You don't have to—"

"I know I don't." His voice held a quiet sort of anger. He jerked on her tie again, and she had to grab it with both hands to keep her robe from popping open. "I want to. Let me."

"Cal." Lucy searched his face for some kind of clue as to what was going to happen next. Knowing what was coming had saved her more than a time or two when things got angry and out of control.

"Do you think just once you could let me give you something without questioning my motives?"

She gripped her robe tighter, the familiar spiral where everything suddenly turned against her reaching out for her. "I'll do whatever you want, Cal."

"Whatever I want?"

She nodded.

"Sit down."

She made to go back to her chair, but he still had a hold of her.

"On my lap." He patted his leg with his free hand.

She watched him, wondering what he was playing at. He'd become all serious and calm as though he was asking her to do something simple or this was some kind of test. He made no move other than the smile that crept slowly across his face.

"Sit down, darlin'."

She lowered herself onto his leg, balancing so she could pop up at any moment.

"Now, put your head right here." He patted his shoulder.

"Why?"

"You said you'd do whatever I wanted. I want to hold you, darlin'."

She lowered her gaze to his shoulder and then felt herself leaning in. His arms came up around her, loose and comforting. It had been a long time since a man had held her. She settled against him, placing her hands on his chest. This was a dangerous proposition. This hope that unfurled slowly, uncertainly.

She trusted him, she suddenly realized. And that was the most dangerous thing she could ever do. Because if she trusted him, she'd let him in. Once he got in, she didn't think she could ever get him back out.

EIGHT

She tucked herself in tight, bringing her legs up and curling into him like a child. Cal held her tighter, dropping his cheek to the top of her head. She was so warm and good smelling. And soft, so soft. Her skin, her hair, her lush curves pressed against him. He inhaled, taking more of her in as though he needed her very essence to survive.

He was an idiot to think that he could ever let her go again.

"Cal?"

"Hmm?"

"Thank you."

"What for?"

"The wedding was really beautiful. And my dress... I've never worn one like it. And the flowers and the decorations... It was all perfect."

"I'm glad you liked it since you picked everything out."

She nudged his shoulder. "You know what I mean. None of it was necessary."

"Darlin', it was all necessary. And worth it."

"It wasn't, but thank you for it anyway."

"You're welcome."

She yawned. "I think I'm too tired for the Jacuzzi."

"Me too. Seems a shame not to use it though. Maybe tomorrow before we leave."

"This is the first time I've ever been away from Poppy. I'm not sure how much longer I can bear to stay away from her."

Running a hand over her hair, he chuckled. "Well then, we'll just have to come back some other time."

Her little hand snaked up and around his neck to play with his hair as he was doing with hers. "Seems kind of extravagant."

"But fun."

"Yeah."

She snuggled deeper into him, and her other hand came around his waist to his back. She was getting bolder. He could sit like this with her forever.

"Cal?"

"Yes, darlin'?"

"Could I…?" She let out a breath that blew hot against his neck. "Could I ask you a favor?"

"Sure."

"Stop sneaking Poppy that sugary cereal. I can't get her to eat the good stuff anymore."

He pulled back to look at her. "How did you know?"

"I can smell it on her, and the other day her cheek was still sticky from it. It's not good for her."

"I was bribing her to like me, but I'll stop."

"You don't need to bribe her to like you. She likes you almost better than she likes me."

"Then the bribes worked. What can I bribe *you* with?" He was close enough to kiss her. All he had to do was lean down a bit.

"You don't need to bribe me either."

"You mean you already like me?"

"Maybe more than I should."

His gaze dropped to her mouth. "How much do you like

me?"

"Definitely more than I should."

"Enough to let me kiss you?"

"Yeah," she whispered. "Just enough."

He lowered his mouth to hers. Her hand at his nape encouraged him to get closer. Then they were kissing. A light, testing kind of kiss as though they were learning each other all over again. And maybe they were. They definitely weren't the same people they'd been seventeen months ago. He kept it easy, enjoying the feel of her at this new angle and the way she sifted her hand through his hair. Everything felt new and a little scary. A fragile kind of peace was building between them. He'd have to step lightly, careful not to trample it the way he'd so carelessly done before.

Reluctantly breaking the kiss, he glanced down at her to gage her reaction. Her lids stayed closed a moment and then she sighed.

"You're really good at that," she whispered, her eyes fluttering open.

Her compliment made him grin. She always kept him a tad off balance.

"So are you," he answered back.

"We should do that more often."

"I agree. We can do it as often as you'd like."

"I think I should go to bed now."

"All right."

She disentangled herself from him, stood, and adjusted her robe. Tucking her arms around herself tight, she looked at him as though he was an unsolvable puzzle. "I'm not sure what to believe here."

"What do you want to believe?"

"I don't know."

"I think you do, but you're too afraid."

"I'm not afraid."

"Then what are you?"

"Cautious. If it was just me…"

"If it was just you, what? What would you do?" he challenged.

She shifted her stance, flipping her hair over her shoulder. "I'd ask you to come to bed with me."

"But you won't because of Poppy."

"If I'm wrong—"

"You're not wrong, and you're not asking me to go to bed with you because you're afraid."

"I am not."

"What are you scared of? What's going to happen if we sleep together?"

"I might start believing in you again."

"You're already starting to believe in me or else you wouldn't have brought up taking me to your bed."

"Never mind. Forget I said anything."

She turned to go, but he grabbed her arm. Trying to pull out of his grip, she shrank from him, a desperate, wide-eyed look on her face.

"Lucy, stop. Settle down."

"Let go of me."

"Okay."

He released her, and she stepped out of his reach, staring at him as though she was trying to anticipate what he might do next.

"When I reach for you—" he began in the gentlest tone he could manage with the rage he felt against her ex boiling just below the surface. If he ever got a hold of that asshole… "—it will be to stroke you, to soothe you, or to get you so hot for me you can't think of anything but having me buried deep inside you. It will never be to hurt you."

"I don't know what you're talking about."

"I've hurt you in a lot of ways, Lucy. I know that. I

have to live with it and find a way to make up for it. But I will never harm you physically. Ever."

"I know you won't."

"Good." But she didn't, not really. It was more about her wanting to believe than the actual believing of it. But it was a start, a place for them to begin. "I swear to you, darlin', that I will do everything in my power to never hurt you again. And I want more than anything to accept your non-offer to take you to bed. You don't know how much I want that. But I won't. Not until we get some things settled between us that only time and new experiences can create."

"What kind of new experiences?" He could tell she was curious. And interested.

"The kind that make you forget and forgive. I'm going to earn your forgiveness if it's the last thing I do. And then you'll forget why you were mad at me in the first place."

"And how are you going to do that?"

"I'm going to woo you."

"Woo me. That's backward, isn't it? Seeing as how we're already married."

"I still have my work cut out for me though, don't I?"

She pressed her lips together. "Hmm."

"I'm up for the challenge."

"Why? I thought this was just a business arrangement. You're paying me to be your wife, for crying out loud. That's not exactly romantic."

"The idea was that I would help you and you would help me. Except you haven't cashed your check. Technically no money has changed hands. By the way, why haven't you cashed it?"

"I don't know."

"Maybe you see the same potential here that I do. Maybe you remember how good it used to be between us.

Maybe you want me in your bed so bad it's all you can think about."

"And maybe it would be a moot point anyway because your head would be too big to fit through my bedroom door."

Lucy was pretty sure this man had gone insane, and then he threw his head back and laughed and she *knew* he had. He certainly wasn't the same Cal she'd been with before. That Cal would've had her robe open and her begging for release within three minutes of her walking into the room. *This* Cal held her gently and asked to kiss her and woo her. She wasn't quite sure what to do with this Cal. The only thing she knew for sure was that she wanted to take him to bed and find out all of the other ways in which he'd changed.

"You are definitely right about that, darlin'. And that's what got me into hot water with you in the first place. But I'm here now, willing to try. What do you say, will you be my girl?"

"Are you asking your wife to go steady with you? You have gone crazy."

"Crazy about you. Come here and kiss me good night."

He slid his hand down her arm and tugged on her wrist. This time she didn't resist him. He brought her to stand between his legs. She put her hands on his shoulders and looked down into the wildest blue eyes she'd ever seen. She was crazy about him too, but it wasn't the same as it had been before. Back then she'd been crazy blind with need for him and just plain all around crazy blind where he was concerned. She wondered if maybe he was more dangerous to her now than he'd ever been before.

He put his hands at her waist, then smoothed them up her back. "Give me a kiss good night." His voice held all the wicked promise of the old Cal, but his words were the gentle promise and boast of the new Cal.

She leaned down and gave him a chaste good-night kiss. He didn't pressure her for more and let her slip away from him toward her bedroom.

"Good night."

"Good night, darlin'."

NINE

It had been two weeks since her husband had asked her to go steady with him and had started to court her. They'd been on seven dates, and he'd come to the door with flowers each time. At the end of the night he'd escorted her to her bedroom door, kissed her good night and then walked across the hall to his room. It was very strange and kind of thrilling.

It also made it hard to keep her mind on planning her first dinner party as Mrs. Cal Sellers. The caterer had already had to break her out of her daydreaming twice during their meeting, and even now Lucy struggled to follow what he was saying. Something about aperitifs and amuse-bouches, whatever they were. She nodded along, trusting that this man knew more about fancy dinner parties than she did. After all, it was his job.

"Mrs. Sellers?"

Lucy looked up to find their housekeeper in the dining room doorway. "Yes, Hazel?"

"There's a delivery at the gate. Were you expecting it?"

"What kind of delivery?"

"Flowers. For you."

"Oh. No, I wasn't expecting it."

"From your husband?" The caterer winked.

"Probably. The flowers for the party aren't supposed to arrive until day after tomorrow, right?"

"Correct."

"Should I let them up?" Hazel asked.

"Yes, please. Thank you, Hazel."

"Now about the table décor," the caterer went on. "I think a long, low centerpiece would set things off nicely. Here's a photo of what I had in mind." He handed her his tablet to look at.

"Oh, that's pretty. Yes, that one."

"Excellent. Then we're all done here."

He packed up his things, and she showed him to the door, uncertain of everything she'd chosen. She wanted the party to be perfect and for Cal to be proud of her. He'd more than held up his end of their bargain, and now she was going to play hostess to the man whose company Cal wanted to buy. The company that could mean millions to Sellers Investments.

As the caterer went out the door, the deliveryman came up the walk carrying the largest bouquet of roses Lucy had ever seen. It was a wonder the man could see where he was going. Cal had outdone himself this time.

"Sign here." He thrust a clipboard at her.

She started to sign her name, except it was the wrong name on the order form. "There must be a mistake. My last name's not Walker, it's Sellers."

The deliveryman thrust the flowers off to the side and grabbed for her, pulling her through the doorway. He put a hand to her throat and pinned her up against the house. "Your name will always be Mrs. Kevin Walker no matter who you spread your legs for."

The shock of seeing Kevin was eclipsed only by the sheer terror of his fingers digging into her windpipe. She couldn't move, thrust back to the days when she lived under his brutal hands and the pain he could inflict.

His grip tightened on her throat as he lifted her. "You're a whore."

She fought for air, her hands coming up to pry at his, her legs scrambling for purchase. He shoved a hand between her legs and squeezed. Spots danced in front of her eyes. She reached out blindly, trying to get at him, and caught him in the face, raking his cheek with her nails. He howled in pain and released her. She slid down the side of the house.

"Bitch!" He smacked her face hard, knocking her flat.

She curled into a ball as he drew his foot back to kick her. Only the blow never landed. A grunt and sickening, bone-crunching sound brought her head up. Sam the nanny stood over Kevin, who writhed on the ground, covering his face with his hands, blood gushing from between his fingers.

"Are you all right, Mrs. Sellers?" Sam asked, keeping his gaze on Kevin.

Lucy put her hand over her stinging cheek. "Yeah. I think so."

"I don't care who you fuck," Kevin said, his voice muffled by his hands. "I want my daughter back."

"She's not yours." She staggered to her feet, the rage against her ex rising inside her. "She's mine. And you're not getting anything but the hell out of here."

"I'm calling the police," Sam said.

Kevin struggled to stand. "You're nothing but a bitch and a whore. I'm going to get my daughter back if I have to kill you to do it."

Lucy got as close to him as she dared. "You'll never get her. I'll kill you before you ever lay a hand on her."

He lunged for her, but Sam leapt, swinging his leg up and connecting with Kevin's jaw. Kevin folded and dropped to the grass, unconscious. Lucy glanced from Sam to Kevin then back again.

"Where'd you learn that?"

"Nanny school."

"You did not learn that in nanny school."

Sam shrugged, then bent to turn Kevin on his stomach and secured his hands with a zip tie. Not exactly normal nanny paraphernalia. Kevin was still out when Sam rolled him onto his back again and checked his pulse.

Sam looked up at Lucy. "You should get some ice on that cheek. It's starting to swell. And you've got a little blood right here." He motioned toward the corner of his mouth.

She wiped at the blood and put her palm to her hot cheek. It would probably bruise too. How was she going to explain this to Cal's business associates two nights from now? How was she going to explain this to Cal?

"We've got a little situation here," Sam said into his phone. "I've got it handled, but you may want to see about your wife."

Lucy waved her hands at Sam. "Don't tell him," she whispered. "I'm okay."

Kevin had invaded their home. The police had been summoned. This was not part of their bargain. Their arrangement might have started out as a business deal, but it was starting to become more than that. The last thing she wanted was for her past with Kevin to invade her present with Cal.

"Her ex showed up at the house," Sam said into his phone. "By the time I heard what was going on he had her on the ground."

Lucy glared at Sam as best she could with one partially swollen eye.

"He got her in the face before I could stop him. He's out cold and cuffed right now. The police are on their way." He held his phone away from his ear. She could plainly hear Cal's string of expletives from where she stood.

When there was a pause, Sam put the phone back to his ear. "No, sir. But she could use some ice, and she'll probably have a shiner." He held the phone out again. "Yes, sir. I understand. I'll give you a full report when you get here." He hung up. "You should get that ice," he said to Lucy.

"You're not really a nanny, are you?"

"Yes, ma'am, I am."

"Then you're not *just* a nanny. What else are you?"

"British Special Forces. Formerly." He pointed to his cheek. "If you don't get that ice, I've been instructed to call you an ambulance. A bag of frozen peas works well."

Sirens wailed in the distance.

"Fine."

She stormed into the house and grabbed the next best thing—a bag of frozen corn wrapped in a towel. On her way back outside she caught sight of herself in the mirror in the entryway. Kevin sure knew how to cause the most damage from the least amount of effort. But then he'd had a lot of practice. She put some spit on her finger and wiped at the blood at the corner of her mouth. She was going to be bruised from her jaw to her eye. His ring had caught her mouth and split the skin, but it wasn't as bad as it could've been. Thank God Sam had been there to stop it.

By the time she got back to where Sam stood over a just-coming-around Kevin, the police were rolling up. They took her and Sam's statements and put Kevin in the back of one of the cruisers.

She was finishing up with one of the officers when Cal arrived. He took one look at her and stalled. His face went pale. She had the makeshift ice pack over the worst of it. Wait until he saw what was underneath.

"That's my husband," she told the officer when they stopped him at the edge of the walk. "Please let him through."

Cal approached her slowly, his gaze never leaving her. He looked...heartbroken. There was no other way to describe it. She'd never seen that expression on him. Tears pinched the backs of her eyes. He gently drew the ice pack down.

"Oh, darlin'," he breathed.

That was all it took. She burst into tears. He wrapped her in his arms.

"I'm sorry," he kept repeating. "I'm so sorry."

She gripped the back of his jacket and held on. This was all her fault. She'd brought this to his home—the police, the drama. It would probably make the news. Not exactly the kind of family values Cal wanted to present.

She pulled back to look up at him. "No. I'm sorry. I brought all of this to you, to your home—"

"Shh. This isn't your fault. I knew what he was capable of, and I didn't adequately protect you."

"What do you mean you knew?"

"Mrs. Sellers," one of the officers interrupted. "Here's my card with the case number." He handed her a card. "If you have any questions, give us a call."

Cal glanced up past the officer and spotted her asshole ex in the back of one of the police cars. Before he thought to do it, he was moving in that direction. He'd never wanted to hurt someone so bad in all his life. He came right up to the car window and banged on it with the side of his fist. He wanted this asshole's full attention.

"You ever touch my wife or come within a thousand feet of her again and I will end you."

"Sir. Back away from the car," one of the officers warned.

"Cal, don't," Lucy pleaded, pulling on his arm. "He's not worth it."

Cal stepped away.

"She's a whore," Kevin yelled. "She's always been nothing but a whore."

Cal went for him but was held back by Sam and one of the officers. "I mean it," Cal shouted. "Stay away from her." He jerked out of their grasp. Wrapping an arm around Lucy, he eased her up the walk and into the house.

He brought her into his office and closed the door behind them. Leaning back against it, he tipped his head up and closed his eyes. The bastard got to her. It was all he could think about the whole way home and then when he saw her and the damage to her face... Son of a bitch! He had one job, *one*—to protect her—and he'd fucked it up.

"I'm sorry." He opened his eyes to look at her.

"It's my fault. I wasn't paying attention... I never dreamed he'd come here. I'm so, so sorry. I should've told you about him. This wasn't part of the bargain, all this chaos and the publicity... Oh, Cal, I'm so sorry. Your dinner party... I've ruined everything." She burst into tears again, and it was like someone twisted a knife in his chest.

He went to her and held her. "No, darlin'. This is my fault, not yours."

She looked up at him with her watery eyes and half-swollen face, and he wanted to punch something. "What did you mean outside when you said that you knew what he was capable of? I never told you anything about him. In fact, now that I think about it, you've never asked about him or my time with him."

"Why in the hell would I want to hear about you and another man?"

She pulled away from him and wiped at the tears still falling down her face, each one like acid on his heart.

"You're avoiding my question, and I know why. You

had him investigated, didn't you?" Her expression changed from disbelief to anger. "Oh, my God. That's why you hired Sam—to protect us. I know he's not just a nanny. He's Special Forces, for God's sake. Well, let's have it." She flung her hands out, then crossed her arms over her chest. "All of it. What do you know?"

"Now, darlin'." He tried to soothe her, his mind running through what needed to be done to insure his wife and daughter's safety. "This isn't the time to hash this out. I need to get Lucas on the line so he can get his guys down here to rework our security."

He'd hire four, no six guards around the clock, with a new security procedure for anyone trying to get through the front gate. Walker had gotten past it too easily. If he could, then anyone could. He'd promised her they'd be safe here. They weren't. None of them were. He moved toward his desk to make a list of everything they were going to need.

"Cal Sellers, you stop avoiding my question and answer me right now!"

He pulled up short and turned toward her. "Fine. You really want to know? Hell yes, I had him investigated. You were a cagey little thing when it came to answering questions about him. I asked you flat out why he didn't have visitation with Poppy, and while you didn't lie, you didn't exactly tell the truth, did you? Otherwise you would've told me about the restraining order and the multiple, *multiple* arrests for beating you bloody."

He stalked toward her, angry with her and her asshole ex, but mostly he was furious with himself. "I saw the pictures of you, Lucy. I *saw* them. So, yeah. I knew what I was getting into with you when I married you and I did it anyway."

Lucy couldn't believe it. She was such an idiot. Cal hadn't married her because he'd wanted her. He'd married her as some kind of community service penance. She'd carried the shame of what she'd been through for months and months, hiding the worst of it from everyone in her life including Lucas and Mi, and now because of Cal's need to know and control *everything*, her life had been broken open for everyone to inspect and judge. They'd look at her with pity in their eyes, and she'd always be a victim. She'd always be the woman who stupidly stayed with a man who beat her.

"You married me *anyway*?" She struggled to keep her emotions in check. "How good of you. You must have been pretty damn desperate to stoop so low. And sneaky too, going behind my back and getting Lucas to investigate me."

"Sneaky? Look who's talking? You've been hiding a hell of a lot from me, haven't you? You can't blame me for going out and getting answers on my own."

Her worst fears confirmed. They knew. They'd seen the photos of her at her very lowest. The degradation. How desperate and sad she must seem to them all now.

She fought back against the rising tide of humiliation the only way she knew how. "Did you ever think that I *have* to hide things from you because I never know when I'm going to walk in on you screwing your secretary?"

"Now we're getting down to it, aren't we? You still don't trust me or believe me when I tell you that I didn't screw her."

"Wanting to screw her and actually screwing her are *the same thing* in this case. If I hadn't walked in on you and stopped you, you would've *actually* screwed her. So why should I trust you when you'd throw everything away in an instant for a ride up a short skirt?"

"I've been here every day trying in every way I know how to show you that you can trust me. I'm not the same selfish asshole I was back then."

"Oh, yeah? If you're trying to earn back my trust, then why didn't you wait and ask me again later about Kevin instead of going behind my back? From where I'm standing, the new improved Cal looks and acts a lot like the old Cal."

He let out a breath, his shoulders sagging. "You're right. I might not have had sex with her, but that doesn't mean I wasn't working my way around to it. I was an asshole to do that to you. I ruined everything between us. It's my fault you ran off and married a man who abused you. And now here we are back together, and you're still getting hurt because of me."

She stared at him, trying to work out what to do with him. The old Cal would've never acknowledged his mistakes and failings. Maybe he had changed. Him acknowledging his part in what had happened between them forced her to look at what was happening between them now. He was right. She should've confided in him from the beginning of this whole thing. He'd offered her a way out, knowing that she came to him with more baggage than a commercial airliner. He'd made a bad bargain when he'd married her, but like he said, he'd known it from the start and had married her anyway. There had to be something recoverable in that.

"Huh." A corner of her mouth tugged up at the irony. "We're a messed-up pair, aren't we?"

Cal nearly dropped to his knees in relief. He hadn't totally screwed things up. She was offering him forgiveness or at the very least understanding. He grasped at it, afraid it would suddenly slip away. "Yes we are, darlin'. Yes we are."

"I'm going to get this out here and now because I don't know where any of this is going. You've made me feel special and cherished with your flowers and dates and kisses good night. I'm starting to believe in you, Cal

Sellers, and it scares the hell out of me.

"I couldn't take it if I walked in on you with another woman again. I don't know what I'd do, but I know I couldn't take it. You darn near destroyed me last time, and I ran to the first person who showed me any kindness. Out of the frying pan and into the fire. It was my choice to marry Kevin. I own my part in that. I'm trying really hard to trust you. I want to trust you, but you can't go off all half-cocked behind my back. If you want to know something about me, then you ask me."

"And you'll tell me the truth? No hedging or skating around or leaving out the parts you don't want to talk about?"

She hesitated, then nodded. "Yes."

"All right then. I won't go snooping around where I don't belong. Come here." He held out his hand to her, and she took it. "I'm going to say this to *you* right here right now. I take my marriage vows to you very seriously. There isn't a woman alive who could tempt me away from you.

"I know I've hurt you, and I paid the price for it when I lost you and had to stand in the back of that church, watching you pledge your heart and body to someone else. I swore if I ever got a chance with you again I'd be the kind of man you deserved and who deserved you."

He put a hand on her good cheek. "I want to kiss you so bad."

She leaned into him, pressing her body right up against his. He got so hard thinking about laying her down on the couch and showing her how much he wanted her and this second chance with her. But he didn't. Instead he waited, like a virgin kissing a girl for the first time, for her to give him permission. It was a humbling thing to have to ask his wife for a kiss and be unsure of her answer.

TEN

Lucy went up on her toes and brushed her lips across Cal's. He cupped her face so he wouldn't be tempted to let his hands wander over her. He wasn't kidding when he'd told her he liked the way she looked now—all womanly curves and large, full breasts. And her ass. My God, her ass. He wanted to grip it in both hands, haul her up against his erection, and show her what she did to him with nothing more than her body pressed to his and his lips on hers.

He broke the kiss and glanced down at his wife. She was so beautiful even with the swelling and the bruising that she took his breath away. "You're a gift I don't deserve. I promise to do my damnedest to make you happy. I want you. And if you ever decide you want me, I promise to make you glad you married me. As many times and in as many ways as you'd like."

"I don't doubt that since you've already proven yourself in that arena."

He grinned like the sinner he was. "And yet I still feel like I have something to prove with you. One of these days, darlin', one of these days, I'll make good on my promise, and when I do, you'll have made me the happiest man alive." He turned her face to examine the bruise just beginning to darken under her eye. "You need more ice. And a hot bath." He leaned in and placed a gentle kiss on her cheek. "I could kill him for laying a hand on you."

"Don't. He's not worth it."

"Did he ever hurt Poppy?"

"No. She almost never came to his notice except when he wanted to brag about her or use her to get me to do what he wanted."

He brought her hand up to his lips and kissed it. "Go up and take your bath. I'll look in on her. I need to make sure she's safe."

"Sam's with her, so I'm sure she is. But I know what you mean. I think I'll go up with you."

They walked side by side up the stairs, holding hands. He felt both excited and nervous around her as if he were on the verge of completing a huge merger that would make him richer than any man had the right to be. He risked a sideways glance at her. How could he have ever looked at another woman, let alone touched her? He'd been the biggest, most arrogant fool to walk the earth back then. He'd learned his lesson. He would do better by her. He was certainly willing to give it his all.

They found Poppy in the playroom with Sam, who was reading her a book. When they walked in, Poppy clapped her hands and broke out into a huge grin. For Cal. The air in his chest expanded, making it hard for him to breathe. She filled places inside him he hadn't known were empty. She was *his*.

"There's my girl." Lucy rushed over and scooped up her baby, showering her with kisses.

Sam got up from the chair and came over to Cal. "I'm sorry I arrived too late," he whispered. "By the time I got there he'd hit her in the face and was about to kick her."

"You stopped him."

"Yes, sir."

"Then you got there in time. I can't thank you enough, Sam, for saving my Lucy. I don't know what I'd do if anything happened to her or Poppy."

"I'll be giving a full account of what happened today to Mr. Vega."

"Could you include your security recommendations? I have some ideas of how we can tighten up, but you're more of an expert than me. I'd appreciate your suggestions."

"Yes, sir."

"Thank you. Why don't you go on downstairs and relax for a bit. You've earned it."

Cal was alone with his girls. He'd watched Lucy be a mother to their daughter many times over the past few weeks, but there was something about watching her now that made him imagine more babies with her. Another two or three, boys, girls, it didn't matter, as long as they greeted him the way Poppy did now, trying to leap out of her mother's arms toward him.

"Come here, sweet pea." He scooped her out of Lucy's arms and held her. "Did you miss me?"

"She could care less who I am when you're around."

"I believe your momma's jealous. Another female's captured my heart, and she just can't take it, can she?"

Poppy grabbed his cheeks so she could rub noses with him. It had become their thing.

"I'm the bringer of food and baths. You're the big giant plaything who sneaks her sugary cereal—don't think I don't know you still do that—and who gives her horsey rides and tickles her."

"Well, darlin', I can't help it if she likes me better."

"It's all that bribing."

"You do what works for you and I'll do what works for me. Why don't you go take that bath, and I'll keep working my wiles on Miss Poppy."

Lucy hesitated. Watching Poppy with Cal worried her. The more attached she got to him the harder it would be if she had to leave.

"All right. I won't be long," she said.

"We'll be fine. Go on." He picked up a book, sat down in the rocker with Poppy, and started reading to her.

As Lucy ran the water in the tub, she couldn't get the sight of Cal holding Poppy out of her head. It made her long for things that might never be. Poppy deserved a father who loved her and who would be there for her. In that regard she'd failed her daughter, she thought as she lowered into the steaming bath water. The first father she'd given her daughter had been neglectful when he hadn't been abusive and cruel. And now here was Cal wanting to fill the role that should've been his in the first place.

But Lucy still wasn't convinced that Cal had made a full one-eighty where women were concerned. She hadn't been joking when she'd told him his cheating a second time would destroy her. She'd been more than halfway to falling in love with Cal when she'd walked into his office that fateful afternoon and caught him between the legs of his secretary, her skirt hiked up, his tongue in her mouth, and his hand up her blouse.

She'd stumbled out of his office and down the hall with Cal on her heels. He'd finally caught up to her in the elevator, stammering excuses and mumbling half-hearted apologies. She hadn't believed a word he'd said then, but now…now she was starting to believe, and that was the most dangerous thing she could ever do.

Because if she believed him, she'd start to trust him. If she trusted him, she'd have to tell him the truth about what happened after she walked out of his office that day. And once it was out, there would be no going back.

With thoughts of Cal and Poppy tumbling around in

her head, she couldn't get comfortable in the tub, so she climbed out and toweled off. It had only been a couple weeks since she and Cal had started spending time together again in this weird married-but-not-quite-a-couple gray area.

She'd watch him when he wasn't paying attention and she'd remember the good times and what it had felt like to have all of Cal's attention. What it had felt like to have his hands on her…and his mouth, his incredibly talented, seductive mouth. He'd seduced her with words and then put all of it into action, backing up his boasts with skill.

The first time they'd slept together had been an accident. They'd been at a launch party for one of the products that would be featured on *Pleasure at Home*. She'd been with the show for a couple of years by then. When she bumped into him at the bar and he offered to buy her a free drink with a wink, she accepted. He was cute, and even though he was her boss's boss and therefore off limits, she didn't hide her interest in him. A couple hours later and they were slipping out the back door and climbing into his Porsche. He took her to his place. Probably to impress her. It had.

Before she knew it they'd been on the stairs to the second floor, ripping each other's clothes off. They'd made it as far as the landing and then he was on top of her, sliding into her, her legs wrapped around his waist. She'd never come so hard, so fast in all her life. Then he'd taken her back downstairs and fixed her an omelet. They'd done it a second time with her bent over the countertop and him driving into her from behind.

She hadn't gotten to see his bedroom until two weeks later. By that time they'd had sex on every available horizontal surface and even a few not so horizontal. It had gone on like that between them for months. He could hardly keep his hands off her. When she'd walked in on him with someone else, she'd been beyond shocked and humiliated. It had brought her world down around her. And then she'd met Kevin. He'd been everything Cal hadn't. Or so she'd thought.

Lucy changed into clean clothes and went down the hall to check on her husband and daughter. She found Cal rocking a sleeping Poppy. He hummed softly. She started to go into the room, but Cal's whispered words stopped her.

"If you were mine, I'd never let you go. If you were mine, I'd make sure you knew how much you were loved and wanted every day." He kissed Poppy's forehead, and Lucy's eyes filled with tears.

This was what every child should have, a father who loved her and wanted her. It was what Lucy should've had and what Poppy should've had all along. She backed out of the doorway, smothering a sob with her hand.

No matter what had happened between them, Lucy realized now that she never should've kept Poppy from her father and Cal from his daughter.

ELEVEN

How was she going to tell him after all this time?

Because she had to. She had to tell him. Not only had she promised him the truth, but she couldn't sit back every day and watch him care for and cradle his daughter and not tell him the truth. When she'd initially agreed to marry him, she was only thinking of keeping Poppy safe. She hadn't expected Cal to dote so much on his daughter. How could she? He hadn't mentioned children at all in the months they'd been together. The words marriage and family had never fallen from his mouth until that afternoon when she'd come to him in an act of sheer desperation.

She'd found out she was pregnant a week after walking into the nightmare in his office. She swore then that she'd never ask Cal for anything. Ever. And she hadn't until she had to ask for her old job back.

But now things were different. Cal was different. And her feelings for him, well, they'd changed too. Seeing him holding their daughter and wishing she was his was more than Lucy could handle. She'd tell him. Tonight.

Her mind made up, she dried her tears and took a really deep breath.

By the time she returned to Poppy's room, Cal had just

put the baby in her crib and was coming back out the door.

"Nap time," he said, with a proud grin. "How're you feeling?" He examined her face. "The swelling's not as bad as it was before, but you should still keep ice on it." He ran a light finger under her eye. "It's already purple. I hate seeing his mark on you."

"I'll be okay. But what about your dinner party?"

"Already postponed. You'll have to change the date with the caterer, but that shouldn't be a problem. There's something I wanted to talk with you about, but I have to get back to the office. Will you be okay?"

"I'll be fine."

He leaned down and kissed her on her good cheek. "I'll see you tonight."

He started for the stairs, but she called him back. "Cal?"

"Yes?"

"I was thinking of maybe trying option number twelve tonight."

"Option twelve..." Cal tilted his head to the side, hardly able to believe what he was hearing. He had no idea what option twelve was, but if she wanted it, then he sure as hell would give it to her. "Oh. Is that right? And just who were you thinking of trying it with?"

"My husband. If he gets home at a decent hour."

He walked back toward her. "I'll see what I can do for you, darlin'."

"You do that."

He gave her a real kiss this time, but not the kind he had planned for her tonight. This one was easy and gentle and full of promise.

"I'll see you tonight," she promised.

He reluctantly turned away from her and headed down the stairs. As much as he wanted to stay, he had preparations to make and a mayor to call about a certain suspect that had been taken into custody today. He also had a surprise up his sleeve for Lucy, one he hoped she would agree to. There was no way he was going to allow what happened today to ever happen to her again.

He stopped to thank Sam one more time for saving Lucy, then left for his office. First order of business: call Lucas. Next order of business: look up option number twelve.

中

Cal spent the rest of the day working his tail off to get everything done that needed done so he could be home at a reasonable time. While option twelve didn't have the same flare as eleven and thirteen, it was still miles away from where he and Lucy were right now. He'd take whatever she was offering. He hoped she would be just as amenable to his suggestions.

That afternoon he'd purchased a handgun for Lucy and arranged for shooting lessons. That way if she was ever attacked again, she would have a way to protect herself. He'd do everything in his power to make sure that asshole kept as far away from his family as possible. To that end, he'd had a long talk this afternoon with the mayor about the need to crack down on crime, especially domestic violence. If the mayor also happened to have a copy of the file Lucas had given him on Lucy's case, well, that might just light a fire under his ass.

Cal drove through the gates of home, looking forward to seeing his family. His family. Who would've thought old rabble-rousing Cal would be looking forward to getting home to his wife and daughter? Poppy had charmed him almost as much as her mother. He adored that little girl. Who could've predicted it? He'd always liked kids…in small doses. But Poppy was different. Everything she did impressed him. Maybe he'd come to that point in life where he wanted a wife and children.

The good Lord knew he was done with the bachelor life and had been for sometime. Now he had Lucy and Poppy to fill the nights he would've spent home alone. He parked his car in the garage and headed into the house. The first thing he heard was Poppy crying. Screaming actually. He dropped his briefcase and tore up the stairs.

Lucy held Poppy's stiff little body as the child reared her head back and wailed.

"What's wrong with her?" he asked, the panic in his voice making it too loud.

"Ear infection. I think. This happened once before. I called her pediatrician, but she hasn't called me back yet."

"Can't you give her anything?"

"I gave her some infant pain medication, but it hasn't kicked in yet, poor bug." Lucy rubbed the baby's back. "I know it hurts, precious." Her cell phone rang.

Cal held his hands out. "Let me have her. You answer that. And it better be that damned doctor." He took Poppy from Lucy and put her to his shoulder where she always seemed to like it best. "There now, sweet pea. I've got you. She's burning up," he told Lucy.

"Fever. I'm going to take this where it's quiet. You sure you got her?"

"We're fine. Go on."

He walked back and forth, rubbing Poppy's back and trying to soothe her. He got her quieted down to long, pitiful moans interrupted by hiccups that tore at his heart. She was so hot and sweaty that she'd soaked his dress shirt. Her red curls lay flat to her head. He kept walking with her, and she eventually fell asleep. He eased down into the recliner and closed his eyes.

Hearing her screams had scared half a year off his life.

Forget the diapers and nighttime feedings. This had to be the worst part about having a child—seeing them suffer and not being able to do a damn thing about it. He didn't think he'd ever felt more helpless, except for when he'd come home and seen the damage on Lucy's beautiful face.

He settled Poppy in the crook of his arm and gently rocked her. Poor little darlin'. Tiny beads of sweat dotted her forehead and pink cheeks. He pulled a blanket through the slats of her crib, then draped it gently over her, worried she'd catch a chill from being wet.

She looked so much like her momma and—he had to admit—her daddy was in there too.

Lucy came into the room. "The doctor's calling in a prescription. Will you be all right if I go run and pick it up? Or should I have Sam do it?"

"They'll probably want insurance information. Why don't you take Sam with you to the pharmacy? And here—" He gently leaned forward and pulled his wallet out of his back pocket. "Here's your and Poppy's new insurance cards."

She opened her mouth to say something, then closed it and stood there blinking at him.

"Something wrong?" he asked.

Lucy didn't think Cal had ever been any sexier than he was in that moment, cradling his sick daughter and talking about things like insurance cards. The man she was looking at now was not the man who'd knocked her up and then thrown his secretary onto his desk. No, this was the kind of man who would stick around, the kind of man who loved and took care of his family.

"Thanks," she said around the tear-filled bubble in her throat. "I'll be back soon. Call me if you need anything."

"Will do."

She left the bedroom, knowing her daughter would be taken care of. Throughout her trip to the pharmacy with

Sam she kept going over her decision to tell Cal about Poppy and what his reaction might be.

It was a strange and exhilarating feeling to have a potential partner to parent with. She'd been on her own for so long it was going to take her a while to adjust. She wondered how Cal would take the news that he was a father. Was he only enjoying playing at being a daddy, or was he developing feelings for his daughter? When he found out he was a daddy for real, would he stay around or would he leave?

She guessed the only way to be sure would be to tell him. Once it was out, she'd know where she stood and could make better decisions for her and Poppy. Either way they had their deal for a full year. By that time Poppy would be nearly two years old, and Lucy would have a tidy nest egg put away. She supposed she could ask Cal for child support if she had to. He'd pay to keep it hushed that he had a child if he didn't want Poppy in his life. If that was the case, they were no worse off than they were now.

It all seemed so logical. So why was she holding out the hope that Cal would want to keep fathering his daughter? And then the second, smaller hope that she and Cal would stay married and live happily ever after?

Now there was a dream.

She snorted, which drew Sam's attention in the car. "Something wrong, Mrs. Sellers?"

They were on their way home from the pharmacy. Lucy had picked up a few other things she thought she might need for Poppy.

"No. Just thinking. Can I ask you a question?"

"Sure."

"Do you have kids?"

He grinned. "Three. All boys."

"You like being a dad? I mean, it must be hard being

away from them."

"Best thing I ever did, and yeah, it's hard. But when we're together, we're really together, you know?"

"Yeah." She didn't, but that wasn't something she wanted to burden Sam with.

She stayed quiet the rest of the ride home. When she got there, Cal was in the same spot and nearly the same position as he'd been in when she'd left, eyes closed.

"Hey," she whispered.

He opened his eyes. "Oh, hey. I fell asleep. Did you get the medicine?"

She held up the bag. "I hate to do it, but we should wake her up and give her a dose so it can start working right away."

He looked down at Poppy. "Isn't there some kind of superstition about waking a sleeping baby?"

"You want her in pain any longer than she has to be?"

"No." He gently nudged Poppy. "Hey, sweet pea, time to wake up and take your medicine. Come on, sweets." Poppy started howling. "Now I see why they say that," he said to Lucy and then turned Poppy so Lucy could drop the medicine into her mouth. "That's my girl. She took it like a champ. Now what?"

"Now you get her to go back to sleep."

"Easy." He rose, lifting Poppy to his shoulder, and walked.

It took only a few minutes before Poppy was asleep again. Cal laid her gently in her crib and backed away.

"Now what?" he asked.

"Now you come with me. I have something I need to talk with you about."

TWELVE

Lucy grabbed the baby monitor, led Cal into her bedroom, and closed the door. She'd been so calm in Poppy's room, but now alone here with Cal, she was a bundle of sweaty nerves. Where to start? Should she build up to it or blurt it out? How did people do things like this?

She wiped her hands on her skirt. "Have a seat." She gestured toward the two chairs by the fireplace.

He sat down and propped a booted foot on his knee. He had a big wet spot on his expensive dress shirt from Poppy's sweaty little body, his hair was messed up and his eyes were half-lidded and sleepy looking. If she hadn't been so twisted up inside from what she was about to tell him, she might've suggested option number eight or twenty-one. They were similar, but option eight added a twist she'd been dying to try and... She was stalling.

She lowered herself into the chair opposite him. There was really no good way to say this so she just started.

"Back when we were together and I caught you with your secretary—"

"I said it before and I'll say it again—I'm sorry. And I'll keep on saying it until you believe it. I'm sorry."

"No, that wasn't what I wanted to talk about."

He shifted in his seat, dropping his foot to the floor and

leaning in. "What is it that's got you so upset, darlin'? Is it Poppy? Is she worse off than you thought?"

"No, it's not that either. Be quiet a minute and let me get this out, okay?"

He nodded but kept watching her with an intensity that was so Cal.

"I left your office that day, and I swore to myself I'd never see you again. No matter what. And then things got very bad for me financially. If it were just me, I'd have sucked it up, been homeless or gone to live in a shelter or something, but I had Poppy to think of. So I put my pride aside and I went to you for a job. I never expected…" her hand fluttered in a helpless motion, "…that you'd offer me marriage. I figured I had a fifty-fifty shot at getting my old job back. The odds were high enough that I had to ask. For Poppy.

"And then Kevin came back." Her eyes began to fill with tears, but she held them at bay. Cal started to say something, but she stopped him with her hand. "It was…still is a life-or-death situation. And again, if it were just me, I'd deal with him however I could, but there was Poppy. He only wants her now because she's the key he uses to get to me. He can't have children of his own, so he was willing to marry me. I thought I was doing what was best for everyone. He agreed to pass Poppy off as his own. But she's not. Kevin isn't Poppy's father. You are."

He was quiet so long, his expression unchanged, she grew nervous, waiting for an explosion that never came. "Aren't you going to say something?"

"Darlin', I know how to do math."

"What are you talking about?"

"I knew she had to be mine by the timing. Unless you were cheating on me, which I couldn't complain about, now could I? I figured she had to be mine. I am much relieved to know you didn't cheat and that she really, truly is mine."

She shook her head. "I don't understand. You *knew*? Why didn't you ever say anything? Why didn't you *do* anything?"

"What could I do? You married that asshole instead of telling me. Your thoughts on the matter couldn't be any plainer. You made it clear you didn't want me in your life let alone Poppy's life after what I did to you. And rightly so from where I was standing at the time. But I kept tabs and helped when I could. I paid for that private room and your expenses when she was born. She has a trust fund and a college fund. She is also listed as one of the heirs in my will, the main heir. I did what I could for her from the outside."

Her heart was pounding so hard she couldn't catch her breath. He knew. All this time. All the while she was taking the beatings from Kevin, he knew Poppy was his daughter.

He scooted forward in his chair. "But now I know her. I've held her and rocked her. She's mine, and I'm claiming her. I won't allow another day to go by in her life without me in it. I'm here, and I'm not leaving."

"So that's it. Everything's solved in your world."

"No, everything's not solved, but it's starting to work itself out."

"What about a year from now when this marriage is over and we go our separate ways?"

"If that's what you want, then that's what we'll do. If it was up to me, I'd make you my wife in every way—not just in name—and the three of us would be a family."

"Why?"

"Well, I thought that was fairly obvious."

"*Obviously* not."

"I'm in love with you." He said it so simply when nothing that had ever happened between them could ever be classified as simple, including her very complicated feelings for him.

"It took you walking out of my life and into the arms of another man for me to realize it. And I swore—" he took her hands in his, "—that if I ever got another chance with you, I'd do everything I could to be the kind of man you can trust and maybe love in return. And then you walked into my office in your tight blouse and even tighter skirt, flipping your hair over your shoulder, all but demanding that I give you your old job, and I knew. That was my second chance, maybe my only chance to have you back again.

"I know it's going to take time to earn your trust and forgiveness. Seeing you with that other man, imagining you with him, watching you create a family with him... I got back some of what I must have put you through, and it nearly brought me to my knees. In one stupid, thoughtless act I lost you and my daughter. I lost everything that mattered before I even knew it could matter. So now here I am getting to know my daughter and wooing my wife. And hoping I can win her back."

"I don't know what to say."

She truly didn't. His declaration left her speechless. Maybe there was such a thing as second chances and do-overs. If he'd been anything in the past few weeks, he'd been consistent, putting his words into action over and over. It was clear he adored his daughter, doting on her and stepping up to be a real father to her. Maybe they could work things out. Maybe she could trust him. Maybe, maybe, maybe.

"You don't need to say anything."

"But I do. When you talk like that, Cal, you make me want everything you said. You make me want to trust you again."

He grinned like he'd been awarded a prize. "I want to

kiss you so bad right now, darlin', that I don't think I could stop once I started."

"I'm not sure I'd want you to if you did. Come here, cowboy." She grabbed him by his still-damp shirt collar. "Kiss me."

Cal put his lips to hers. This kiss was like none they'd ever shared. Their first kisses had been feverish and hungry, their recent kisses had been tentative and testing, but this kiss...this kiss was sure and hopeful, and it outshone any other kiss. He dropped to his knees in front of her chair and brought her right up against his body, her legs on either side of his hips. The feel of her... There was no holding back. He let his hands wander, relearning her curves.

He trailed a line of kisses across her jaw and down her neck. She sifted her fingers through his hair and held him as though she never wanted him to stop. He made thorough work of kissing her, setting everything free that he'd kept pent up. He wanted her more than he'd ever wanted a woman in his life, more than the first time he'd had her. This was *the* first, the most important first. She was letting him back into her heart and maybe her body. He grew wild for her, desperate for the feel of skin on skin and her hands on his body.

Gripping her ass, he rocked against her. She worked at the buttons of his shirt. He followed suit, undoing the buttons of her blouse, exposing her an inch at a time until he was looking down at the creamy swell of her breasts spilling out of the cups of her bra.

He bent his head to her beckoning flesh, cupping her breasts in both hands. She'd always been more than a handful, but now after having his child, her body had become a lush wonderland of new curves to explore. God, he wanted her. He pressed his erection against her so she could see for herself how much. She answered with a moan and dug her heels into his backside, grinding against him.

He peeled back a cup of her bra and then the other, and her breasts popped free from their confines. Bending back, she guided him to where she wanted him. He was only happy to oblige, drawing her nipple into his mouth and sucking hard.

"Ahh," she gasped.

He wanted to be inside her so bad he thought he'd die before he'd get the chance. Slipping a hand between her legs, he felt how wet she was through her panties. He had to touch her, dip his fingers into her slickness. He slid his hand into the waistband of her panties, stroking into her with one then two fingers. She arched back farther as he worked her, drawing out her pleasure toward orgasm.

She began panting, and he knew she was close, so close. He drove his fingers into her as he wanted to drive his cock into her, over and over, not letting up until she broke on a low moan, clutching his head to her breast. He nuzzled her, working his way back to her mouth, and kissed her, a long, slow promise that this was only the beginning. There would be more, so much more between them.

"Cal?"

"Hmm," he answered as he kissed the slopes of her breasts.

"That wasn't in the option agreement."

"We'll add it." He moved his fingers inside her again. "How about number five? I'm feeling number five real strong, darlin'."

"Five?" She gasped.

"It's the one where I put my mouth where my hand is now."

"No. Just your hands. I want your mouth here and here." She cupped one breast and then the other, rolling her nipples between her thumbs and fingers.

"Jesus, darlin'," he breathed.

He gripped her panties and ripped them in half, exposing her. Running his hands up her pale thighs, he couldn't believe what a lucky bastard he was to have her wanting and willing. He widened her legs, using both hands on her, rubbing her clit and stroking her deep. Gazing up at her, he touched his tongue to her nipple. Her arousal was intoxicating, and he couldn't stop watching her reactions as he pleasured her. The sounds she made, the scent of her, he was sure he would come right here with his mouth on her and her hand in his hair, urging him on.

She brought her other hand up to her breast and rubbed her nipple. The first gasps of her impending orgasm drove him mad. This was his Lucy, wild and wanton and so uninhibited. He picked up the pace, slipping three fingers inside of her and working her until her hand fisted in his hair and she cried out.

He slid his fingers out of her and laid his head on her stomach. His dick throbbed so hard he thought it might explode any minute. If he touched her again, he'd lose it for sure. He couldn't hear her moan one more time without being inside her.

This time wasn't for him though. It was for her. He wanted to show her what he couldn't say, that he hadn't had a woman since he'd had her. That he'd loved her when he'd cheated on her, but instead of telling her, he'd sabotaged it because it scared the hell out of him. She scared the hell out of him. Her and her power to make him drop to his knees and beg her to take him back. And that he was weak, so very weak when it came to her.

He'd known about his daughter, but instead of doing what he normally would—barge in and take over everything—he'd let her go, thinking that was best for her and her mother. He'd thought about Poppy a lot, wondering what she looked like, how she was growing and if she was happy.

He hadn't lied when he'd told Lucy that he wanted his daughter. Whatever happened between the two of them, he'd be in Poppy's life. He wasn't letting her go. Ever.

Lucy stirred, sifting her fingers through his hair and scattering goose bumps over his skin. "Are we going to take this to the bed?"

He looked up at her, past her breasts spilling out of their cups, and he wanted to answer yes. God, yes. "I think," he said, kissing each of her breasts, "that we've made a very good dent in the options."

"What about you?" She tried to reach down and grab him, but he moved before she could put a hand on him.

"My pleasure, darlin', was in pleasuring you..." he ran a finger over one breast then the other, "...and finally seeing these..." he bent and licked one of her nipples and she shuddered, "...and putting my hands and mouth on them."

"But don't you want to have sex?"

"There isn't anything I want more in this world. And I mean *anything*."

She scooted up, trying to pull her skirt back down. "I don't understand."

The old him would've nailed her to the chair, but the new him wanted her to want him as much if not more than he wanted her. For that he would wait. Even if it killed him.

He stilled her efforts. "Do you know how incredibly sexy you are all laid out like a feast for a king? I could look at you like this all day long."

"But you don't want to have sex with me. Is this some kind of game?"

"I'm not playing here." He took her hand and put it on

his crotch. "Does this feel like a game to you?"

She moved her hand up and down, and he had to grab it between both of his to get her to stop. "Darlin', if you do that, I'm going to embarrass myself."

She retracted her hand and went back to putting her clothes to rights. "I don't understand you, Cal Sellers. I don't understand what this is or what you want from me."

"Did I leave you wanting? Because if I did, then you should shove your skirt back up, and I'll make you come so hard the staff will think I'm killing you up here." He rose onto his knees and bracketed her with his hands on the arms of the chair. "Don't think for one second, Lucy, that I don't want to fuck you into next week. And then when I'm done, fuck you again and again until my name is the only thing you say and my face is the only one you connect with pleasure."

She gasped, her eyes widening, and he thought for a moment that he'd scared her with his intensity. But no, she was *excited*. Her full breasts heaved, and her cheeks were flushed. She watched him with the same hunger he felt for her. Oh yeah, she was turned on.

"I'm going to think about the sound and feel of you as I jerk off tonight. And then tomorrow and the next day and the day after that, however long it takes until you trust me completely, I'm going to walk across the hall to your room and make you come over and over again. And then I'm going to go back to my room and get off on everything I've done to you. When the day comes that you trust me, that you truly believe I've changed, that's the night I'm going to take you to bed and make you my wife."

THIRTEEN

Every night for nearly a week, Cal had gone to Lucy's room and gotten her off in increasingly inventive ways. Then, just as he'd said he would, he'd gone back to his room and jacked off, remembering everything he'd done to her. This had seemed like a really good idea when he'd originally come up with it. But the memory of Lucy naked, legs spread, her face flushed, and lips parted chased him into the days. More than once he'd gone into his private bathroom in his office and gotten off thinking about the way she looked and the sounds she made when she came.

Tonight he had something special planned for her. Owning a company that sold adult toys had never been handier than it had in the past couple of days. One of the boxes he'd stuffed inside his briefcase for her contained something he wasn't sure she'd ever considered trying. Which made him want to try it all the more.

He found Lucy playing with their daughter on the living room floor, where Lucy helped Poppy pound colorful balls with a hammer until they dropped into holes, rolled down shoots, and popped back out again, eliciting a shriek of joy from Poppy. Dropping his briefcase on the couch, he sat on the floor next to his two favorite girls.

He bent and kissed the top of Poppy's head. "Hey there, sweet pea." Then he gave Lucy a long, lingering kiss. "Hello, darlin'."

She blushed and dropped her gaze to her lap. So she'd thought about him while he'd been gone, or at least the things he'd done to her the night before. He'd been quite inventive, if he did say so himself. It hadn't been a hardship to research different ways to pleasure a woman. He thought he'd been experienced in it before, but now every night with Lucy had been like a master class in getting a woman off, and he hadn't even scratched the surface of all there was to know and do.

"Hi," she said, her blush deepening. "I wanted to talk to you before dinner and Poppy's bedtime ritual."

"Go on."

"You don't have to come to my room tonight."

He frowned, his mood turning. He'd already failed in wooing his wife, and it hadn't even been a week. Where had he gone wrong?

"If that's what you want," he said, flattening his voice so she wouldn't hear his disappointment.

She watched him closely from under her lashes, her body stiff as though she was bracing for something. "It's just that I got my period today, and I'm not really feeling like doing, you know, things."

Oh, was that all? He suppressed a relieved sigh and leaned in to kiss her cheek. "Not to worry. Is there anything I can do for you, darlin'? Are you feeling very sickly?"

"I'm okay."

She kept watching him in that odd way, and then it hit him. She was expecting him to react the way her ex would. It brought back the memory of the night she'd agreed to marry him and her insisting on adding the last option to their option agreement, the one that made everything in it totally and completely optional. Goddammit. She was probably going to be on pins and needles the rest of the night, wondering if he'd keep his word or not, wondering if he was going to force himself on her. Fucking hell. His chest tightened, thinking of everything she'd been through, and it got hard to breathe, like he'd been punched in the gut.

He traced the barely there bruise under her eye. He wanted her to remember the difference between him and her ex. He would cut off his own hand before he'd ever put a mark on her like that asshole had.

"This is almost gone. I'll be glad when I can look at you and not see what that bastard put you through. I only hope one day you can look at me and not expect me to turn on you like he did."

"I don't."

"No, darlin', you do. But that's okay. It's part of your healing and the trust we're building between us."

"I don't know what to say when you say things like that to me."

"There's nothing that needs to be said." With his finger he stroked from her temple to cheek. "Eventually you'll just know..." he put his hand over her heart, "...and feel, and nothing will ever have to be said because it will just be. I'm not like him. I might hurt you in other ways, but I'll never hurt you physically, and I'll never, ever force myself on you."

"I know that. Don't be ridiculous."

He could've chased her denial until he cornered her and forced her to admit what she could hardly admit to herself, but that wouldn't get them anywhere. So he changed the subject.

"I brought you a present." He grabbed his briefcase.

"You don't have to get me things."

"This is really for me, but I'm hoping you'll like it too."

He opened the case and pulled out the *other* present he'd brought home for her.

"Cal, you did not get me a gun."

"I did, darlin', and I arranged for you to have lessons on how to load it, clean it, and shoot it. I want you to be able to protect yourself." He'd wanted to give it to her sooner, but it had taken awhile to find the right teacher for her, someone who would be discreet and understanding of their situation.

"I don't want a gun in the house with Poppy. What if she gets a hold of it?"

"Well, that will be part of your lessons—proper handling and safety."

She thrust it back at him. "No."

Instead of taking the box from her, he picked up their daughter and sat her on his lap. "I understand your position. I really do. But let me ask you this—what if Kevin gets in here again? What if I'm not home and Sam's not here? What if he gets past our security and there's no one to protect you—to protect Poppy—except you? How will you do it? Because I'm telling you, darlin', if that asshole gets in here, I want you to be able to put a bullet in him."

Lucy looked down at the box in her shaking hands and couldn't come up with an argument against it. If she'd had a gun the last time she saw Kevin, she would've used it. In a minute. Without a thought. She'd have shot him and kept on shooting him until she ran out of bullets, and then she'd beat him with the gun until her arm got too tired to swing anymore.

She clutched the gun to her chest. "When's my first lesson?"

"That's my girl. And this is my girl," he said to Poppy as he lifted her above his head, making her giggle.

Poppy sure did adore her daddy and had pretty much

from day one. Cal had taken to fatherhood as though he'd never missed a day in her life. More than once Lucy had wondered what would've happened if she'd told Cal about her pregnancy when she'd found out she was expecting. Where would they be right now? Would they have gotten back together? Did Cal resent her for the months he'd spent away from his daughter? Did he regret not being there for her birth?

"When's dinner?" Cal asked, drawing her out of her musings.

"In about fifteen minutes."

"I'm going to change and come back down to play with Poppy." He sat Poppy back down and put the hammer in her hand. She immediately went back to whacking a ball into the hole.

"And that's what I'm going to do when boys come knocking on my front door wanting to court you. Thump them upside the head." He ruffled Poppy's hair and then went upstairs to change.

Lucy couldn't help but stare at him as he walked away. The backside of Cal was one of her very favorite sides of him. She blushed all over again, remembering of all the things he'd done to her over the past several days. And not once had he asked for anything in return or made a move to do more than see to her pleasure. If she was honest, she'd admit that there'd been times when she wished he'd drop his pants and drive into her. She missed the feel of him on top of her and the way he'd watch as he thrust in and out of her.

She shook her head to stop those thoughts. She'd only frustrate herself since he wouldn't be visiting her tonight. She rubbed her tummy. Her cramps had gotten worse after having Poppy. The over-the-counter pain meds helped but didn't take away all the pain.

She thought about what Cal had said, that she

expected him to behave like Kevin had. He'd conditioned her to expect the worst, and she'd usually been right. Kevin hadn't cared if she was on her period, sick, or if she was in the mood. When she'd been on her period, he'd force her facedown on the bed or wherever they happened to be and did what he wanted. It had gotten to where she'd hated sex. Even when she hadn't resisted, Kevin had still managed to make her feel ashamed and dirty.

He'd complained about how fat she'd gotten after having Poppy, pinching her breasts and the rolls at her waist. She'd tried really hard to be a good wife to him, to be quiet and timid the way he liked. She'd dressed in the clothes he preferred and worn her hair the way he wanted her to. And it was never enough. The slightest thing would set him off, and then he'd start in on what a horrible wife and mother she was. The insults quickly escalated to threats. If she didn't move fast enough or address him with respect, he'd grab her and shake her, twist her arm behind her back or smack her around.

He *enjoyed* hitting her. When he'd come around later with his apologies, it was the look on his face as he'd hit her that helped her remember how much he loved to hurt her. She accepted his apologies and promises to never do it again, knowing he didn't mean them. Hit, blame, apologize. Over and over they repeated the same cycle. Until she'd finally gotten out.

She glanced at the box in her lap. She'd like to see the look on Kevin's face when she pulled a gun on him. She'd like to humiliate him and make him suffer the way he'd humiliated and hurt her. And then she'd put the gun to his head and blow his brains out. Just thinking about it brought a smile to her face.

Poppy crawled over and whacked the box with her hammer.

"No, no, sweet girl. No whacking mommy."

Cal came back into the room. "She's aggressive. I like that." He lay down on his belly on the floor to be eye level with Poppy. "But no hitting people. Unless they're boys wanting to take liberties before they've put a ring on your finger and made you their wife. Maybe not even then."

"I think having a daughter is karmic retribution for all of the liberties you've taken with women who weren't your wife."

"I think you're right. Add to it that my wife is the only woman I want to take liberties with and it's definitely ironic if not some kind of retribution."

"With all the ironic karmic retribution you've racked up, you're bound to have only daughters and no sons."

"As long as I'm having them with you, darlin', I don't care which I have." He grabbed a ball that had gotten away from Poppy and handed it back to her. "Here you go, sweet pea. I'd have ten daughters if they all came out looking like you," he told Poppy.

Lucy snorted. "You say that because she looks exactly like you."

"You think? I think she looks like her pretty momma."

"The only thing she got from me was my grandma's red hair."

"Nah, she's every inch you."

"Thank you for the gun."

He glanced up at her. "I'd rather give you diamonds or pearls, but that's not what you need."

"Is it wrong that I hope I get a chance to use it?"

"No, but honestly, darlin', I hope you don't. I hope that bastard stays locked up where he can't get to you or Poppy."

"Still." She lifted the lid of the box and was surprised at how utilitarian the gun looked. "It's kind of ugly."

"But effective, and that's what we're going for here."

She lifted it out of the box, weighing it in her hand.

"Not as heavy as I thought it would be."

"Easy there." He pushed the nozzle away. "First lesson in gun handling is to assume the gun's always loaded. It's not, but if you approach every gun as if it was, you'll be much safer."

She gripped it in both hands and aimed at an ugly vase across the room, resting her finger lightly on the trigger.

"Now that's about the sexiest thing I've ever seen," he said.

"I'm not going for sexy, I'm going for scary."

"Scary sexy then."

She sighed and put the gun back in the box. "Maybe I'll be more frightening once I've had lessons."

"No doubt."

FOURTEEN

Cal hung up the phone and let out a string of curses. Kevin Walker was free on a technicality. Free to come after Lucy and Poppy. Goddammit. He poured himself another whiskey. He hated having to tell Lucy she was back to looking over her shoulder and worrying about when and where that asshole would show up next.

Taking a sip of his drink, he leaned back in his chair to think. Lucy would start her lessons tomorrow, and the security measures he'd ordered from Lucas's company were in place, including an extra bodyguard inside the house and a patrol outside. What else could he do to protect his family?

His family. A few weeks into his marriage and he was already counting on it holding. He was crazy in love with his wife and crazy in love with his daughter and pretty sure he was just plain old crazy for having thrown it all away the first time around. This was his second chance, and he wasn't going to blow it.

He downed the rest of his drink. He couldn't wait for the time when Lucy slept beside him every night like a real married couple. The visits to her room had been fun, but there was something missing from their encounters. It was more than Lucy's fears and lack of trust, it was something deeper, something just beyond his reach.

He headed for the stairs and bed, checking in on Poppy as part of his new routine. She was curled up on her side, her little fist in her mouth. As he'd done so many times before, he thanked God for her and Lucy. They'd brought more to his life than he'd ever expected and turned his house into a real home. His world had been redrawn and colored. It was full in a way it had never been before. He didn't think he could ever go back to living without them.

Easing the door closed, he turned toward Lucy's closed door. He'd gotten used to being with her before turning in for the night. It was more than a physical thing between them. He'd already confessed his love for her, and even though she didn't say it, he had an inkling she might feel the same. As with everything between them, it was going to take some time and effort, but it was worth it. They were worth it.

He went to his room and made a valiant attempt to sleep. Although he'd slept in his own bed every night after visiting Lucy, tonight it felt big and empty, and he didn't have the smell of her on him or the memories of being with her to help him slip into slumber.

She'd made it clear that she didn't want him to visit her tonight. Their relationship was at a tipping point. She was starting to trust him and maybe even rely on him a little. While the sexual play between them had been hot, they left him feeling incomplete. It had nothing to do with his lack of physical release. He wanted more, something deeper. He'd give anything to have her snuggled up next to him right now. After a few more minutes he gave up and made the trek down the hall past Poppy's room.

He knocked on Lucy's door and waited for her to let him in. It was a little like looking over the edge of a cliff right before he jumped off. Maybe the bungee cord would hold and she'd let him in or else it would snap and she'd shut the door in his face.

The door cracked open and Lucy appeared, wearing plaid, flannel pajama pants and an oversized T-shirt. With no bra.

"Yes?" she asked.

"Can I come in?"

"Cal, I told you I'm not feeling well. Maybe in a few days."

"Is there anything you need?"

"No. I'll be fine. I just need some sleep."

"That's why I'm here. To sleep. That's all I have in mind tonight. I promise. It seems as though I've grown used to being with you."

Lucy watched him, rubbing her crossed arms. "You're drunk."

"I'm not drunk. I had a drink."

"I really just want to be alone. Can't you understand that?"

"If that's what you want, darlin'." He started to turn away.

"Wait."

He held his breath, watching her face as a myriad of emotions moved across it. He'd give anything to know what she was thinking. Would she take a chance and trust him? Had he shown her enough times in enough ways that she could?

"I can't give you want you want," she said.

"All I want to do is sleep with you. Sleep as in close my eyes and snore and when I wake up in the morning see your beautiful face on the other pillow."

She eyeballed him for a few seconds more before she gave a short nod. "Sleep. And that's all."

He would've whooped if he didn't think it would get him kicked out of her room. "That's all I've got planned." He walked to the foot of the bed. "Which side do you prefer?"

"This one." She went to stand on the side closest to the door.

He went to the opposite side of the bed. "Good choice."

This felt like a moment for them, one of those little things that changed everything after it. They both climbed in on their respective sides. He turned toward her, but she faced away, so he eased up behind her and put his arm around her.

Her whole body went tense, and it was as though her breathing had stilled too. He snuggled deeper into her, and she let out a sound he'd never heard her make before. Instantly he backed away to his side of the bed.

"What did I do?" he asked.

"Nothing."

"That was not a nothing response to a little cuddling."

"I don't like it...like that."

"You don't like cuddling like that?"

"I don't like anyone behind me." She scooted closer to the edge away from him.

He rolled to his back and stared up at the ceiling. It took a moment for him to think about what she'd said and not said. With Lucy it was one clue wrapped in a thousand layers of things she couldn't bring herself to say. She didn't like it like that with someone behind her. He suspected she wasn't talking about cuddling. She was talking about sex and sex in that position. He sifted through some of his most amazing memories of doing it with Lucy just that way, including one of the first times they'd been together. She'd liked it then, but now...

He turned his head and looked at her stiff form, curled up in a ball, clinging to the edge of the bed. This wasn't what he had in mind when he'd imagined sleeping with his wife tonight.

"Lucy?"

"What?"

"Will you turn over and look at me?"

"Either go to sleep or leave."

He took a deep breath. He couldn't put the question out of his mind, but at the same time he dreaded the answer. "Lucy, what did he do to you?"

"You know what he did. You saw the photos. And you saw firsthand what he can do."

"Why can't I cuddle you from behind?"

"Damn it, Cal. Shut up and go to sleep."

"Did he make you do things you didn't want to do? Sexual things?"

"Why do you want to hear about it? Is this something you're going to get off on later?"

He put a hand on her shoulder to try to get her to roll toward him. "I think you should go see a counselor, someone you can talk to."

"I don't want to talk about it."

"You'll never get past it if you don't."

"Stop pushing me on this."

"Darlin'—"

She whipped toward him so fast he jerked back. "You want to hear about how he raped me? Or how when he wasn't raping me, he was sodomizing me or making me suck him off? You want to hear about how it didn't matter what I did or didn't do, I would always have to put up with him sticking his dick in me whenever he felt like it? You want to hear about the time he made me strip naked in front of his friend and how he held me by the hair while he did me from behind and his friend stuck his dick in my mouth?

"You want to hear about the *other* photos he took of me? You want to know how he threatened to kill Poppy if I didn't do what he said? Or how he locked me in the house every day with no money, no phone, and no way out? You want to hear about how sometimes he liked to tie me up and—"

"Stop!"

"No, you wanted to hear about it, Cal, so here it is. All of the ugliness. He especially liked to force me facedown on the bed or the floor with my arm twisted behind my back—"

"No more, Lucy."

"That's why I don't like anyone behind me, cuddling or otherwise. You're just going to have to live with that and get over your hurt little feelings." She flopped back over and sucked in a sharp-sounding breath.

He lay there listening to her trying not to cry, his chest aching like he'd been punched in the solar plexus, feeling like the biggest ass in the world. He'd had no idea. No fucking idea at all about what she'd been through. He thought he knew, but his imaginings didn't come close to her reality.

He swiped at his eyes and climbed out of bed. What was he doing here, playing at being a husband to her? He knew nothing of her or how to help her. All the while he'd been thinking only of what he wanted, painting an image of them getting over Lucy's past like it was some little bump in the road. She'd been brutalized and raped. He didn't know anything about that, couldn't even come close to imagining it. All of his money, his power, his success was nothing, meant nothing.

He went down on his knees next to her. "I'm sorry." His useless platitude boomeranged around her and came back at him, echoing hollowly in his head. He cleared his throat and tried again. "What can I do?"

"Nothing. Go to bed." Her words were flat and unforgiving.

He laid his forehead on the edge of the bed. "Let me do something for you."

"There's nothing to do. It's already done."

He punched the mattress. Useless. He was totally useless to her. There was no fixing this for her. All of the money in the world couldn't take away everything she'd lived through.

He found her hand and slipped it into his. "You're safe here. You and Poppy will always be safe here. No matter what happens between us, you will always have a safe home. I promise you. You'll never have to be afraid again." He kissed the back of her hand and tucked it under her chin. "Good night." He started from the room.

Her hand snaked out and grabbed his leg. "Don't leave me."

The last thing she needed was another man, especially one as worthless and idiotic as him. "Lucy…"

"I've never told anyone any of that."

"Why did you tell me?"

"Because you asked. No one ever asked, they just assumed. He looks so normal. No one would ever believe."

"I believe."

She moved over to make room for him next to her. "Don't leave me."

How could he? How could he ever leave her alone and defenseless against that monster again? He got between the covers, careful not to touch her or move in any way that she might consider a threat. But then she did something so wholly unexpected it made his breath catch. She picked up his arm and put it around her, laying her head on his shoulder and snuggling up next to him. Why would she seek the touch and closeness of a man after what she'd experienced?

"Now you're going to treat me differently, aren't you?" she asked.

He shook his head, unable to get words past the clog in his throat.

"Liar."

Lucy wished she'd never said anything about what Kevin had done to her. She'd told Cal the worst of what had happened to her physically, but there were no words for what it had done to her on the inside. The past few weeks with Cal were the most normal—or as close to what she remembered of normal—she'd felt in a long time.

She disgusted him now. She knew it by the way he held himself away from her and how he wouldn't look her in the eye. He'd never see her as the Lucy she'd been before. He'd never flirt with her or touch her without thinking about what she'd been through.

"Kiss me," she dared. It felt as though everything between them was riding on what he would do next.

"Darlin'..."

She leaned up and looked down at him in challenge. "Do it. Prove to me that you don't see me differently now. An hour ago I wouldn't have had to beg you. You would've had me flat on my back, pressing your erection against my leg and making me feel how much you want me."

"I don't think—"

"That's the problem. You're thinking. I don't want thinking Cal. I want hornier-than-hell Cal. I want the Cal who pushed my skirt up and made me feel like a woman, not a victim."

Lucy slipped her hand in his shorts and stroked his flaccid penis.

He grabbed her wrist. "Don't."

"Cal, I want to."

"No."

She yanked her hand out of his pants, ashamed of her desperation and of what must think about her now. He didn't even want her to touch him. Would he ever look at her the way he used to? Or would he always see what she'd been through?

His gaze locked on to hers. "When I knocked on your door, I made a promise to you—no sex. Just sleep. I intend to keep that promise, Lucy, and not because of what you told me."

"I don't believe you."

"Believe this—I want you. Every minute of every day. What I don't want is for you to ever feel as though you have to service me."

"That's not what—"

"No? When I walked in here, you were very clear about what you wanted and what you didn't want. I'm pretty sure giving me a hand job wasn't on your want list." His tone softened as he stroked her cheek. "You want to know what I see when I look at you?"

She nodded.

"I see a strong, beautiful woman who went through hell and back. I see my wife and the mother of my child. I see a woman who has no idea how incredibly sexy she is. You have more power than you realize. He left you memories you don't know what to do with, but he didn't take anything from you. Not as far as I can see."

"You're just saying that."

"No. I'm not. You might not believe me now, but someday you will." He leaned in slowly and brushed a kiss across her lips. "I think it's time we do that thing I promised and go to sleep. Poppy will be waking up in a few hours."

He held out his arms for her, and she snuggled into his side with her head on his chest.

He turned out the light. "I love you."

She couldn't move, afraid to break whatever spell Cal was under. Of all the things he'd ever said to her, what he'd just proclaimed had to be the most hopeful thing she'd ever heard. She felt the weight of his words like a blanket wrapping itself around her and working through the cracks in the walls she'd built just to survive another day. He loved her. He really, truly loved her.

After a few moments his breathing evened out. He was asleep, so it was safe to say what she'd wanted to tell him for days.

"I love you too, Cal Sellers," she whispered.

She could've sworn she felt him smile in the darkness.

FIFTEEN

Over the next week Cal came to her room each night, knocked on her door, and waited for her to open it and invite him in. Lucy had gotten used to sleeping in his arms. She'd taken him into her body just about every way, but somehow taking him into her bed felt more intimate than any of the sexual stuff they'd ever done. By the end of the week she was ready to once again renew their sexual relationship.

So when he knocked on her door that night, she answered it completely naked. His mouth fell open, and he stared at her.

"Are you going to come in or not?" she asked, trying hard not to feel insecure.

Cal hadn't seen her fully naked since she had Poppy. There were other changes to her body like the burn on her shoulder and the scar on her hip where she'd gotten cut when Kevin had pushed her down and she hit the corner of the glass coffee table, breaking it. If she'd answered the door to him fully dressed, she might have chickened out.

He moved so fast into the room he created a breeze. She closed the door and leaned back against it, trying to strike a seductive pose, but she wasn't all that sure she pulled it off. He was still staring at her as though he couldn't stop. He *liked* what he saw. That revelation gave her courage she couldn't have mustered on her own.

"I was thinking," she said, sauntering toward him, "that we'd try option number forty-seven."

He bobbed his head.

"You don't have any idea what option number forty-seven is, do you?"

"No, but I like the way it starts out."

His words emboldened her further. "So I could tell you that it's the one where you stand on your head—"

"There's an option where I stand on my head?" He shook his head. "Never mind. I don't care." He shucked his boxer shorts and stood before her, ready for any option. "Where do you want me?"

"On the bed."

He backed up, never taking his eyes off her, until his calves hit the edge of the bed. He sat down. "Now what?"

She walked toward him, adding a little extra bounce to her step that made her breasts jiggle. He seemed to like that. A lot.

"Jesus, darlin'," he breathed, his gaze focused on her chest.

"Number forty-seven is the one where we can't use our hands."

He looked up at her then. "No hands? At all? What if I want my hands here?" He put his palms up as if to cup her breasts. She felt it as though he'd actually touched her. "What if I want to slide my fingers here?" He turned one hand and made a forward motion with two fingers pretending to stroke into her with them. She clenched her thighs together, his phantom touch making her throb for the real thing.

She put a knee on the mattress between his legs and grabbed her breasts, presenting them to him. "Are you saying that you only want to use your hands on these? I'm disappointed in you, cowboy. I thought you were more creative than that."

He leaned forward, his gaze on hers, and licked one of her nipples, giving her an exquisite chill. "Oh, darlin', if this is a challenge, I'm up for it."

"Mmm." She raised her knee, stroking up then down the length of him, eliciting a groan from him. "I see how up you are."

"Shall we make a wager?"

"On what?"

"Who will use their hands first."

"What's the wager?"

He leaned in and licked a circle around her belly button. She was already wet and dying for his hands on her, and they hadn't even kissed yet.

"Winner gets to pick the next ten options," he answered.

"Five."

He glanced up at her and traced the under slope of her breast with his tongue. She sucked in a breath.

"Not very confident, are you?" he asked.

"No, I'm curious to find out which option you'll choose first. I don't want to wait ten nights to find out."

"Darlin', I'd be glad to do all ten of your options tonight."

"Now who's not very confident they'll win?"

"Even the loser wins in this bargain."

She bent down, forcing him to lie back, and placed her hands on the bed on either side of him. Brushing her nipples up the length of his body from groin to chest, she answered, "True. It's a win/win wager."

"Jesus, darlin'. Do that again."

She obliged, pressing her breasts together and stroking his penis with them. He stacked his hands behind his head and watched her. On the third downward stroke she licked the head, swirling her tongue around it. He moaned and started to reach for her, but pulled the gesture before he touched her.

"Come here, darlin'. I want to kiss you."

"Mmm, not yet." She worked him some more until his hips lifted off the bed and he growled at her to stop. "What? Don't you like what I'm doing?"

"I want to be inside you when I come."

"But you were just bragging about doing it ten times tonight."

"I lied."

He somehow made a move with his legs that flipped her onto the bed next to him. In a second he was on her, pressing the full length of his body to hers, his mouth covering hers in a kiss that let her know how much he wanted her. She wrapped her legs around him, bringing him right where she wanted him most. He changed the angle of the kiss, and suddenly she was hot and desperate for the feel of him inside of her. She pressed her hips up then down, rubbing her clit against him. Close, so close.

He pulled his mouth from hers and looked down at her. "This is the stupidest option on the list. I want to touch you so bad. Here…" he rocked his hips, sliding himself against her slickness, "…and here." He bent his head and drew one of her nipples deep into his mouth.

She fisted the sheets as he kept up the pace and then she came, her arms going around him and holding him to her.

"You lost," he said, a self-satisfied smile lighting up his face. He rocked back and thrust all the way into her.

She froze, then pushed at him. "Get out! Get out of me!"

It took Cal a second to comprehend what she was saying. He was finally inside her, finally home. When her words hit, he pulled out of her and backed away, up and off her entirely until he was standing beside the bed looking down at her panicked face.

"What?" he asked. He'd been right there. What had he done wrong?

"You can't be inside of me like that."

Putting his hands on his hips and closing his eyes, he took a deep breath. In, then out, until he felt like he had some kind of control over himself and wouldn't jump back on top of her.

"Okay," he said after a while. "We don't have to do this." But Jesus God he wanted to. More deep breathing.

She moved...to the other side of the bed. The cold hand of despair reached down inside of him and fisted in his chest. He'd screwed this up. She'd trusted him and he blew it. Completely. He'd never get her trust back. He realized she'd pulled something out of the nightstand drawer and was handing it to him.

"—this on," she said.

He looked at what was in her hand. A condom. She wanted him to wear a condom. Relief flooded him first. He hadn't totally fucked this up. And then confusion set in. What in the hell?

"Why do I have to wear a condom? There hasn't been anyone else since you."

She withdrew her hand with the condom, and he could've hit himself upside the head for his stupidity. He should've just put the damn thing on and asked her about it later.

She got very nervous then, crossing her arms over her body. "I'm not going to be totally in the clear for another two months. Anyone I'm with has to wear one."

He couldn't wrap his head around what she was getting at. "Clear of what? Aren't you on the Pill or something?"

"Yes, but the Pill doesn't protect against HIV."

She said it like he was stupid or something, which at the moment he sort of was. And then it hit him, and he took a step back.

"Your son-of-a-bitch ex gave you HIV?"

"No. I don't know. I won't know for a while. I'm not in the clear yet. Neither is Poppy."

"Poppy...?" He reached a hand out to the bedpost.

"He was with his other wives. And while I was pregnant..."

She let that hang in the air between them. All of a sudden his legs wouldn't hold him anymore, and he collapsed onto the bed. Dropping his head into his hands, he cursed her ex and this whole fucking situation.

"I'm sorry," she said.

He could hear the anguish in her voice. None of this was her fault, and yet here she was paying the price. His idiocy in his office had led to this. All of it could be laid at his door. Once again she'd left him speechless and with the overwhelming feeling that nothing between them would ever be fixed. It certainly would never be the same as it had been *before*.

Before he'd thought himself cock of the block and thrown her away like she was nothing. Before she'd found out she was pregnant with his child. Before she'd married that bastard who had done unspeakable things to her.

"I wish you would've told me before you answered the door like that." It was all he could think to say because it would've changed everything.

"I'm sorry."

More deep breaths. He had to know everything now. Right now. He couldn't walk the minefield of her past without some idea of where not to step. "What else?"

"What?"

"What else do I need to know? What else haven't you told me?"

"That's it."

He nodded. Okay. He could handle this. He could handle anything for her.

"I take medication that reduces the chance that the virus will set in," she said. "But it doesn't protect you one hundred percent during sex or oral sex. So I have to ask you to wear a condom during sex and you can't go down on me and I can't give you a blowjob without protection. I can't do everything with you that I want to because he might've given me an incurable disease. I'm dirty." Her voice broke on the last word.

He glanced at her over his shoulder. It was the only movement he trusted himself to make.

She tried to cover herself with the edge of the sheet. "He made me feel dirty, and now I can't stop feeling that way. And I don't know why you want me. I'm not normal. I don't know if I can ever be normal. I'm just so tired of feeling dirty. I'm tired of being broken and dirty and ugly."

She sucked in a hiccupped breath. "And I hate the way you're looking at me right now because it makes me feel like you'll never look at me the way you used to. Always what happened to me will be all you see, and I can't take it. I can't stand that I have to make you wear a condom because being with me could kill you. And I hate that it could kill our daughter. And it's my fault."

Her words ate at him, digging at his insides until all that was left was a sharp ache for what she'd been through. So that was why she never let him go down on her. He'd figured it was a new aversion having to do with what her ex had done to her. The bastard had ruined so many things for her and here she was trying to take the blame for something that simply wasn't hers to take. "It's my fault."

"How in the hell is it your fault?" she asked, her misery

punctuated with anger. "Does everything always have to revolve around you?"

"If I hadn't been so stupid and fucked around with my secretary, all of this would never have been. All of it. So yeah, I'm taking the blame because it's mine to take."

He stood across the wide, yawning gap of the bed from her, knowing nothing would ever be as it once was between them. "I swore the day you walked out of my office that I'd be better and do better. But I can't stand what happened to you. I can't stand it. It's all because of me. And I try to find a way to fix things, but then I turn around and they're so much more fucked up than I thought, and I wonder if they can ever be fixed at all.

"And then you hand me a condom and tell me that what I set in motion not only hurt you deeply, but it could kill you *and* our daughter. And I can't fucking fix that!"

"Who asked you to fix it?"

"What am I supposed to do with it?"

"Live with it just like the rest of us."

He held out a hand. "Give me the condom."

She put a knee on the bed and tentatively reached across the space to lay it in his palm. He took it between two fingers and looked at it. It wasn't like he'd never worn one. Except for those couple of times with Lucy—one of which he guessed had led to Poppy—he'd always been diligent about protection. This condom represented more than their past, it represented a potential future of medication and medical tests and suffering.

All of Cal's imaginings of more babies with Lucy dried up along with the saliva in his mouth, and he couldn't form the words that would tell her it was okay. It would be okay. Because it wasn't fucking okay, and maybe it never would be.

He set the condom on the nightstand. "Do you still want to do this?"

"Do you?"

Yes. And no. He wanted to show her that he didn't see her the way she saw herself. But he didn't think he could get it up with everything she'd said still laid out between them. She could die. Poppy could die. He'd just gotten them back, and now he could lose them.

He realized she was waiting for his answer. She was still naked, standing on the other side of the bed, watching him with that look. He hated that fucking look almost as much as he hated her ex.

"Lay down," he ordered gently.

She hesitated.

"I won. I get to choose the next five options. Lay down on the bed, darlin'."

She did as she was told, watching him with wide blue eyes. He moved to the other side of the room, grabbed the desk chair, and set it at the foot of the bed. The perfect viewing spot.

"Stay there. I'll be right back." He went into his bedroom and grabbed the things he'd need. As he came back into her room, her gaze latched on to what he held in his hand. Her intrigued look surprised him. "You like this?"

"Yes."

"Do you want it?"

"Yes."

She sounded a little hesitant and a lot curious. Good. She was going to like what he had in mind for her. After all, it was the option she wanted to try the most.

"Fix the pillows so you're propped up higher," he told her. "That's good. Are you comfortable?"

She nodded. There was so much trust in her expression he nearly lost his nerve. He had to get this right for both of them and somehow live up to the faith she placed in him.

He set the one item on the bed next to her. Her gaze followed his movements. He leaned over her and gently placed the weighted nipple clamps on each of her nipples, adjusting the tension until she closed her eyes on a little moan.

He took his seat at the foot of the bed. Their gazes locked.

"Widen your legs," he commanded. "Wider. Now bend your knees. Drop them back so you're wide open. That's it. How're you feeling?"

"Good." Her voice was wispy now, full of expectation.

"*This,* darlin'…is option number thirty."

SIXTEEN

Option thirty.

Cal had asked her which options were her favorite on their wedding day, and Lucy had listed option thirty last even though it was the one she most wanted to try. After what she'd been forced to tell him, he'd chosen her favorite option instead of one of his own.

She lay on the bed naked, her legs wide for him. He'd placed a chair at the end of the bed, which added an extra dimension she hadn't anticipated.

"Do you trust me, darlin'?"

She nodded, her eyes wider than they'd been before.

"I'm going to sit here. I'm not allowed to move or touch you. I can't touch myself. And you're going to do everything I tell you to do, got that?"

"Yes."

"Good girl. Now we're going to start with you licking your fingers. Rub them over your nipples in small circles."

She did as he asked, her nipples pebbling

"Pinch them."

She took her nipples between her fingers as he'd commanded, feeling the pull deep inside. Arching her back, she pinched harder, letting out a moan.

"I love it when your cheeks flush like that. Do you like

it? Do you like touching yourself?"

"Yes," she panted.

"I can tell. Are you pretending it's me, or is it just you?"

"It's me."

"You're so damn sexy, darlin'. You're making me so hard. Feel your body, how soft and voluptuous you are. Your body drives me insane. Are you wet?"

"Yes."

"How wet?"

"Not enough."

"Stroke yourself. Slide your fingers up then down. That's it."

Her breathing grew more rapid. She could see he was enjoying this, the watching. She dipped her fingers down and up, slipping into her slickness, teasing herself. Fully flush with arousal now, all she wanted to do was come.

"Arch your back a little more so the weights pull," he ordered.

She did as he asked, lifting her torso so that the weights tugged her nipples, and it was so close to how it felt when he had his hands on her that she groaned, moving her fingers faster.

"Now pick up the vibrator and switch it on."

The phallus was larger than she would've chosen for herself and had a rabbit-shaped thing at the base. She switched it on, and the ears vibrated.

"The other switch. Turn that on too."

She did, and the beads in the shaft spun while the shaft itself thrust up and down. She gasped in anticipation.

"Slide it inside you. Slowly."

She used the fingers of one hand to widen herself and inserted the vibrator as deep as it would go. She was overwhelmed with sensation. The thrusting action stroked her while the vibrating ears hit just the right spot.

"Look at me, darlin'." He was fully hard, sitting at the edge of the chair, watching her. "Do you know what I see when I look at you?" She shook her head. "I see a woman so unbelievably beautiful and sexual I want to bury myself deep inside you and pound into you until you scream my name. Do it. Move it inside you as I'd move."

She did as she was told, finding a rhythm that rocketed her toward orgasm. Opening her legs wider as the sensations built, she put her other arm above her head, pushing her breasts higher. The clamps bit down, plunging her closer to the edge.

"Faster. Harder. That's it. Fuck yourself. Come for me, darlin'. Come."

The vibration slammed into her from the front as the thrusting head hit her deep, and she went off, throwing her head back and coming so hard she cried out. Never had she felt anything so intense in her life. The orgasm rolled through her, wave after wave of ecstasy. Nothing existed outside of her and the pulsing between her legs. She switched off the vibrator and threw it on the bed. Chest heaving and limbs tingling, she went completely limp.

"Goddammit if that wasn't the hottest thing I've ever seen."

She'd forgotten he was there. She turned her head to the side so she could look at him. "Thirty is *the best* number."

"I'm going to have it tattooed on my ass."

She laughed. "Oh, man. I needed that."

He got up from the chair, his penis hard and jutting, and lay on his stomach next to her on the bed. He kissed her shoulder right next to her scar. "You're so damn beautiful, darlin', that sometimes I can hardly breathe when I'm with you. Like right now. Your cheeks are pink and you look happy. Are you happy?"

"I think so. If happy is a loose-limbed kind of numb feeling in my arms and legs."

"That's orgasmic happiness."

She looked into his blue eyes and smiled. "Yeah. I think I am happy. More now than I used to be."

"I still have four more options, you know."

"Four." Laughing, she rolled toward him, the nipple clamps making a tinkling sound as she moved. "Are you planning on using them all tonight?"

"No. Just one more."

"Which is that?"

"This is one that I put on the list, but if you're not comfortable with it, then I'll choose another one."

"It's not one where I have to bend ways that normal people don't bend, is it?"

"Nope. It's one we've done before, so I know you can do it."

She thought of all the ways they'd had sex in the past. There were a couple she wasn't so sure if she could revisit.

"What is it?"

"Thirty-three."

"Which is that?"

"It's a really good one. In fact you can leave these on." He lifted the chain of one of the nipple clamps. "I know how much you enjoyed them."

"How does it work?"

"I lay on my back and you straddle me...backward."

The reverse cowgirl. She wasn't sure how she felt about it.

"Or you can face forward if you'd rather," he offered.

He'd chosen number thirty as the first option he'd won. He'd done it for her. The least she could do was try number thirty-three. It would give her that deep penetration she liked without having him directly behind and on top of her. She could set the pace.

"Okay," she said. "I'll try it."

Cal leaned over and kissed her. It took everything he had not to pounce on her and drive into her without any finesse whatsoever. The way she'd come completely unwound, her legs spread, head back, crying out, he'd had to squeeze his dick to keep from coming right then and there. He'd chosen number thirty-three, hoping she could get off the way he knew she liked it best and yet put her in control. His motives weren't entirely altruistic. He'd have a fine view of her ass as she bounced up and down on top of him.

He wound the chain of one of the clamps around his finger, tugging on her nipple, and then sucked on it. She arched back, leaning into him. He ran his hand over her hip and then between her legs. She was still so wet from pleasuring herself that his fingers slipped easily into her. Widening her legs for him, she tilted her pelvis, giving him deeper access. He knew she was getting close to coming again, and damn it, so was he. He'd been on the verge since he'd told her to spread her legs and touch herself.

Fumbling on the nightstand, he located the condom and rolled it on. With no finesse at all, he shifted so that he was between her thighs. He broke off the kiss and looked down at her.

"I don't care what number this is. I want to see your face." He eased himself into her little by little, watching her the whole time, until he was fully seated. "Oh, God. I can't…"

He began to move within her, thrusting without any skill. It had been *so long* since he'd been inside her. She wrapped around him, hugging him to her. He lost track of everything except the feel of her and his impending orgasm. He chased it, driving hard into her until it hit. He threw his head back and grunted, then collapsed in an unceremonious heap on top of her.

As his heart rate slowed and his brain re-fired its engines, he realized she was crying. He pushed himself up and looked down at her. She was smiling, but tears leaked out of her eyes and into her hair.

"Darlin', what's wrong?"

"Nothing's wrong." She sniffed.

"Then why the tears?"

"Because it's been so long since I came during sex. I missed it."

He put his forehead to hers. "Jesus, darlin', don't say things like that."

"It's true. God, Cal. That was so good. I don't care if it was in the option agreement or not. Plain old vanilla missionary sex works just fine for me."

He gave her a gentle kiss. "Me too, darlin'. Me too. Any way I can be inside you works for me."

"I missed you."

"I missed you too."

"I'm counting this as one of your five even though it's probably not in the option agreement."

"Oh, are you?" He rolled them over so she was on top. One of the nipple clamps had fallen off. He released the other one and threw it on the floor, then he bent his head and kissed each of her breasts. God he loved her breasts.

"Yeah."

"So you're making the rules around here now?"

She leaned forward, brushing her nipples across his chest. "Got a problem with that?"

"No, darlin'. When you do that, I don't have any problems at all with that or anything else in the world."

"Could I ask you a favor?"

"You could ask for anything from me right now and I'd likely give it to you."

Her lips curved into the kind of smile she used to give him. Even if she weren't naked and lying on top of him, that smile would get her whatever she wanted. It had been too damn long since he'd seen it.

He cupped her face. "What can I do for you?"

"Can we keep things the way they are?"

"What do you mean?"

"You haven't exactly been subtle about wanting me to share your bed every night. I'm just not sure I'm ready to move across the hall."

"We can keep them any way you want. I kind of like having to walk across the hall and ask permission to come into my wife's bedroom. Keeps me honest."

"Are you sure?"

"There's only one thing I'm completely sure of, darlin'. And that's if nothing at all changed between us and we stayed exactly the way we are right now, I wouldn't have a thing to complain about."

"You're only saying that because I'm naked and laying on top of you."

"Like I said. Keeps me honest."

SEVENTEEN

It was the night of the dinner party when Lucy would really earn her stripes as Cal Seller's wife. She'd chosen what she thought was the perfect dress and had her hair and makeup professionally done. The house was spotless, the decorations flawless. The food was more than delicious—it was exquisite. Even Poppy had a new outfit for the occasion, a cute little red, black, and white dress with white tights and shiny new black Mary Jane shoes.

Lucy stood in the entry hall, ready to greet her husband as he came home from work. She hoped with everything in her that he approved of what she'd done. This dinner was important not only to Cal but to Lucy as well. He'd offered her marriage as a way out of her situation based on her ability to pull off the kind of corporate affairs wives of her caliber were expected to perform. Only she'd never hosted a dinner party, and she'd certainly never choreographed a six-course dinner for four.

Twisting her hands together, she checked the time again. Twenty minutes. Twenty minutes until their guests arrived, and their host had yet to make an appearance. What would she do if he didn't come home before their guests got here? How would she entertain them?

The front door opened, and Cal appeared. "I'm late. I'll be right down." He barely gave her a glance before he ran past her up the stairs, briefcase in hand.

Halfway up the stairs, he turned. "Damn it." He made his way back down and gave her a brief kiss, then headed upstairs. "I'll be five minutes, no more."

She stared at her husband's retreating form, wishing he was standing next to her so she would at least know what to expect before their guests arrived. She made her way into the kitchen to check yet again on the preparations. All seemed to be in order as the caterer shooed her away. She found herself back in the entryway, alone, waiting for people she'd never met yet had to impress.

She checked her reflection for the third time in the past few minutes. The hairstylist and makeup artist had made her look like someone she hardly recognized, a better, prettier, more presentable version of herself that perfectly matched the expensive dress she wore. She was a long way from the trailer parks and apartment complexes she was used to. Washed, waxed, made up and done up, she felt the part. She knew how to charm people. She knew how to present herself in the best possible light, and she certainly knew which fork to use and when.

She could do this.

Straightening her spine and lifting her chin, she imagined herself greeting the President of the United States and the First Lady. If she was worthy of them, she was certainly worthy of a good old boy from Tennessee and his wife. Even if they were billionaires and were often photographed doing ordinary things like wrangling steer and organic gardening.

Oh, my God.

She was so out of her depth. She didn't know the

difference between millionaires and billionaires. To her they were 'aires miles out of her reach. What had Cal been thinking, putting her in charge of a dinner party where she was expected to not only entertain but to charm them over to her side...to Cal's side, where he could convince them he was the one to buy their company and grow their business? She knew *nothing* of these people.

As far as she was concerned they may as well live on opposite sides of the galaxy, let alone the state. She checked her reflection in the hallway mirror for the fourth time. Too much blush! She looked like a harlot. This would never do. She'd embarrass Cal, and the deal would be dead before discussions even began.

She rushed toward the bathroom as Cal thundered down the stairs. He caught up to her halfway there.

"Where are you going?" he asked. "They'll be here any minute."

"I need to fix—" Oh, damn. The doorbell. "I'm wearing too much blush. Stall them." She started for the bathroom again, but he gripped her elbow.

"No, you don't. You look perfect. In fact... Come here."

"There's no time!"

"Darlin', if you don't come here, I'm not going to answer the door.

"*What?*"

"Thought that'd get your attention. Come here." He hooked her hand into the crook of his arm. "You're perfect. Let's greet our guests."

She stared at him like he'd lost his mind because clearly he had, and then the doorbell rang again and she realized it was she who had taken a turn for the worse. She had guests to greet. *Oh, Lord, help me please*, she prayed. There was no way she could get through this night successfully without some kind of divine guidance.

Cal opened the door to a rather ordinary-looking couple about twenty years older than they were. For some reason that made Lucy feel better. The wife's dress was of a similar color as her own, and the man appeared to be more interested in their house than he was either her or Cal.

"Hello, Joel," Cal said smoothly. "This must be your lovely wife, Anne. Please come in."

He held the door open for them. The wife's attention was focused more on Cal than on either her husband or the home they'd been invited into. She spent way too long greeting Cal and hardly gave Lucy a glance as she was introduced. Lucy had her number. Anne Gleason was a woman who had married young for money, produced the proper heirs, and was now free to pursue her options. Lucy was going to make sure that Mrs. Gleason knew that Cal wasn't anyone's option but hers.

"A pleasure to meet you." Lucy held out her hand to Mr. Gleason only to be crushed into a hug so fierce it left her breathless.

"Mrs. Sellers. Lucy," Mr. Gleason said, holding her away from him with both hands on her arms. "I've heard so much about you." His gaze raked her from head to toe, and by the time he was done, Lucy was desperate for a shower.

So this was the man they had to charm into agreeing to sell his company to Cal's. Cal hadn't mentioned anything to her about him being a letch.

Cal dropped an arm across Lucy's shoulders, drawing her in close. "My wife and I are pleased to welcome you as our first guests as husband and wife. Isn't that right, darlin'?"

Lucy picked up where her husband left off. "It's such a pleasure to have you in our home. Please, won't you come in?" She guided them to the living room where a tray of hors d'oeuvres had already been set up. "May I offer you a drink?"

Mrs. Gleason lowered her shawl, revealing an unexpected plunging neckline. "What do you have?" She settled herself into the sofa, arms draped across the back.

Lucy suddenly realized that Anne's entire outfit was nearly see-through, with little peek-a-boo cutouts that barely covered her areolas. But Mr. Gleason didn't seem to notice his wife's outfit. His eyes were glued to the front of Lucy's dress, which was much more modest in comparison to Mrs. Gleason's.

Lucy sat next to Anne on the couch and crossed her legs.

Instead of sitting in the chair opposite the couch, Mr. Gleason squeezed in next to Lucy, making her scoot over to avoid being sat on.

Cal came forward, reaching a possessive hand out to Lucy. "Darlin', why don't you go and check on dinner while I see to our guests?"

She took his offered hand, leaving Mr. and Mrs. Gleason alone on the couch. "Please, help yourself to an appetizer. I'll be a minute," she told her guests.

Cal followed her partway to the kitchen and leaned down close to her ear. "You stay next to me and we'll be just fine."

Lucy wasn't so sure. The Gleasons seemed to have differing objectives for the evening, and they had nothing to do with business.

"I'm up for some kinky things," she said to her husband. "But wife swapping isn't one of them."

"I'm telling you right now, darlin'," he whispered so just she could hear, "I'm the only one who's going to be taking that dress off you tonight."

She flushed under his gaze as memories of the past few nights came into her head. They'd knocked off Cal's remaining options from their bet, including the reverse cowgirl. At first it had been difficult for her to enjoy it, but then Cal had stroked her from her shoulders down to her waist, over her hips and across her thighs, and she'd felt how much he cared for her. The next thing she knew she'd rocked them both to completion, tossing her head back and crying out Cal's name.

Tonight it was Lucy's turn to choose an option. Just thinking about it made her nipples hard and her panties wet. Why should she be the only one who was uncomfortable?

"You know when you say things like that, cowboy, it makes me so wet."

"Jesus, darlin'. I love it when you talk like that. Makes me want to push you up against the wall, lift your skirt up, and see for myself how wet you are."

"That's exactly the option we'll be scratching off the list tonight."

He groaned and turned back to his guests. She chuckled and headed for the kitchen, making a show of checking on dinner even though she knew everything was being taken care of. After a few moments she rejoined Cal and the Gleasons in the living room with a fresh tray of hors d'oeuvres. Joel still sat on the couch, drink in hand. His wife stood next to Cal at the bar as he fixed a drink. She leaned forward, and her breasts practically fell out of her dress and onto Cal's arm.

"Come sit next to me," Joel said, patting the couch.

Lucy sat and held out the tray to him. "Would you care for an appetizer?"

"Thank you." He chose one and popped it into his mouth. "Delicious. Now you."

Before Lucy realized what he meant to do, he was pushing a Brie and crabmeat puffed pastry into her mouth. She was still chewing when he reached out and brushed his thumb across her lips.

"A crumb," he said and then licked his thumb.

Lucy swung her panicked gaze toward her husband, but he was busy making another cocktail with Anne pressed up against him as though she was interested in learning how it was done. Or else the whole front side of her had been superglued to Cal.

"You have a lovely home," Joel said, drawing her attention back to him.

"Thank you."

"You'll have to give me a tour after dinner. I'd love to see the upstairs."

"Oh, it looks a lot like the downstairs. Except with beds."

He put a hand on her thigh. "Then I'm sure I'll love it even more."

"We shouldn't hog all of the hors d'oeuvres." She popped up off the couch, making his hand slide away. "I should see if Anne and Cal would like some too."

"Excellent idea." He rose as well, placing a hand on her back where the cutout on her dress opened up to bare skin.

With her hands full of the tray, there was nothing she could do except put up with it as they made their way across the room. A sick knot twisted in her belly. This man didn't seem to care if she was interested in him or not. As soon as she could, she turned so that his hand fell away, offering the tray to Cal and Anne.

"Care for an appetizer?" She could hear the strain in her voice.

Cal must have heard it too. "Darlin', why don't you put that tray down, and I'll mix you a drink." He handed Anne her cocktail, forcing her to move back or end up with her drink down the front of her dress. "Here's your Slow Comfortable Screw, Anne."

Lucy couldn't believe the woman's nerve.

Cal leaned on the bar toward her. "What can I get for you, darlin'? How about a Harvey Wallbanger? A Screaming Orgasm? I can also do a Long Slow Comfortable Screw Up Against the Wall." He winked. "But only for you."

Lucy bit the inside of her cheek to keep from smiling, then cleared her throat. "I'd love a Long Slow Comfortable Screw Up Against the Wall. But only from you."

The rest of the evening went well, Lucy thought. Anne and Joel continued to flirt with them, but after Cal's drink offering they weren't as persistent. Cal insisted on showing their daughter off to them, which brought out a different side to Anne that Lucy appreciated. They had motherhood in common if nothing else.

Cal closed the door after waving goodbye to their guests and leaned back against it. "I think that was the most interesting dinner party I've ever attended."

"I'm not sure interesting is the word I'd use, but it was certainly the most unique."

"You know, darlin'..." he eased away from the door and came toward her, "...you really held up your end of the bargain tonight. The food was delicious. You were a gracious and generous hostess. Not to mention the fact that you look amazing in that dress." He hooked a finger into her neckline and pulled. "Every time you bent over I got to look down it."

"You and Joel. I think next time I'll wear a turtleneck."

He let go of the front of her dress, trailing his finger up to cup the back of her neck. "Did you enjoy yourself despite the rudeness of our guests?"

"I actually did. I especially enjoyed my cocktail. I don't think I've ever had a Long Slow Comfortable Screw Up Against the Wall."

He backed her up until she met the wall. "I'm feeling

challenged to remedy that, darlin'."

"You already did once tonight." She brought her arms up around his neck. "I'm counting on you to do it again."

"This is a wall," he said, moving into her. "And you're up against it."

"We're in the middle of the house."

"The caterers have gone. The staff is in their quarters. We're alone and up against a wall."

"I'm not wearing any panties."

"It drives me crazy when you talk like that," he growled.

Cal put his mouth to hers, finally able to do what he'd been dying to since he came home and saw her in this dress—mess her up. Wedging his leg between hers, he changed the angle of the kiss, grinding his thigh against her. Her gasp fanned the flames inside him to the point that he struggled for control. When she went for his belt buckle, making quick work of it, he fought to keep from shoving up her skirt and driving into her without any ceremony at all.

Kissing a path down her neck, he found the zipper at the back of her dress and drew it down. The lower the zipper got, the lower the front of her dress dipped until the sleeves slipped down her arms and she pulled them free. A flick of his fingers and he had her bra hooks undone, and it too slid down her arms.

He caressed her breasts with both hands, fondling her nipples. She went wild for him, reaching for his zipper. He felt cool air and then her hands on him. He loved the way she touched him, caressing up and down. Fisting her dress in one hand, he raised her skirt. The naughty minx hadn't lied. She was bare and wet, so unbelievably wet for him. Slipping one then two fingers into her, he groaned at how wet she was for him. She widened her legs, her head tilting back to give him access.

He nipped and kissed her neck, which he knew drove her mad. She thrust her hips against his hand, clutching at him and moaning as she drew closer to climax. He wanted to be with inside her when she came. If she kept stroking him like that it would be over before they got started. He reached a hand into his front pocket and came up with a condom, which he handed to her. She ripped open the packet with her teeth. So damn sexy when she took charge. Rolling the condom on him, she drove him insane, stroking him nonstop.

He shoved her skirt all the way up, gripped her ass in both hands, and lifted her up against the wall. Pinning her with his body, he grabbed his dick and found her entrance. He thrust up as he brought her down until he completely impaled her. God the feel of her.

He began to move in sharp, deep thrusts. She threw her head back and gasped. He knew she was close, but not as close as he was, so he slipped a hand between them and rubbed her clit. She went off, digging her nails into his shoulders. He followed her, burying himself inside her.

Dropping his forehead onto her shoulder, he struggled to regain his breath and keep them from sliding down the wall to the floor. She'd wrapped her legs around his waist, sifting a hand through his hair as she liked to do.

"And that, darlin', is a long slow comfortable screw up against the wall."

"Mmm, it's also option number fifteen. Very sly of you to put a condom in your pocket."

"Very sly of you to not wear any panties. When did you take them off?"

"Right after dinner. When did you get the condom?"

"When I went to get Poppy."

"How smart we are."

"I don't know about smart, darlin'. More like horny.

Ever since your dirty talk about being wet, I've been semihard all night. Through cocktails, dinner, and dessert all I could think about was this." He kissed the curve of her neck. "And lifting your skirt up. Have I told you how much I love that you hardly ever wear pants?"

"I can wear skirts around you."

Jesus. When she said shit like that, it stabbed him right in the chest.

"Maybe I'll take to going without panties too," she added.

"In that case you're going to find your skirt up around your waist a lot."

Her laugh was the most magical thing he'd ever heard. She was laughing more often these days than she had when they'd first gotten married.

He reluctantly pulled out of her. She unwound her legs, and he eased her down until her feet hit the floor. She looked thoroughly ravaged and so damn sexy he wished he had another condom so he could put her back up against the wall and go for round two.

"I'll be right back, darlin'. Why don't you go on upstairs and put that dress back on."

"But we're going to bed."

"But not to sleep. That dress had me tied up in knots all evening. I'm not done with it yet."

EIGHTEEN

☿

"Relax your shoulders," the instructor at the shooting range told Lucy.

Lucy had finished her gun-safety class and was much more comfortable with a firearm in her hand than she'd been when she'd begun the class. The sound of it firing didn't make her flinch as much as it had when she'd first started coming to the range. She'd even managed to land most of her shots on the target. She glanced down the range at Cal, who was too busy concentrating on his target to notice her watching him. He'd shot guns since he was a kid, so he was a lot more at ease than she was.

"Good," the instructor said. "Now widen your stance a little. That's good. Go ahead."

Lucy sighted down the barrel, focusing on the target. This time she imagined it was Kevin trying to take Poppy from her. She fired. Then again, until the gun clicked empty.

She pulled her headphones off.

"That was good. More aggressive. I'm afraid to ask whose face you saw on the target," the instructor said as he recalled the target from the back of the range.

"My ex."

"I have one of those." He grinned at her. "Her face

sometimes appears on my targets too." He pulled the target down and handed it to her. "Nice job. You're improving, but I'd still like to see you get in some more practice."

Most of her shots had hit the paper, and a few had torn holes through the target body. She *was* getting better.

"Next time we should do a simulation. Shooting at the black shape of a person isn't the same as shooting an actual person. The simulation gives a more real-life kind of scenario where you have to choose who to shoot and who not to shoot."

"That sounds like a good idea."

"See you next time, Mrs. Sellers."

"Thanks, Jake."

Lucy packed up her gun as she'd been taught and put it in its case. She'd clean it when she got home. Cal was still shooting, so she went into the attached store to wait for him. She was admiring a pearl-handled gun in the display case when a man came up next to her and wrapped his hand around her forearm.

"I want my daughter," a voice growled in her ear.

Kevin.

He squeezed so hard on her arm that her knees buckled. She tried to twist away, but he countered her move so that she ended up hurting herself more.

"If I have to kill you to get her, I will."

"That's the only way you'll get her."

She swung her gun case and caught him in the side of the head. He stumbled, releasing his grip on her. She tried to swing it again, but he blocked it then grabbed her arm before she could bring it around a second time.

He hauled her up and got right in her face. "You fucking cunt. You'll pay for that."

He shook her, then released her so suddenly she had to grab the display case with both hands to keep from going down. Her gun case clattered to the floor. When she turned, Kevin was gone.

"Are you all right?" A woman helped her stand. "I can't believe he came at you like that. Somebody call the police."

"I'm okay."

"Are you sure, ma'am?" one of the store employees asked.

"I saw the whole thing," the woman told the clerk.

Another employee, this one a young man, came over. "He drove off, but I got part of the license plate."

"The cops are on their way," another man said.

"I'm okay, really," Lucy tried to reassure them.

"Come and sit down, miss." The older employee took her by the elbow and directed her to a chair at the end of the counter. "You're looking kind of pale."

A little group formed around them.

"What's going on?" She heard Cal before she saw him.

"This lady was attacked right here in the store," a man told Cal.

Cal elbowed his way into the group.

"Nothing—" Lucy started.

"This man came out of nowhere," the woman interrupted. "He grabbed her, but she swung her case and got him right upside the head. And then he shook her and knocked her over."

"Then he ran out," the young store clerk filled in. "I got part of his license plate." He nodded like he was proud of what he'd done. "And Bud called the police. They're on their way."

Cal knelt next to his wife. "Lucy?"

"It was Kevin." She tried to suppress the shudders that went through her. "He threatened to take Poppy."

"You hit him?" Cal asked her.

"Yeah," Lucy said. "I surprised him. I hit him before he

could hit me. " The realization of that washed through her. She'd struck back. She'd swung her case without thinking and hit him in the head. She'd always been too terrified of him to lash out. The retribution would've been too great. But this time, *this time* she'd surprised him and went after him. She hadn't let him get away with hurting her.

"Good for you." Cal took her hand in his, still kneeling at her side. "I hope that asshole has a bitch of a headache because of you."

Cal seemed proud of her, but she couldn't see past being Kevin's victim yet again. She hadn't done much more than scare him off. If only she'd had her gun out...

Sirens screamed in the distance, coming closer. She'd screwed up things for Cal. The media would get wind of this like they had the incident at their home. So far Cal was getting the bum end of this bargain they'd struck. He was supposed to be cultivating the reputation of a family man. Instead his personal life drew the worst kind of publicity. The gossip hounds had been all over their first run-in with the police. This would only make matters worse.

She shot up out of her chair. "Let's go."

"Darlin', we need to document this."

"No. Let's go home. I want to see Poppy."

"But the police are already here, ma'am," the store clerk said.

Cal pulled out his cell phone. "I'll call Sam to let him know what happened and to make sure she's okay."

"All right."

The police came in and took statements from the witnesses. The security camera had caught the whole thing on tape. By the time they were finished with the police it was nearly dark.

Lucy stared out the window as Cal drove them home.

One of the smaller local newspapers had sent a photographer and reporter to the gun store and had gotten the scoop of the month when they found out that billionaire Cal Sellers and his wife had been involved in what had happened. Their photos were probably already up on the Internet. Just what Cal needed—another scandal.

"Are you all right, darlin'?"

"I'm fine."

"I know you better than that. What's going on inside that pretty little head of yours?"

She really didn't want to point out what a bad bargain he'd struck when he'd asked her to marry him, but it was true. If he was smart, he'd divorce her and marry someone without all of her baggage and drama. She'd let him visit Poppy. Cal and his daughter grew closer every day, and the fact was she loved seeing them together. Poppy deserved a daddy, and Cal was the most devoted she'd ever seen. She could never separate them now.

"If you want to divorce me, I wouldn't fight you. We could work out a schedule for Poppy. I won't ask for anything from you. I'd just need a little money to find a place and get settled. I'd pay you back every penny. The sooner the bet—"

Cal jerked the steering wheel to pull over and slammed on the brakes. He shoved the car into park and turned in his seat to look at her.

"Our deal was for one year, Lucy. One year. That's the bargain you struck. I've kept up my end of the deal, why aren't you willing to keep up yours?"

"That's the thing. I'm not keeping up my end of the deal. It's not fair to you that your wife lands you on the five o'clock news. That wasn't part of our bargain. You wanted a wife so you could present yourself as a stable family man, not a wife who regularly has brushes with her ex that require police presence." She swiped at the tears that fell, hating herself even more for bringing so much drama to the situation. "I'm an embarrassment to you, not an asset. I struck the bargain with you, thinking I could hold up my end. I'm not. And I'm sorry."

"From where I'm sitting you're more than holding up your end of our bargain." He took her face in his hands and smoothed his thumbs across her cheeks to dry her tears. "I hate that you blame yourself for what Kevin does. You're not to blame any more than Poppy is. It cuts me in two sitting here watching you cry over that asshole. He's not worth it."

"As long as Kevin keeps coming around, I'm a liability to you, not an asset."

"When I add up all of my assets, I count you and Poppy as the most valuable. Now dry your eyes and let's go home to our daughter. And I don't want to hear any more talk about divorce and liabilities."

He kissed her forehead, then put the car in gear and pulled back onto the road. He'd said pretty much what she'd expected him to say, but she couldn't help the feeling that he didn't quite believe everything he'd told her. She knew he didn't like all the negative publicity. It had already begun to affect his business. She'd heard about the contract he didn't get and at least one investor had backed out of another project.

He said he didn't regret their marriage. She was sure there were things about it he didn't regret, but she was sure there were other things he did. Like the fact that she still didn't share his bedroom even while she welcomed him into her bed. Every night he knocked on her bedroom door and asked to be allowed in. She'd told him he didn't have to anymore, but he'd just shaken his head and insisted that he did and he would until he knew she trusted him.

Another way she was letting him down. He was right. She didn't completely trust him. She was beginning to wonder if she ever would fully trust anyone ever again. And when their year was up, would he decide that it was more trouble than it was worth to keep asking his wife for permission to sleep with her? If the press ever got wind of their unusual arrangement, what would that do to his reputation?

She grew as frustrated with herself as she knew he had to be. It seemed as though every step forward led to two back. He denied she was damaging his business as he dried her tears, but she didn't believe him. It was one more way in which they lied to each other. Everything was okay. They were working through her issues. Things were getting better.

Only they weren't.

Yeah, the sex was great, but was it enough? How much longer before he got tired of carrying the burden of their marriage? How much longer before he got tired of begging her to be a real wife to him? And how much longer before he decided he was done with their marriage, done with her?

NINETEEN

Cal hung up the phone and cursed a blue streak so broad he was sure his momma heard it all the way across the state. Another investor out. At this rate the project wouldn't start on time. He was down two investors and barely managing damage control with the others. It seemed they were fine with him when he was the playboy businessman who generated scandalous headlines, but not with a man who'd had a secret baby and then hastily married the child's mother who was being victimized by her ex.

The press had dug through Lucy's past, and soon it would come out that she'd married a man who was already married, who'd beaten her and was still harassing her months after she'd left him and married yet another man—Cal. It was one thing, apparently, to leave a string of mistresses in your wake and another to let a woman with a sordid past drop a baby on your doorstep and coerce you into marrying her. At least that was how the press was spinning it.

His publicist, Charity, had been wearing holes in the carpet in front of his desk most of the day, strategizing with him on how they were going to contain this mess and maintain his reputation for being a sharp-minded businessman who didn't put up with anyone's bullshit. More than once he'd caught her looking at him from under her lashes, no doubt wondering like everyone else how a woman like Lucy had gotten her hooks into him when every socialite in Texas hadn't been able to snare him.

The whole thing pissed him off to no end. Lucy was his wife. Poppy was his daughter. He was taking care of his responsibilities and building a life with the woman he loved. And damn it all if he didn't love her so much he could hardly catch his breath sometimes. She scared the shit out of him at the same time as she made him gladder than any man had a right to be. He looked forward to going home at the end of the day and hated to leave at the beginning.

He didn't give two shits what anyone else thought of him, but it killed him what they were saying about Lucy. More importantly, it would kill her to know what they were saying. She was smart enough to have picked up that he was having business problems and considered herself a liability to him. When she'd offered divorce in the car the other day, he'd about lost his shit. The last thing he wanted was a divorce. They'd find a way to work through this.

That bastard Walker would be caught, and the publicity surrounding them would die down, and everything would go back to normal. Or at least a semblance of normalcy. Lucy moving her things into the master bedroom had become a symbol to him of them having a real marriage. Instead he still visited her every night like a boyfriend, coming across the hall and knocking on her door for a sleepover. Not that he was complaining. Hell no.

They'd come miles from where they'd started. And while there were still times when she'd panic and make him stop or pull out, there were other times when he glimpsed the old Lucy. His Lucy. In those moments she'd drop her head back and enjoy what they did together. Uninhibited and wild, letting her intense sexuality free, was when she was the real Lucy. He'd come to live for those moments and tried to invent new ways to make them come out.

They were building something unexpected and necessary together, and he hated the thought that people on the outside would try to tear it down before they'd gotten a chance to explore it. And he hated that he was going to have to ask Lucy to go in front of a camera to tell her side of the story. His publicist, Charity, had thought she'd be great in an interview with her girl-next-door looks and his baby on her hip. They'd film it at their home to really highlight the family-man image Cal needed to show the public to rebuild his reputation.

He glanced down at the script on the desk in front of him. Lucy would have to memorize her part to make sure she stayed on message, Charity had said. And to make sure she didn't ad-lib something they didn't want broadcasted. When he'd proposed marriage to Lucy, he had no idea he'd be asking her to do more than the occasional dinner party or charity event. He certainly hadn't expected her to be the key to potentially saving Sellers Investments.

His reservations about having her do this interview ran as deep as his need for her to do it. She was still so fragile. He worried what the pressure of it would do to her. Charity and the board might not like it, but if Lucy said no to the interview, then she wouldn't do it. Consequences be damned.

"What about this one?" Charity held up a matching blue blouse and skirt. The color reminded him of Lucy's eyes.

"I like it. And that pink set too."

Charity had had his assistant, Felicia, pick up several outfits for Lucy to try on and decide which she was more comfortable in for the interview. He was relieved to see that there was no frilly fifties-style apron or string of pearls to really drive home the wife-and-mother point.

"What have you got for the ball?" he asked.

Charity showed him a half-dozen dresses. In the end he told her to send them all to the house for Lucy to select one for the annual Dallas Young Professionals Ball. Cal was set to give the keynote speech this year. As his wife she was expected to attend and be properly dressed. He'd already purchased a sapphire-and-diamond necklace and earring set that matched her engagement ring for her to wear at the event and instructed Charity to choose dresses that would go with them.

He only hoped Lucy wouldn't think all this work had been done for her because she couldn't be trusted to turn up in something appropriate. Who was he kidding? That was *exactly* why all this work had been done on her behalf. His publicist wanted Lucy to wear a dress that would be—in her words—flattering, yet modest, appropriate, yet cutting edge, tasteful, yet elegant. Whatever all that bull meant. All he really wanted was for Lucy to look and feel beautiful. And if the dress showed a lot of cleavage, he'd be extra happy, but he had a feeling that tasteful meant a lack of exposed skin.

As soon as Charity left he gathered up his things, anxious to see his wife and daughter. Felicia knocked and then entered the room, shutting the door behind her.

"What is it, Felicia?" Cal asked.

"I know you're about to head home, but Mrs. Gleason is here. She says it's urgent."

He snapped his briefcase closed and set it next to his desk. "Send her in."

He finished setting his desk to rights as Felicia went to get Anne Gleason. He wondered what could be so all-fired important that she needed to see him at six o'clock in the evening without her husband. This couldn't be good.

Anne swept into the room, wearing one of those dresses that tied around the neck and pushed a woman's breasts up to her chin. He had to give it to her, she had nice tits, but they didn't hold a candle to Lucy's. Still he looked. He was a guy after all, and she'd put them out there to be looked at.

"Cal, darling. Thank you for seeing me without an appointment."

She hit him with her whole body, wrapping her arms around his neck and giving him a full-on kiss on the lips. Behind her he saw Felicia's scowl before she shut the door. Shit.

He unwound Anne's arms and pushed her back. "What can I do for you, Mrs. Gleason?"

She had the nerve to pout as she stroked the lapel of his suit jacket. "Now, Cal, I thought we were friends. When you call me Mrs. Gleason, it makes me think of my mother-in-law, and she was an awful bitch. Call me Anne."

He pulled her hand off him and gestured for her to have a seat in one of the chairs on the other side of his desk. "Please have a seat...Anne."

Instead of doing what he wanted her to do, she propped her hip on top of his desk and leaned forward so he had a clear view down the front of her dress. She wasn't wearing a bra.

"I'm so glad you could see me. I wanted to thank you again for the lovely dinner at your house," she said.

"Your thanks belong to Lucy. She did all the work. I'll be sure to pass them along to her again."

"Joel was quite taken with her. It was Lucy this and

Lucy that all the way home. He's become a bit obsessed. So I've come to invite you to dinner in our home. Just the two of you. We've got a wonderful wine cellar, so you might want to plan for an overnight stay so you can thoroughly enjoy yourself."

"I'll arrange for a driver that evening. What night are we talking about?"

"Oh, the sooner the better. How about this Friday, say around seven? Dress casually. I'm thinking of having Indian food. We'll sit on pillows on the floor. It will all be very decadent and intimate."

Lucy was going to hate spending another evening with the Gleasons, especially in a setting they couldn't control. But he really couldn't afford to say no. Buying Joel Gleason's company would give him what he needed to not have to depend on investors for future projects. And he was looking forward to the day when he wouldn't have to deal with investors.

"Let me check with Lucy to make sure we don't already have plans, and get back to you."

She clapped her hands together. "Lovely. I hope you can make it. I have something *very special* in mind for us." She winked and hopped off his desk, making her breasts jiggle. Before he could stop her, she planted another kiss on his lips, then walked out the door with a wiggle of her ass.

He wiped his mouth with the back of his hand, then rubbed off her lipstick with one of the hand-stitched handkerchiefs Lucy had made him. If the way Anne behaved was any indication, they were going to be spending the evening getting backed into corners and swatting away hands. There was no way he was going to subject Lucy to that. He'd have to find another way to persuade Joel to sell him his company.

Lucy stared at the gorgeous clothes scattered across her bed and hanging from the back of the closet doors. There was no note, just a comment from their housekeeper Hazel about how they were for her from Cal. Six evening gowns with matching shoes and bags and four different skirt-and-blouse combinations with accessories. What could they be for? She'd already bought what she thought was a nice dress for the Dallas Young Professionals Ball next week. Did he not trust her judgment?

She hadn't spent as much on her dress as these dresses must have cost, but hers was still nice. And it fit. Fitting had been an issue in the dressing room and the reason she hadn't bought the dress she'd really wanted. That and the money. She couldn't bring herself to pay more than she would've if she'd been using her own money instead of Cal's. It just didn't feel right to her.

There was a knock on her bedroom door. She opened it to find Cal filling up the doorway. Her body reacted before her mind could with a stuttering in her chest followed by a flush that brought a tightening of her nipples and a wetness between her legs. If he threw her on the bed right now, she'd be ready to take him. It was as though her body recognized him as her mate and prepared itself for him. She'd never felt this with any other man except Cal. It both frightened and thrilled her.

"Hello, darlin'." He leaned down and kissed her cheek.

She loved how he called her darlin' with that long, slow drawl of his like a long, slow, full-body caress. Heat flashed through her again, and she was sure her cheeks were as pink as her blouse.

"Hey there, cowboy. How was your day?"

"Better now that I'm home. Can I come in?"

She opened the door wider, inviting him in. She loved

how he asked her permission, putting her in control. He'd said he liked it and that it kept him honest, but she had a suspicion he wasn't confident he'd get a yes every time. That had to be the most attractive thing about this new Cal. This man who was her husband and lover had given her the gift to heal at great personal risk.

"Ah." He shoved his hands in his pockets and rocked back on his heels, surveying the clothes scattered across the bedroom. "I see the delivery arrived."

"I'm assuming there's a reason you did this."

"It wasn't so much me as my publicist, Charity. She seems to feel that the right clothes make the right impression."

"I see. So until now I've been making the wrong impression?"

He pulled his hands out of his pockets and held them palms up. "No, darlin', not at all. That isn't why these clothes are here."

"So why are they here?"

"The dresses are for the ball. Charity says that as my wife you have to look the part, especially now with the negative publicity because of your asshole ex."

"I already bought a dress though."

"Sorry. I didn't know that." He walked over and examined three of the dresses that hung from the back of one of the closet doors. "I did have one requirement that it looks like Charity somehow managed to fulfill."

She crossed her arms over her chest, feeling insecure about this Charity fulfilling any of Cal's *requests*. "What was that?"

He pulled a long, thin, lidded box from the inside pocket of his suit jacket and held it out to her. "They had to go with these." When she didn't immediately take it, he extended it out farther. "Go on. Open it."

She accepted the box, frowning over the expensive gold

lettering from an upscale jeweler downtown. "What is it?"

"Open it."

"It's not my birthday."

"I know."

She pulled the ribbon off and lifted the lid. Nestled inside was a fine filigree pendant with pearls, sapphires, and diamonds on a long, thin chain and a pair of earrings that perfectly matched. She couldn't stop staring at them, tracing a finger over the intricate design that matched the engagement ring he'd given her. It was too extravagant and too expensive for someone like her, but she loved it. She absolutely loved it.

"Do you like them?"

She'd almost forgotten he was in the room. She'd been so taken with the beauty and intricacy of the design and the thought that something as beautiful as these could belong to her.

"They match your ring, except that I had pearls added. They're Poppy's birthstone."

He sounded nervous. She glanced up to find him watching her with a look so intense her breath caught. He expected her to reject them, to reject him.

"I know," she said. "They're absolutely beautiful. But why?"

He let out a breath as if he'd been holding it waiting for her answer. "I wanted you to have something pretty."

"These aren't pretty, they're absolutely gorgeous."

His mouth curved up into a smile as his confidence fully returned. "I'm glad you like them." He lifted her left hand. "I know colored stones aren't what's fashionable, but the sapphires reminded me of your eyes."

Damn it! When he said things like that, it made her eyes all watery.

"Hey, are you crying?" He pulled his handkerchief from his pocket and handed it to her. "Are those happy tears?"

She nodded and sniffed, dabbing at the corners of her eyes with his handkerchief. "You always know what to say to make me turn into a watering pot."

"Come here, darlin'." He took her into his arms and rubbed her back. "I'm glad you like the jewelry. That's stressful stuff for a man."

"I like how you included Poppy in it." She sniffed back more tears. "I'm sorry I didn't tell you when I was pregnant with her. I'm sorry you weren't there when she was born and for all the months since. You're a really good father."

"Aww, Jesus, darlin', when you talk like that... I didn't deserve to be a father to her, but now I think I might. I'm trying real hard, and the truth of it is, she's the best thing I've ever done, however accidentally and messed up I did it. I'm glad I've got this chance with her and with you."

"Me too."

She pulled back enough so she could go up on her toes and kiss him. As with everything with Cal, things got out of hand quickly, and before she knew it he'd backed her up against the dresses on the closet door with a knee between her legs, one hand on her breast and the other lifting up her skirt. Poppy started crying, and his hands fell away.

He put his forehead to hers and let out a breath. "Damn, darlin', you've get me going from zero to sixty in about two seconds." He kissed her hard on the mouth. "I'll go get her." He left to tend to his daughter.

She'd grown accustomed to having a real parenting partner since their marriage. Poppy lit up around her daddy. It was a treasure to watch the two of them together. She was starting to think that maybe things could work out for them. And that got her tearing up again. She unfolded Cal's handkerchief to dry her eyes and froze. Lipstick. Red lipstick on the handkerchief she'd hand embroidered and had given to him. And he'd used it to wipe lipstick off. Off of what? And whose lipstick was it?

"Here she is." Cal came into the room holding Poppy. "Sam said she heard my voice and started crying for me."

He turned his face and kissed their daughter, and she saw the smudge of red at the side of his mouth. Her heart kicked out a ragged beat, and she flushed for an entirely different reason. This was how it had started the first time. Little signs that Lucy had ignored or made excuses for. In the end all of her denial couldn't excuse the secretary Cal had bent over his desk and almost screwed. Hell, maybe he already had, and that scene in his office was one of many times he'd cheated on her. She only had his word to go by, and she wasn't sure how good that word really was.

Now he was back at it. She'd been right not to trust him. Her mother had trusted her daddy even when he came home reeking of perfume with love bites on his neck. The last thing Lucy wanted for herself or for Poppy was a recreation of her childhood. Poppy would never hide in her room while her father fucked another woman as soon as her mother left the house. And she sure as hell didn't want to ever look the other way like her mother did.

She reached up, swiped the lipstick off with her thumb and showed it to him along with the stained handkerchief. "Looks like you didn't get rid of all the evidence. You're getting sloppy."

TWENTY

"Oh, that." He chuckled. "Anne Gleason stopped by my office to invite us to dinner."

"And you kissed her."

"*She* kissed *me*." He narrowed his eyes at her. "What are you implying?"

"It's not like there's no history here."

"We're not having this out in front of our daughter."

He left the room. Lucy stewed like an overfilled pressure cooker. She didn't have the self-confidence she'd had the first time she'd caught Cal cheating, but what she did have was a limit for how long she'd listen to him stammer and make excuses as to why he fell face first into another woman's cleavage. Or why he couldn't seem to keep his lips off another woman's lips.

He came back and closed the door behind him. "You're right. There is a history here, but it's ancient history. I'm not cheating on you."

"Yet? Or not at all?"

"Not at all."

"What am I supposed to think when I find this?" She shook the lipstick-stained handkerchief at him. "How would you feel if you found evidence that I'd been with another man? How would you feel if you *walked in* on me with another man?"

"Before or after I punched him in the face?"

"I told you when we started this that I couldn't take you cheating on me again."

"I'm not. I wouldn't."

She stared at him, trying to find the truth in his expression. He hadn't gotten to where he was without perfecting his poker face. But he wasn't doing it this time. He stared straight back at her, and she could see the regret mixed in with something else—desperation. He not only wanted her to trust him, he needed her to. Her eyes teared up for a whole other reason.

She started to dab at her eyes with the stained handkerchief, then pulled the gesture in disgust and threw it on the ground. "I believe you."

He sagged in visible relief. "It's the truth, darlin'. I haven't touched another woman since you stormed out of my office and out of my life. Every time I started to think I could be with someone else, thoughts of you would pop into my head, and everything in me would freeze up. No matter how many women I dated after we split up, none of them were you. None of them tossed their hair over their shoulder and jutted out a hip like you do. None of them made me feel both humble and like a conquering hero like you do. And I knew if I took them to bed that none of them would make that sound you make when I first thrust inside you.

"Or make me come so hard I think I might just die from it. And none of them would ever make me want to drop to my knees and beg to be believed. Because if you don't believe me, we're over. And I can't be without you again, Lucy. I just can't. So I'm thanking God you believe me. And I'm thanking you for giving me this second chance with you."

She was sobbing now, covering her face with both

hands, as he dropped to his knees and wrapped his arms around her waist.

"I won't screw this up. I won't."

She cradled his head against her chest and cried harder. She was right to trust in him. She knew how aggressive Anne Gleason was toward Cal and how she hadn't hid her desire to sleep with him. His words played over and over in her head. He hadn't been with another woman since they'd split up? She could hardly wrap her mind around it. He'd gone without for seventeen months while she'd given herself to someone who had ruined her life and was still ruining it.

She cried for the time they'd lost together and the mistakes they'd made and for the sheer joy of finding each other again after all they'd been through. She couldn't seem to stop crying until Cal lifted his head to look up at her and she bent to kiss him. The rising tide of sorrow and regret inside her spilled over, catching fire and morphing into something else altogether.

And then she was kissing him for an entirely different reason that had nothing to do with the past and everything to do with the future, their future together. She dropped to her knees in front of him, yanking on his shirt, desperate for the feel of him under her hands. She managed the first couple of buttons and then just pulled the whole thing over his head. Her blouse hit the floor next to his shirt.

Cal let her have her way, shoving at his clothes, then hers. She believed him. When he'd never given her any reason to in the past. He'd lied back then and hid things from her and offered up the worst kind of betrayal. And she'd taken him back, taken him into her bed and her heart again. It was all he could think about as he laid her down on and crawled between her wide-spread legs, as he rolled the condom on and lowered himself over her.

He entered her slowly, watching her face and the way she dropped her head back and arched into his entry. He thrust hard into her just to hear the sound she made when he was fully seated. God he loved her. He pulled back and then came at her again a little harder, and then again and again, building the pressure between them until he was sweating from the effort and she was crying out so loud he was sure the whole house heard her.

When he finally let loose, rocking deep into her, it did feel like he might die. There was no other moment more perfect than being inside Lucy. He'd live inside her if he could.

Her hot breath blew on his cheek as he lay on top of her. He knew she was looking at him, but he couldn't quite meet her gaze yet. The rawness of being inside her, of pressing himself into her, was still too new. He needed another moment before he could look into her eyes without tearing his heart out of his chest and laying it at her feet.

When he had control again, he turned his head to look at her. Her face was pink, her full lips were red, and her tear-filled eyes were so blue they rivaled a winter sky.

"I won't screw this up," he told her, his voice as scraped out as he was.

"I know." She smiled at him even as the last tear slid down her cheek and into her hair. "Will you help me move my things across the hall? I want to sleep with my husband in our bed. Tonight."

༺༻

Cal lay in bed that night, listening to his wife wash her face and brush her teeth in the bathroom, feeling like the luckiest man in the world. She trusted him. She finally trusted him. Ironically it had taken another woman's lipstick on him to do it. No more walking across the hall to knock on her door and the sickening feeling low in his stomach at the thought that she might not let him in. But now, now he didn't have to worry.

They'd spent the rest of the evening moving her things and then played with their daughter on the big bed before reading her a story and putting her to sleep for the night. It had felt real and right. They were a family in every sense of the word. He stacked his hands under his head and stared up at the ceiling he hadn't seen in weeks, not exactly sure how he'd accomplished it.

Lucy came out of the bathroom dressed in some kind of flimsy see-through thing that had him sitting up in bed so he could get a better look. She wasn't wearing a damn thing underneath.

"What do you think?" She spun for him, and the fabric flew out around her.

He had trouble forming any thoughts except for ones he couldn't repeat. It was like someone had wrapped all of his favorite things in gauze so that he couldn't quite see them.

"It was a gift from Mi." She held the dress out at the sides, looking a little unsure. "I was supposed to wear it for our wedding night."

"We can pretend tonight's our wedding night."

"But do you like it?"

"It's a tease. Come here and let me rip it off you."

She laughed. "Don't you dare tear it. It's too beautiful."

"Then you better take it off before you climb up here, darlin', because I can't be responsible for my actions once your knee hits the mattress."

She looked down at herself, smoothing her hands over her body, and then she lifted the skirt and pulled the whole thing over her head. Instead of joining him, she went into the closet.

He strained to keep her fine ass in view. "Where are you going?"

"To hang it up. I don't want it ruined."

She came back out wearing nothing but the jewelry he'd given her. He decided right then and there that he'd buy her a whole shop full of jewels if she came to bed dressed just like that every night.

She climbed up next to him, which was a bit of a struggle for her. He made a note to get a step for her or else buy a whole new bed she didn't have to strain herself to get into. The only exerting he wanted her to do in bed was with him. She straddled him and flipped her hair back over her shoulders so that her breasts were fully exposed.

"I was thinking," she said, "that we could try option number two." She pulled a scarf from underneath one of the pillows and wrapped it in her fists, tugging on it to make it snap.

He ran his hands up her thighs. "Whatever that option is, I'm on board."

"It's the binding option, the one where I tie you up."

"However you want me, wherever you want me, I'm there."

She looked at the carved wooden headboard with a frown. "There's no place to tie your hands to."

"Hmm, that is a problem. What if you tied my hands together and I have to keep them above my head no matter what? And then tomorrow I'll have a new bed delivered with a step for you to climb up and a wrought-iron headboard you can tie me up to any time you like."

"That seems awfully extreme for just the one option."

While she'd been deciding what to do, his hands had wandered up her thighs to her breasts, and he rolled her nipples between his fingers. She moaned and arched her back.

"If you've got your heart dead set on that option, then there's only one thing to do—buy a new bed." He leaned up and replaced one of his hands with his mouth.

"We don't...ooohhh...need a new bed." She fell forward, catching herself with one hand on the headboard, giving him better access.

He could've spent all night on her breasts. They were so sensitive that one touch had her rubbing herself against him. He could feel her slickness, smell her heat as she moved. He barely touched her, and yet she was so ready for him. He drifted a hand down her back to her ass and slipped a finger into her from behind. She moved up and down, pleasuring herself on his hand. With his other hand he slid a finger in from the front. She went wild then, bucking up and down. He added two more fingers, and she groaned, her breasts jiggling with her movements. He leaned up and caught her nipple between his lips and sucked hard.

She came on a long, low moan, her head back, lips parted, her hair a wild mess around her. He released her nipple and laid back to watch as her orgasm rolled through her. She was so goddamned beautiful he could hardly believe she was his.

She collapsed onto his chest as her orgasm faded. "I'm never, ever going to tie your hands up. They're too good. That thing you just did with them. Oh, my God."

"I don't know about that. That no-hands option we tried a while back was pretty damn great."

"This was better."

"I'm not done with you yet, Mrs. Sellers. This is our wedding night." He rolled them so that he was on top. "We have to consummate our marriage to make it legal and binding."

"Mmm, binding."

He adjusted the pendant he'd given her so that it fell

between her breasts. "We'll get to the binding. But first I want to make love to my wife. This would be option number thirty-seven."

She ran her hands into his hair. "And what happens in this option?"

"This is the option where I ruin you for all other men."

"That might have already happened about three minutes ago."

"That was nothing. Just an appetizer."

He kissed her as he'd wanted to on their wedding day, sealing their vows. And then changed it, kissing her deep and long. Running a hand down her body, he mapped her curves, caressing her waist as it dipped in and her hip as it flared out. Long, slow movements down then up her leg. He repeated the motion over and over, his hand skimming her inner thigh and the underside of her breast, but never giving her what she wanted.

Her hands were all over him, relearning him as he was her. He kissed a trail along her jaw and down her neck. She shifted, nestling him between her legs. He wanted to go slow, but she had her hand on his ass and her knees bent so she was wide open. She kissed him like she more than wanted him, she needed him.

He broke the kiss and looked down at her. Her eyes were so blue, bluer than the stones between her breasts, and she was smiling up at him. No hesitation, no fear, she was his Lucy once again. He bent and kissed the slope of each of her breasts, gliding his tongue in circles until he was tracing around her nipples. She held his head in her hands, making little moaning sounds. He pulled her nipples into his mouth, one and then the other. By the time he glanced up at her face, she was squirming under him.

She grabbed the condom off the nightstand and rolled it on, taking her time about it. He'd get her back for that.

While she was busy torturing him, he slid two fingers into her. She sucked in a breath. He gently stroked her clit, easing her legs wider apart. He kissed her, mimicking the thrusts of his hand. She clutched at him, and he knew she was close so he slowed down.

This wasn't going to be one of their mad couplings. He wanted to show her with his body what he felt for her and how she made him feel when he was with her, inside her. She gripped his ass and tilted her hips, trying to get him to hurry it along, but he kept up the slow, agonizing pace until he felt her give over to it. Her head dropped back, exposing her neck for him to kiss, so he obliged her.

He positioned himself at her entrance, and for a brief moment he hesitated. And then he saw his ring on her hand and everything they were, everything they would be, slid into place for him.

"Look at me," he told her.

Her lashes fluttered open. Their gazes locked as he eased into her. When he hit deep, she made that sound that drove him mad, and he nearly lost it. He had to take several breaths to hold on to some kind of control. And then he pulled back and slid into her again. Stroking in and out, he kept the pace where he wanted it, but not quite where she needed it. He watched her expression change as she drew close to coming.

"I want you to look at me. I'm the one inside you." He drove into her harder, watching as her lips parted and she drew nearer to orgasm. "I'm your husband." He pumped faster into her, and she bit her lip, digging her nails into his back. "And I love you."

She sucked in a breath and came, still biting her lip. He thrust into her once more, jerking as he too found release and collapsed on top of her. This time he faced her, waiting for her to turn her head and look at him.

She finally did, her gaze roaming over his face as if

seeing him for the first time.
"I love you too," she whispered.

TWENTY-ONE

Cal proudly escorted his wife into the Dallas Young Professionals Ball. The ballroom had been decorated in an under-the-sea theme. Blue-green lighting made it feel as if they were underwater. They weaved around seaweed that sprang up from the floor along with anemones and other sea life. Decorative fish hung from the ceiling, and the fabric on the walls seemed to wave as if affected by a current.

Lucy had chosen a royal-blue floor-length dress that tucked in at the waist and showed a reasonable amount of cleavage. It was his favorite of all the dresses Felicia had dropped off for Lucy to choose from. Lucy's hair was piled up on her head, exposing her creamy white skin and the necklace and earrings he'd given her. She was by far the most beautiful woman in the room. He couldn't take his eyes off her. A lot of other men couldn't either, he noticed.

Lucas had arranged for them to have bodyguards disguised as guests. One male and one female, so that when Lucy went anywhere—even to the ladies' room—she was never alone. Cal wasn't about to take another chance that her bastard ex could get to her. Poppy was at home, well protected by Sam and the security team that regularly patrolled the grounds of their estate as well as in-house staff whose sole purpose was to protect one tiny redheaded little girl.

Cal scanned the room and nearly groaned out loud when he spotted Joel and Anne Gleason headed their way.

He leaned down to whisper in Lucy's ear. "If either of them offers you a drink, don't take it. I wouldn't put it past them to roofie us."

Lucy glanced sharply up at him. "They wouldn't."

"You want to take that chance, darlin'? The only thing we drink tonight we get from the bar ourselves."

"Cal, Lucy, how wonderful to see you," Anne said.

She air-kissed Lucy and tried to go for Cal's lips, but he successfully dodged her and planted a kiss on her cheek instead. He shook hands with Joel and watched very closely how he greeted Lucy. Joel gave her a chaste kiss on the cheek, but his gaze was glued to her chest.

Lucy tried to hide her revulsion for the Gleasons, especially after Anne had attempted to kiss Cal on the mouth. Again. She didn't consider herself a violent person, but she'd have no problem pulling her gun from her purse, hoping Anne would get the point that Cal was hers.

"I never did hear back from you about dinner," Anne was saying. "We'd love to have the two of you over. What about the weekend after next? Do you have plans?"

"A friend of mine owns Sur La Mer downtown. I could get us a table," Cal offered.

Anne waved away his suggestion. "No restaurants. I insist on returning the hospitality."

"I've just acquired a case of Château d'Yquem," Joel said. "We haven't had an occasion to open it yet. Don't disappoint my wife. She loves to play hostess."

Joel couldn't have laid down the ultimatum any stronger. This was a hurdle she and Cal would have to jump in order to make the deal Cal needed so badly.

"We'd love to," Lucy agreed, despite her feelings for the Gleasons. She knew Cal still hadn't persuaded Joel to sell him his company. "Thank you so much for the invitation."

"It's settled then," Anne said. "Dinner at our place a week from Friday at six o'clock."

Joel rubbed his hands together, his gaze firmly fastened on Lucy's cleavage. "I've been looking forward to showing you my collection of taxidermy from all over the world, Cal. We've got a lot to discuss you and I."

Lucy wanted to ask why anyone would want to collect dead animals, but she could see that Cal was nearly at his limit for politeness.

"Oh, look. Mimi Vanderclark is waving us over," Lucy said. "I'm so sorry to have to leave you," she told the Gleasons. "But Mimi is an old family friend, and if I don't say hello, I'll never hear the end of it. Won't you excuse us?"

They said their goodbyes to the Gleasons, and Cal led them across the room where Lucy had pointed.

"Who's Mimi Vanderclark?" Cal asked.

"I made her up. I'm awful, aren't I?"

"No, you're brilliant."

They were waylaid by some business associates of Cal's, a couple of whom recognized Lucy from her days as the cohost of *Pleasure at Home*. Everyone seemed interested in speaking with her. There were a lot of questions about them and the rumors running through the media. Cal extricated them from those situations and maneuvered them around the ballroom so that by the time they found their table, Lucy was pretty sure she'd met everyone in the room.

Cal pulled a chair out for her and waited for her to be seated before he took his seat next to her.

"Have I told you how beautiful you look tonight?"

"Only about eighty times."

"All I can think about is getting that dress off you."

"I don't know why. It's not like I'm wearing anything underneath it."

He groaned, leaned in to nip her earlobe, and proceeded to tell her exactly what he wanted to do to her once he got her dress off. By the time he finished, she was sure she'd flushed from her neckline to her forehead. She had to take several gulps of water before she felt like she had herself under control.

The MC began the program with a handful of corny jokes about businessmen, which earned him pity laughs. The awards ceremony was filled with names of people Lucy had only ever heard of or read about on TV or online. Every time one was announced, Cal would lean over and tell her something unrepeatable about them. A few times she had to cover her mouth to keep from laughing out loud and embarrassing Cal.

After that, dinner was served. It was surprisingly good for a banquet dinner. And then Cal told her how much it had cost per plate, and she knew why. Lucy was surprised to be having such a good time in a room full of people she had absolutely nothing in common with. The dinner conversation wasn't nearly as boring as she'd expected.

Cal nudged her arm to get her attention away from the woman next to her. "How do I look?"

She examined him, which wasn't a hardship. "You look great. Very handsome."

"Good. I'm on next, and they're about to announce me."

As soon as the words were out of his mouth, his name was called and he stood to a round of applause that kept going until he quieted the crowd from the podium. The audience seemed to enjoy Cal's speech, laughing at his jokes and nodding along with his observations. Lucy was so proud of her husband she could burst.

A siren pealed, interrupting Cal midsentence. A mechanical voice came over the loudspeakers, warning that this was a fire alarm and telling everyone to exit the building.

"I guess my speech was too hot," Cal joked, then motioned for Lucy to stay where she was, standing next to their table.

All of a sudden there was a lot of shouting and people rushing toward the doors. Smoke billowed from the overhead vents. Someone pushed Lucy, knocking her forward and into the swelling crowd that grew more frantic to get through the only open exit at the back of the room. She struggled to stay on her feet, but as the air got thicker, hits came from every side. She glanced back at the podium, hoping to catch sight of Cal, but he was gone.

A lick of fear slithered up her spine. Where was he? She'd worked her way out of the funnel of the crowd and out into the fringes of the room. Alone. She looked around for the two bodyguards Cal had hired, but they were nowhere in sight.

A hand grabbed her arm, yanking her back against a hard form. "Remember…" Kevin's harsh murmur in her ear sent her heart skidding, "…I can get to you anywhere. Any time." He released her, shoving her back into the mass of people, hurdling her closer to the exit.

She pushed blindly into the swell, knocking into people to get away. By the time she reached the double doors that led to the hallway, panic crawled all over her like biting ants. She had to get to Poppy. She had to make sure her daughter was safe.

Cal caught up to her just as she reached the street door. He wrapped an arm around her waist, pulling her into his side. She grasped fistfuls of his jacket, hanging on to him for more than the steadying effect he was having on her senses. He was safety. He was everything she'd come to rely on, everything she needed in this world.

"I've got you, darlin'. You're all right."

"Kevin's here. He's here."

"I saw. I can't believe the balls of that son of a bitch."

He ushered her past the fire trucks and police to their waiting limo and practically shoved her inside. As soon as he shut the door, enclosing them in the protective cocoon of the car, she grabbed for him again, climbing him to get closer.

"Hey." He held her tight, his face buried in her shoulder. "You're okay. I've got you now. It'll all be okay." The subtle tremor in his voice made a liar out of him. "He can't get you. He's not going to get you."

"He did. He does. Over and over he gets to me." She was sobbing now, beating her fists against Cal's chest. He let her. "And he'll get to Poppy too. You can't stop him. No one can stop him. He gets arrested then set free. You hire guards. He gets around them. He keeps coming." She collapsed, shaking, her voice as weak as she felt. "He just keeps coming."

Cal let Lucy have her rage. When he'd witnessed her bastard ex grab her, he'd leapt over a table to get to her, but by the time he got there, the asshole was gone and Lucy had been in a running panic for the door. He'd caught up to her too late. Every goddamned time he was too late. She was right. Walker kept coming and would probably keep coming after Lucy and Poppy until someone stopped him. Or put a bullet in him.

He didn't know what to say to soothe her, could hardly wrap his head around the terror of seeing that bastard's hands on her and the utter helplessness of watching her break down in his lap. It was his fault. All of his damn money couldn't give Lucy the one thing she needed more than the mansion she lived in and the jewels that lay against her skin—safety. He could hire a thousand bodyguards, arm her until she buckled under the weight of the guns, and use his connections until he burned through every favor owed to him, and it still wouldn't be enough.

"I'm sorry," he offered, knowing it was no kind of consolation for what she'd been through.

"I need to see Poppy."

"We're on our way home. I'm sure she's fine. Probably sleeping."

"I need to see her. Right now."

"I'll call Sam and check in." He pulled his phone out of his pocket and hit Sam's speed-dial number. Sam picked up on the first ring. Cal put the call on speakerphone. "Hey, Sam. How's Poppy?"

"She went down like a champ."

Lucy took the phone. "I want to see her."

"Hang on," Sam said. "Let me call you right back."

Lucy stared at the phone without speaking. Cal couldn't quite get a read on her. Her emotions seemed to be all over the place. Was it any wonder with the hell her ex was putting her through?

His phone rang again. Lucy grabbed for it and answered. Sam held a finger to his lips, then turned the phone so they could see the outline of Poppy sleeping peacefully in her bed, lit by only the nightlight in her room, her breathing deep and even. Lucy let out a tense breath and ran a finger over the image of their daughter.

Then the camera was back on Sam as he made his way out into the hall. "What happened?" Sam's voice had a different tone now, all business. He must have suspected they'd run into trouble at the ball.

"I'll tell you about it when we get home. Thanks, Sam. Really," Cal said. "I mean it. Thanks."

"I'd say I was just doing my job, but making sure that little girl is safe feels more like a mission than a job. See you when you get here." Sam ended the call.

"See, darlin'. She's just fine."

"She's not fine. None of us are fine. He started that fire to get to me. What if someone was injured or killed?"

He pried the phone from her hand and threw it on the seat next to them. He cupped her face, wanting her complete attention. "Let me get something straight for you right now. Nothing that asshole does or did is your fault. Got it?"

"*All* of it is my fault. I brought him into my life. I stayed too long with him. I put our daughter in danger—"

"Damn it! Stop it!"

She stiffened, and her eyes went wide.

"Shit!"

He released her, and she crawled off his lap and as far away as she could. It took every ounce of self-control he had to stay where he was and not follow her and grab her. The way she stared at him...like he was that bastard who'd beaten and raped her. Fuck it all! He struck the window with the side of his fist, and she flinched.

"I told you I would never hurt you." He couldn't keep the anger out of his voice. The whole thing was just so fucked up.

"I know."

He watched the way she hugged herself, rubbing her arm where Walker's hand had been, huddling in the farthest corner of the car from him. If he thought he was angry before, it was nothing compared to this new rage. The sharpness of it sliced at his control.

"When you cower from me... I can't fucking take it."

She continued to stare at him as though he would leap on top of her at any moment. The last thing she needed was to be trapped in the back of a car with an angry, out-of-control man. He grasped for some calm to smother the rage that clawed at him.

"I'm sorry."

She blinked in rapid succession, her body stiff, her lips pressed tightly together.

He took a deep breath and tried again. "You're safe here. You're safe with me." Only his tone was off. He'd ended up yelling what should've been soothing.

Her small voice came to him from across the car. "Don't shout."

"What?"

"Don't shout at me." This time stronger.

He laughed even though there was nothing funny here. The fury at what she'd been through was always there, lapping at his insides and leaving scars he didn't think would ever heal. He thought he'd learned to live with it. But there she was, still cowering like a wounded puppy, waiting for the next strike, telling him to stop his shouting, and he realized that he hadn't managed his rage at all. He'd ignored it, hoping it would go the fuck away.

Every time she'd flinch if he came at her too quickly or shrink from him if he showed an ounce of anger or impatience, he'd flush hot, infuriated for her, and at himself, her ex, the whole goddamned situation. It had gotten harder and harder to control his emotions around her until he felt like he was walking on cracking ice, staring into the abyss beneath it, expecting it to pull him under.

He let out a heavy sigh. "I'm trying."

"Try harder." Her chin came up a fraction of an inch. "Or I'll make the driver stop the car."

"Then what?"

"I'll get out."

"And then what?"

She wrinkled her brow, pressing her lips together. She shook her head, and he noticed that half of her hair had come down. He ran his gaze over her, noting a tear at the hem of her dress and that she was missing a shoe and an earring. Things he could replace. If only he could replace her memories and experiences as easily.

Her expression opened up, slowly returning to the Lucy he'd known before. "No, I'll kick *you* out of the car."

"What if I refuse to get out?"

"You won't."

"Why?"

"You just wouldn't."

He sat back in his seat, the boiling-hot mess of emotions slowly draining from him. Maybe she did know the difference between him and that asshole. Somewhere deep inside she knew the difference. At least he hoped to hell she did.

"You're right on that, darlin'. I'd get out if you told me to. I'd do just about anything you told me to do." Did she know? Did she have any idea the power she held over him? He reckoned if she did, she'd never truly believe it.

"I'm sorry," she said.

"I swear to Jesus if you say that one more time, I *will* get out of this fucking car. I'm the one who should be apologizing. I'm sorry."

"Do you realize that since we got married you curse more?"

Did he? He supposed it was because there was so fucking much to curse about. "Does it bother you? I'll stop."

"Maybe if you saved it for the bedroom."

He let out a half laugh. "You want me to talk dirty to you, darlin'? You'd like that?"

She nodded, a naughty gleam in her eyes. "Isn't that one of the options?"

"If not, we'll add it."

She smiled, and it was like the first rays of sunlight

across the open water, lighting up everything inside him. She sat up, and her fear seemed to fall away. "I do know you're not like...him. I know it in my heart—" She placed a hand on her chest. "But it's going to take time for my head to catch up. I'm—" She made a noise at the back of her throat. "I *regret* that you're the one paying the price for what he did to me."

"Darlin', that's the same as saying you're sorry, and I told you to stop apologizing to me for that asshole. He'll get what he's got coming to him. Don't you worry about that."

"You think so?"

"I know so. Now come here." He held a hand out to her. "I want to hold my wife."

She came right to him, which was something of a relief. He realized that a part of him still expected her to reject him. Maybe he wasn't the only one who needed to relearn how to react. His confidence where she was concerned had taken a hit of his own making. As she curled up in his lap, laying her head on his chest, he swore he'd do everything in his power to protect her and what they were building between them. She'd gifted him with so many things—their daughter, their new life together, and tentative forward moments like this in which he could imagine them together forever.

As the limo pulled through the gates of their home, he swore he'd kill the bastard who was trying to take all of that away.

TWENTY-TWO

Lucy prepared for the interview with *Dallas Women Today* magazine the way she used to gear up before cheerleading her high school's football games—extra deodorant, Vaseline on her teeth, and double-stick tape on her blouse so she didn't show anything she didn't want shown. Cal had been called out of town unexpectedly to handle problems with a merger or something or other. He'd promised he'd be home in time for the interview, but as it grew closer to the time when the crew was supposed to arrive, the chance that he'd make it grew less and less probable.

Since the night of the ball there had been a subtle shift in their relationship. If she'd asked Cal about it, he'd only deny it. But she felt it. Something had changed between them that she couldn't quite pin down what it was. Nothing was missing that had been there before and nothing had been added. It was more of a rearrangement of things, a slight resorting and reorganizing.

If she had to put a finger on any one thing that had changed, it would be the way Cal seemed to hesitate for a fraction of a second before he spoke to her or reached for her. Almost as though he had to think twice about what he did with her. And then he'd say or do what he'd normally say or do and she'd wonder if it had been her imagination. He was still the same Cal just with a half-second delay.

Earlier that day she'd gotten the best news she'd received in a long time. She was officially HIV free, as was Poppy. She hoped that bit of good news might shake loose the doubts that seemed to lurk at the back of her brain. She and Cal didn't have to use condoms anymore if they didn't want to. And they could do other things. Cal had said more than once how he couldn't wait to go down on her. One night he'd described so vividly what he would do to her with his mouth that she practically came right then and there. And she could reciprocate. They could finally cross off option number four.

"Mrs. Sellers?"

Lucy had been so fixated on her sexual daydream that she hadn't heard their housekeeper, Hazel, come into the room. She had a feeling that wasn't the first time Hazel had called to her from the doorway of Lucy's bedroom.

"I'm sorry, Hazel. What is it?"

"Priscilla Barnes from *Dallas Women Today* is here with a photographer for your interview. Miss Preston has them setting up in the living room."

"Thank you. I'll be right down."

Lucy gave herself one last look in the mirror, then squared her shoulders and followed Hazel down the stairs. Cal's publicist, Charity Preston, had arrived early that morning with a small crew of hair and makeup people. Everything Lucy was wearing had been chosen by Charity and deemed appropriate for Cal Sellers's new wife. Lucy must give the right impression. Appearance was everything to Charity. Even if it was fake, which described perfectly how Charity's hair and makeup people had made Lucy look.

Before entering the living room, Lucy took a deep

breath and let it out slowly. Then she swept into the room as Charity had shown her how to do and walked straight up to Priscilla Barnes, offering her hand.

"Ms. Barnes, it's a pleasure to meet you."

The woman gave her a funny look.

"*I'm* Priscilla Barnes."

Lucy swung around to find Charity glaring at her as she stood next to a woman who was clearly Priscilla Barnes...twenty-five years older and without all of the retouching of the photo Charity had shown her of the woman. Oh, crud. There was no making up for this. Charity had drilled into Lucy how important it was that she greet Priscilla just so and give her as much attention as possible. Lucy had failed on both accounts. Miserably.

"Of course," Lucy stammered as she made her way over. "I'd know you anywhere. Please forgive my mistake." She held her hand out to Priscilla, catching Charity shaking her head out of the corner of her eye. Crap. She'd messed up again. Priscilla was a germaphobe. She hated shaking hands. Lucy quickly disguised the gesture as an all-encompassing sweep of her hand around the room. "Welcome to my home, Ms. Barnes."

Priscilla ran her gaze over Lucy, then the room in general. After what felt like forever, her pale blue stare returned to Lucy, pinning her to the carpet with its directness. "You have a lovely home, Mrs. Sellers. You must be very proud of yourself."

Of all the insulting things! Not that Lucy should be proud of her home, but of the way in which she'd acquired it, insinuating that she'd attained it by lying on her back. Lucy wanted to tell the insufferable cow that she *was* proud, proud of the way she was able to hold back and not coldcock the bitch.

Charity must have seen something in Lucy's face because she stepped in smoothly with, "Mrs. Sellers, why don't you have a seat on the sofa." She beckoned the makeup artist. "Wanda, can you give Mrs. Sellers a little touch-up?"

Charity steered Priscilla away from Lucy by asking the woman a question about where Priscilla had just returned from vacation. A question Lucy had been coached to ask. Lucy hadn't been in the room half a minute before she'd botched the whole thing. She dropped onto the sofa and lifted her chin so Wanda could sweep a makeup brush across her face.

Lucy had one job. One. To make Cal look good. She couldn't seem to do that one simple thing. He'd asked her to do this interview in the hope it would present Lucy to the Dallas business community as his wife and earn her some much-needed good press. And she'd gone and mucked it up big time. How was she going to make this up to him?

The front door opened and closed, and Cal came striding into the living room. He spotted Lucy and paused for that half second before heading toward her. Lucy caught Priscilla's raised eyebrow and Charity's pressed lips as she stood to greet her husband. So they'd noticed Cal's hesitation too. Great. Just great.

"Sorry I'm late, darlin'." Cal bent and kissed Lucy on the cheek. He put his mouth to her ear and whispered, "You'll be fine."

Cal gave her elbow a squeeze and turned to make his way toward Priscilla and Charity. "Damned if you don't get prettier and prettier every time I see you, Priscilla. I hope you're not giving Charity too much grief over the setup here."

"No, Cal, it's fine. I understand perfectly why your new bride would want to show off her new home." Priscilla sent Lucy a smile that dripped with the condescension she'd laced through her words.

"Now don't go blaming Lucy." Cal returned to his wife and brought her over into their group. "This was all my idea." He looked down at her with all the love she felt from him in their most private moments, and it made her cheeks heat. "I want the world to see what I see when I look at her. She's the best wife and mother a husband could ask for. And that's never more apparent than when we're in our home."

The real reason was because they could control the environment and who had access to Lucy. But if Priscilla Barnes knew that, she'd know how real the rumors were about Lucy. The last thing they needed was more fodder for the rumor mill.

Lucy pasted on her best *Pleasure at Home* smile and hugged her husband around the waist. "And you're the best father and husband a wife could ask for."

"Darlin', that's hardly true, but I love you for saying it." He kissed Lucy's forehead.

"Well." Priscilla clapped her hands together. "Shall we get started then? Or do the two of you need a...moment?"

"What I have in mind for my wife will certainly take longer than a moment." Cal winked at Priscilla, which seemed to have little effect on the woman.

They were doomed. This whole scheme to redeem Lucy in the public's opinion was going to backfire on them. She should call this whole thing off right now and save herself the humiliation of what Priscilla would write about her. And about Cal.

Charity cleared her throat. "Mr. and Mrs. Sellers, why don't you have a seat on the couch." Charity motioned toward the chair next to the sofa. "Ms. Barnes. Can I get anyone anything before we get started? A beverage maybe?"

"Nothing for me," Priscilla said before lowering herself gingerly onto the chair. She placed her hands in her lap over her tablet and narrowed herself, as though she was trying to touch as little of the chair as possible.

"Lucy?" Cal asked.

Lucy shook her head and arranged her skirt so that it lay smoothly in her lap. "Nothing for me, thank you."

"We're fine, Charity." Cal unbuttoned his suit jacket and stretched back, placing an arm around Lucy.

"I can see you're still in the honeymoon phase of your marriage," Priscilla began, tapping her tablet to life. "How did the two of you meet?"

For all of her ferociousness and judgmental behavior, Priscilla Barnes conducted the interview like a professional. It was almost as if all the questions had been given to her in advance and were slanted strongly toward making Lucy look good. Priscilla lobbed so many slow-pitched questions Lucy's way that Lucy forgot why she was supposed to keep her guard up. After a rough start, Priscilla seemed to really warm toward Lucy.

Maybe warm was too generous a word. Priscilla had stopped looking down her nose at Lucy as if she were the source of whatever horrid mysterious scent Priscilla thought she smelled. Even Charity had relaxed back in her chair. Lucy began to think that maybe she hadn't messed things up for Cal after all, that maybe this interview would be the boon they needed for Cal's reputation.

Priscilla powered off her tablet. "That's all I have. Thank you for being such interesting interview subjects. Marcus." She motioned for the photographer. "Why don't you get some posed shots of Mr. and Mrs. Sellers? Then maybe we can convince them to bring in their daughter for some family photos."

Wanda moved in with her makeup brushes. When she was finished, the photographer directed them how to sit and where to look and began snapping away.

After a few moments, Priscilla called a halt. "And now

the little girl."

Lucy started to stand, but Cal motioned her back down. "I'll get her."

Charity got a phone call that she left the room to take, leaving Lucy alone with Priscilla.

As soon as Charity was out of the room, Priscilla pounced like a hundred-and-twenty-pound cat dressed in Chanel. "As I understand it, you got married as a business arrangement, a deal just like all the others he negotiates on a daily basis."

Lucy couldn't hold back her surprise. How did Priscilla know that their marriage had started as a business deal? Lucy looked around the room for some help, but the only other people in the room were the photographer and Priscilla's assistant huddled together discussing the next shots.

"I..." Lucy began.

"I also understand that he's asked for a paternity test on the child."

Lucy jerked back as though the woman had slapped her. Cal wanted a paternity test?

"And that there was no prenup. Rather clever of you, *Mrs. Sellers.*" Priscilla said the words *Mrs. Sellers* in a tone that branded Lucy a whore. "Although if the child turns out to not be his, you might have some trouble on your hands." Priscilla leaned forward and delivered a shot that went straight through Lucy. "All of your bedroom tricks might not be enough to hold on to him, but I'm sure you'll be able to console yourself with half his fortune."

Lucy gasped so loud the other two people in the room turned her way. Cal reentered the room with a big smile on his face, carrying Poppy. "She said my name."

"How wonderful," Priscilla said as she rose to her feet. "She's just darling. But isn't she a little young yet to be talking?"

Lucy sat, unable to move, pinned to the couch by Priscilla's words. If Priscilla knew about them, then it was all going to come crashing down around them. Cal would never redeem his reputation if Priscilla wrote about their arrangement in the magazine. It would be all over Dallas about how his marriage wasn't real, that it was a business deal. Or worse, that he'd paid Lucy to be his wife. He'd become the butt of cruel jokes. He was better off with a reputation as a playboy than as a man who paid women to be with him.

"I distinctly heard her say 'da'," Cal said.

"Babies make all kinds of gibberish sounds." Priscilla leaned in for a closer look at Poppy, no doubt checking to see if there was any resemblance between Cal and his daughter. "What lovely red hair she has." But Priscilla didn't sound like she thought it was lovely. More like a smoking gun that confirmed her suspicions about Lucy.

"She gets that from her momma's— Darlin', are you all right?" Cal brushed past Priscilla to get to Lucy, making the woman jump out of the way to avoid any contact with Poppy.

Lucy cleared her throat and put on a smile that hurt almost as much as the knot twisting her gut. "I'm fine. Just a little warm." She stood up. "I'll be right back." She dodged Cal and didn't look at Priscilla as she passed the bitch. She had to get a hold of herself before she broke down in front of Priscilla and really gave that viper a story to publish.

She tried to close the door to the downstairs bathroom, but Cal caught it and stopped her. "Are you feeling all right, darlin'? You're as pale as porcelain."

"I'm fine." She jerked on the handle of the door, fine pricks of sweat popping out all over her body as her mouth filled with saliva. "I'll just be a minute."

Cal dropped his hand, but the look on his face told her

that he didn't believe her for a second. Lucy got the door closed and locked seconds before she heaved into the toilet. She reached over and turned on the tap to help disguise the noise. When she got herself under control, she flushed the toilet and rinsed her mouth out.

One look in the mirror and she knew there was no way Cal was going to let this go. He'd know for sure something was wrong. Her skin had gone white beneath the heavy makeup, and her hair had slipped out of some of its pins. She did her best to fix it, but without a brush and some hairspray her efforts did little to hide the fact that she wasn't well.

What was she going to do? There wasn't any kind of spin Charity could put on this that would make it palatable. Lucy could imagine the title of the magazine article—Local Businessman Buys a Wife. Once the story broke, it would be all over for them. Cal would be humiliated. Ruined. A laughingstock.

Did Cal really not believe that Poppy was his? He could pay for a thousand paternity tests, and they'd all come out the same. Poppy was as much Cal's as she was Lucy's. Why hadn't he told her about his doubts? Had he already had the test done? Or was he only thinking about having it done? The one thing that hadn't changed in the last week or so was Cal's feelings toward Poppy. He'd been just as affectionate, just as smitten as ever, if not more so. Was he planning on telling her about the test? Or was he planning on having it done secretly and only mention it if the results came back that he wasn't the father?

Cal took matters into his own hands and unlocked the door with the spare key. He slipped into the bathroom and found Lucy sitting on the toilet lid, her head in her hands.

He dropped to his knees in front of her, pried her fingers away, and tilted her chin up so he could get a good look at her. "Darlin', what's wrong? What happened?" She blinked up at him, her big blue eyes filled with tears, and it felt like someone had skewered him right through the chest with a hot poker. "Darlin'..." he breathed, hardly able to get the words out. "What is it?"

"She knows."

"Who knows?"

"Priscilla Barnes." A tear slipped through her lower lashes and slid down her cheek, and that hot poker twisted inside him. "She knows about our marriage. Our bargain. Do you really want to get a paternity test? Because you can get one. You can get a thousand of them if you want to. Poppy's yours." More tears streaked down her face. He swiped at them as fast as they fell. "I swear to God she's yours, Cal."

How in the hell had Priscilla Barnes found out about their bargain? He hadn't told anyone, and he knew Lucy hadn't either.

"Oh, darlin'. Is that all?" He tried to make light of it, but he knew as much as Lucy likely did that he was going to take a hard knock when that article hit the newsstands. He could kiss that deal with Gleason and Hadley Investments goodbye. All of his plans, his careful work...gone.

He held her face and put his forehead to hers. "I know she's mine. I don't need any test to tell me that. And even if she weren't, I wouldn't care. I'm so in love with that little girl you'd have a hell of a time separating me from her."

"But what about that deal you've been working on? Marrying me was supposed to improve your reputation, not make it worse. All I've done since we got back together is make things worse for you. I can't even have sex right," she sobbed.

"Darlin', we have the rightest sex that's ever been attempted, let alone accomplished."

"You know what I mean. I can't do the things you want. I can't be the way I was before. I'm broken, and now I'm breaking you."

"The only way you could break me was if you left me."

"We never should've gotten married."

He sat back on his heels, the fury he carried around every day rising up inside him. He would destroy Priscilla Barnes for making Lucy feel this way, for making her cry. "Stay here. Don't move. I'll be right back."

He left the bathroom and went down the hall to his office. Punching in the number for Phil Davies, the publisher of *Dallas Women Today* magazine, Cal tipped some whiskey into a tumbler and managed to get two swallows down before Phil picked up.

"Phil, Cal Sellers here." He charged ahead without waiting for the man to respond to his greeting. "Priscilla Barnes is in my living room. She seems to be operating under the misconception that she's writing for a grocery-store tabloid."

"Sir?"

"Now I can handle the first part of my problem myself. I'm counting on you to handle the second."

"Yes, sir."

"I knew you were the right man for the job. Give your wife my best. Good night."

"Good night, sir."

Cal punched the End button on his cell phone and drained his glass. He didn't throw his weight around often, preferring to let his employees handle their jobs, but every now and then it paid to remind his employees who signed their paychecks. Sellers Investments' ownership of *Dallas Women Today* magazine wasn't well known. He doubted Priscilla Barnes had any idea she'd walked into her employer's house and insulted his wife in the most egregious way possible.

He set the tumbler on his desk and strode back out into the living room, where Priscilla stood a fair distance from her assistant. It took them a moment to realize he'd entered the room.

"I hope your wife is feeling all right," she all but sneered. "Those sudden bouts of *illness* can be difficult."

Cal took her by the elbow. "We've kept you too long. I'm sure you have a lot to do, so don't let us take up any more of your time." Behind him he could hear the photographer and the assistant quickly grabbing their things.

"But—" Priscilla began.

"Thank you again for coming," Charity added, going along with what Cal wanted. She'd worked for him too long not to know when he'd had enough. "We look forward to reading your article." She handed Priscilla her coat and opened the front door.

Priscilla appeared to be so startled by Cal rushing her out the door that she didn't get another word out until she was standing in the driveway and Cal was closing the door on her and her crew. "Thank you, Mr. Sellers. And thank your wife—"

Cal slammed the door on the woman, then rounded on Charity. "I told you that Lucy was not to be alone with that bitch."

"She wasn't. I was in the room the whole... Oh shit. I had to take a call. I was only gone a couple minutes."

"Oh shit, is right." Cal reopened the door and gestured for her to leave. "You're fired."

"But Mr. Sellers...Cal..."

"Goodbye, Charity."

On the porch, Charity turned around. "I'm sorry. I never thought..."

"And that's why you're fired." He slammed the door hard enough to rattle the vase on the entryway table. Then he went in search of his wife.

TWENTY-THREE

⚥

Cal found Lucy in the last place he expected to find her—their bedroom closet. She was throwing clothes into a suitcase. The fury that had been simmering ever since he figured out what Priscilla had done to Lucy would've boiled over if not for the biting panic that kicked him in the chest.

"You're not leaving me." He hadn't meant to blurt that out, but there it was—his worst fear.

"I think it's best for everyone involved."

She was so calm, and it was that calmness that scared him more than anything. He could handle the potent emotional brew that seemed to pour from her whether she was happy, sad, or mad. But this serene acceptance ate at his control. He caught a skirt she tried to toss into the suitcase in midair and threw it to the floor.

"I said..." he stalked toward her, backing her up against the clothes hanging in the closet, "...you're not fucking leaving me."

"Cal..."

A part of him registered her fear, but the other part of him—the part where anger had taken up residence and festered—overrode any instinct he might have had to pull back and rein in his emotions. "We have a deal. One year."

She put a hand on his chest, twisting so her body was partially turned away. It was a defensive move meant to expose as little of her as possible, like a boxer would.

"You promised me one year, Lucy, and you're going to give it to me."

He was crowding her now. She leaned back into the clothes hanging behind her. He shoved the hangers aside, exposing more of her. She wasn't going to hide from him, from this.

When he saw the look on her face, all the fight went out of him. He wasn't that man. He wasn't a bully. He damn sure wasn't like her ex. "I'm sorry." He gave her some room, backing away. "Please. Don't leave me."

She looked up at him from over her shoulder. "I was supposed to help your business reputation." She tilted back a little more, her tone not as calm as before, but at least she didn't sound frightened. "Not hurt it. *That* was the deal."

"Yeah, that was the deal. But do you know what else was part of the deal?"

"What?"

"Keeping you and Poppy safe."

She shifted her feet, turning so she faced him fully once more. "No, it wasn't. I never asked for that."

"It was in our vows."

"Those weren't real. They were just part of what we had to do to seal the deal."

"Maybe they weren't real for you, darlin', but they were damn real for me."

"I don't know why you'd want me around for another week, let alone the rest of the year. I've ruined everything. Priscilla Barnes is probably right now typing up that article, and it's going to ruin you." She made air quotes. "The Great Cal Sellers Buys a Wife."

He shook his head. He'd been so caught up in Lucy's upset he hadn't paid enough attention to what had happened downstairs. He held up a hand. "Wait a minute. What exactly did that bitch say about our deal?"

"What do you mean?"

"Come out of there. I can't have this conversation with you half buried in dresses."

He helped her climb out of the clothes racks and sat next to her on the little sofa thing in the middle of the closet. How much did Priscilla Barnes know about their deal? Did she know that he'd been paying Lucy the whole time they'd been married? Had she somehow tricked Lucy into admitting it?

"What did she say?" he asked. "Exactly. I want to know the exact words she used."

"Well..." She tilted her head to the side. "She kept using the words 'I understand'—I understand this and I understand that. She called our marriage a business arrangement, a deal just like all the others you negotiate. And then she congratulated me on marrying you without a prenup. But you have to know I would never take your money or this house."

"I do know that, darlin'. Although if you did ever leave me, you may as well take everything I have with you because without you I'd have nothing."

"Jesus, Cal. How can you say stuff like that to me after everything I've put you through?"

"Because it's true."

She put a hand on his cheek, bringing his face closer to hers. "I don't want to leave you. But I also don't want to keep making things worse for you." She dropped her hand in her lap on a sigh. "I don't know what to do. I can't stay and I can't leave and I can't fix what I messed up for you."

"Priscilla Barnes's threats have nothing to do with you. You didn't cause what happened today, but I think I know who might have. What did she say about Poppy?"

"Just that she *understood* that you wanted a paternity test. And then she insinuated that all of my bedroom tricks wouldn't be enough to hold on to all of the things I gained by marrying you, like your house and your money, if Poppy wasn't yours."

"She hasn't experienced your bedroom tricks."

She smacked him on the arm. "Be serious."

"I am serious. There's this one thing that you do—"

"I think you should get a paternity test."

"Why in the hell would I do that?"

"Because it would put all of the rumors to rest once and for all about Poppy."

"I haven't gotten to where I am in business and in life by chasing down and quashing random rumors. And I'm not going to start now. No. No paternity test."

"Fine. Then I'll get one."

"You can't get one without a DNA sample from me."

She tossed her hair over her shoulder and gave him that look that sent a shot of lust straight to his groin. "Oh, I can get a DNA sample from you, cowboy."

"Well, damn, darlin', is that a threat or a promise?"

"It's a fact." She climbed onto his lap and wrapped her arms around his neck, her skirt sliding dangerously high up her thighs. He followed it with his hands. "I bet I could get more than one from you in the next hour if I really wanted to," she bragged.

"Prove it."

"Right here in the closet?"

"The closet, the floor, the bed. I don't care where."

She kissed him, and that last sliver of fear dissolved as he slid his hands all the way up her skirt to grab her ass and pull her closer. He didn't know what he'd do if she'd gone through with it and left him. He didn't care what that dried-up bitch thought of him or of Lucy, but he sure as hell cared that it bothered Lucy. She'd been through so goddamned much. The last thing she needed was to worry about what anyone outside this closet thought of them.

He worked a hand up her blouse and popped the hooks on her bra. The feel of her. The fullness that more than filled his hand. Those little sounds of pleasure she made when he did something she liked. He could spend all day every day lying naked with her and exploring her body. All of those uncharted spots. All of those abundant curves.

He'd been so caught up in her that he hadn't noticed her hands had been busy too. She'd unbuttoned his shirt, and she now had her hand on his zipper...then on him. She stroked him slowly...so slowly. Groaning, he pushed up into her hand.

"Option number four," she whispered next to his ear, then she went to her knees in front of him. She bent and licked his cock, sending a shudder through him.

"Yes. Okay. Sure. Whatever you want."

Her smile... Jesus. She leaned forward and took him into her mouth. Deep. He dropped his head back and tried not to think about her full lips sliding up then down the length of him. It had been so long since she'd sucked him off— What the hell?

"What are you *doing*?" He moved back, causing his dick to slip out of her mouth. Her mouth...damn.

She ran her tongue along her lower then upper lip, like a cat licking cream. "It's called giving head."

"I know what it's called. I thought you couldn't do it."

"I couldn't until I knew I was cleared. Poppy's and my final tests came in. Both negative. Now do you want to talk or—?"

Lucy found herself squeezed in the fiercest hug she'd ever had.

"Are you both really okay?" he asked, his voice muffled in the side of her neck.

"Yes. We're both fine. This wasn't exactly the way I wanted to tell you…"

He lifted his head and looked at her. "I don't care. I'm just so damn glad you're both all right."

"We're fine."

"Really?"

"Really."

"In that case…"

In one swift move Cal changed their positions so that she was the one lying on the couch with him on top. He pushed her skirt up, grabbed a hold of her panties, and pulled them off, throwing them over his shoulder.

"If I recall, darlin', option number four is a mutually beneficial option. I get to finally put my mouth here." He slid a finger down her slickness. "Already wet."

"And I get to put *my* mouth here." She reached for him, enjoying the *ugh* her touch elicited. "This couch may not be the best place for this."

"Wrong." He bent and licked her. "You're right where I want you."

He set his mouth to her, slipping one then two fingers into her, stroking deep. She arched back, giving in to him. How could she do anything else? Within a matter of minutes she was so close to coming she thought she'd die if she didn't. Her breath hitched as he slowed then stopped altogether.

"What are you *doing*?"

"Punishing you."

"Punish… What for?"

"For threatening to leave me."

"God, Cal, can we talk—?"

He rubbed her clit with his thumb in practiced strokes.

"Ohh, yesss," she moaned.

He slipped his fingers inside of her again, curling his middle finger so it hit just the right spot… "Promise me."

"Yes."

"You won't leave. Don't even threaten to leave me. Say it." He caught her nipple between his fingers. "Say it and I'll make you come so hard you'll think you've died."

"No, Cal," she panted. She was close. *So* close. "I won't leave... I won't leave you."

He licked her clit, then sucked, increasing the pace of his hands. Her orgasm barreled toward her. She was all sensation. The prickling heat...that tense fingernail edge...the ecstasy of that half-second right before...and then it hit. She screamed, her body bowing under the onslaught. He cupped her, holding the sensations in and drawing them out. She distantly felt her body. It was below her somewhere, heavy and spent. Cal was saying something to her, kissing her neck, her breasts. And then he pressed into her little by little until he hit deep.

The pleasure built again, slower than before. She didn't think she could sustain another orgasm. But the feel of him inside her, on top of her, around her, it was all too much. He mumbled something...endearments and naughty words. The dirtier he talked, the quicker she came back around until she was on the edge of orgasm, urging him on with her cries and her fingers gripping his bare ass. She came on a long, low moan, and he quickly followed, driving deep into her.

"Jesus, God, darlin'."

She let out a heavy sigh. "Yeah."

"Are we dead? Did we kill each other?"

"If this is death, then it beats life by miles."

His chuckle vibrated through her. He traced a finger around her nipple, making the skin around it pucker. "Well, I did promise to make you come so hard you'd think you'd died."

"And you nearly killed us both."

He rose up on his elbow to look down at her. "You're

going to keep your promise to me."

"Or what? Every time I try to leave you'll get me naked and make me come so hard I can't walk let alone walk out the door?"

"No." He dropped his gaze to where his hand lay on her breast. "This started out as a business deal, but that's not what it is anymore, is it?"

"Definitely not. Unless you make love to everyone you do business with."

"Hell, no. Although if I did, more deals might go my way."

"*All* the deals would go your way." She fisted a hand in his hair and brought his head down for a slow-winding kiss that she hoped told him more than she could ever say with words. About how much he meant to her. How much she loved him, wanted him, *craved* him. And how grateful she was to have him in hers and Poppy's lives.

When they parted, he gave her a look that she'd never seen on him before, and then it was gone and in its place was his usual wicked grin. "Keep kissing me like that and you're going to get your second DNA sample."

"I wasn't kidding when I told you I think you should get that paternity test."

"Darlin', don't talk about paternity tests while I'm still inside you. You'll jinx us." He shifted to lie next to her.

"You don't want another baby?"

"Sure I do. I thought maybe you'd want to wait till Poppy's a little older."

She shrugged. "I'm on birth control, but if it happens, it happens. I actually would like to wait. Maybe until next year."

"Until we're past our one-year mark?"

"Something like that."

He lifted her chin with his finger so she had to look up at him. "Something like what? Be honest."

"I guess I just want to make sure we're as strong as we can be before we bring another child into the world. And that it's a safe world."

He studied her for a moment, his wild blue eyes searching for something. Maybe that tiny seed of doubt she still carried where he was concerned. He'd changed a lot since they'd been together before. In big and in small ways. The memory of him bending his secretary over his desk still haunted her sometimes, only now the memories were of people she hardly recognized anymore. They weren't the same people they'd been the first time around.

They wouldn't make the same mistakes.

"I want to make sure Kevin can't hurt us ever again," she said. "I can't bring another child into this nightmare."

"I agree." He looked like he was going to say something more, but then nuzzled her neck instead. "About that second DNA sample..."

TWENTY-FOUR

"Lucy, let's go," Cal hollered up the stairs. "We're going to be late if we don't leave in the next five minutes."

"I'm coming!"

Ten minutes later Lucy came barreling down the stairs, her shoes and purse in one hand and two presents in the other. Cal met her halfway and relieved her of her packages.

"Two presents?"

She slipped her shoes on. "One for Crosby and one for Mi."

Cal eyed the packages as he held the front door open for his wife. He knew Rob Crosby, the director of *Pleasure at Home*, had specifically requested no gifts. "What did you get for Crosby?"

"Scotch."

"Good call."

He helped her into the car, and then they were finally on their way to the party. He'd lied when he'd told her they had five minutes, padding their timing by fifteen minutes. And it was a good thing he did. He hated being late, even to a retirement party/baby shower.

"I can't believe Crosby's retiring. I thought for sure he'd keel over in his director's chair at ninety-three while yelling at one of the grips."

Cal had promised Crosby he wouldn't tell anyone the real reason Crosby was retiring early—he had terminal cancer and wanted to spend his last days with his family. It hadn't been an easy thing, making that promise to his friend or keeping it. Lucy had worked with Crosby for two years. If she knew he was keeping this info about Crosby from her, she'd be very upset with him. And the last thing he wanted was his wife upset with him.

Things between them for the past few weeks had been really good. Incredible. The article about Lucy had been published with a completely different slant than he imagined Priscilla Barnes had had in mind. But then, her name hadn't appeared in the byline.

They hadn't heard a thing from Lucy's asshole ex, and Cal had begun to wonder if maybe he wasn't gearing up for something. Of course he didn't share his concerns with Lucy. She had started to hope that maybe Walker had lost interest. Lucas had been keeping an eye out, and so far Walker hadn't shown up on any police blotter or in any morgue. He was still out there...somewhere.

They drove up to the TV station where *Pleasure at Home* was filmed, which looked like every other office building in the industrial park it was located in. Lucy jumped out of the car before Cal threw it into park, excited to be seeing her old friends again. He angled out of the car and slid on his Stetson, pulling it low to shade his eyes. He got the presents out of the backseat and jogged to catch up to his wife.

"I'm thinking we need to get you out of the house more often, darlin', if you're this starved for company that you'd leave me behind to carry your packages."

Lucy slipped her arm through Cal's. "It feels like forever since I've seen Mi, and it has absolutely been forever since I've seen Crosby and the rest of the crew. I have good memories here, Cal. Working here was one of the highlights of my life...other than having Poppy."

"And marrying me."

"Well, yes. And that too. Of course."

He laughed. She always made him laugh. And kept him honest.

They entered the studio to find the party in full swing. Lucy broke away to greet her friends. Cal spotted Lucas off to the side leaning against the wall. After handing the presents off to one of the production assistants, he headed for his friend.

Cal had met Lucas so many years ago, he'd lost track of how long they'd known each other. Lucas was Cal's opposite in just about every way, but somehow their friendship worked. Cal had learned long ago not to question the why of it. He was so damn lucky to have a friend like Lucas.

"Hey," he said.

"Hey," Lucas replied.

"Where'd you get that beer?"

Lucas reached into the cooler next to him, pulled out a beer, and handed it to Cal.

"Thanks. Looks like the wives are glad to see each other."

Across the room Lucy and Mi were embracing and crying like they hadn't seen each other in years.

"Mi's been so busy training Elisa and getting ready for the baby she hasn't had much spare time."

"I hear your sister's a natural at selling sex toys," Cal teased.

Lucas made a face. "I owe you a punch in the throat for hiring her."

"She's a grown woman. Attractive. Smart. The audience loves her. You should be happy. With Elisa taking over the show, Mi will have more time to spend with you and the baby when he comes."

"You're not the only one to notice my sister's attractiveness," Lucas grumbled.

Cal tracked his friend's gaze across the room to where *Pleasure at Home*'s new director, Ian Kershaw, stood talking to one of the cameramen. Only Kershaw's gaze wasn't on the man in front of him—it was firmly latched on to Elisa's ass. Cal could hardly blame the man. Lucas's sister had caught Cal's eye a time or two back in the day. Tall like the rest of the Vegas, Elisa had long dark hair, exotic looks, a nice firm ass, and a rack any man would love to get his hands on. And it looked like that was exactly what Ian Kershaw had in mind.

Cal chuckled. "Like I said...she's a grown woman."

"Don't you have some kind of rule about romance in the workplace you could enforce?"

"It'd be hypocritical of me, seeing as how I slept with Lucy when she was the host of *Pleasure at Home*." Cal tipped his beer toward Lucas. "And of you too, since I do believe you were in my employ when you took up with Mi. Moved her right into your house *and* your bed."

Lucas shifted his feet. "That doesn't count. Damn. He's coming our way."

Ian Kershaw made his way across the room to where Lucas and Cal stood. Elisa followed his movement, *her* gaze firmly on *Kershaw's* ass.

"Looks like the attraction's mutual." Cal clapped his friend on the shoulder and laughed. "Be nice. Kershaw could end up being your brother-in-law."

"Fuck off," Lucas muttered.

"Hello, Mr. Sellers." Ian held his hand out, and Cal shook it. "Thanks again for the opportunity here at *Pleasure at Home*."

"Call me Cal." He gestured toward Lucas. "Have you met Lucas Vega, Mi's husband...and Elisa's brother?"

"No, I don't believe we've met." Ian shook Lucas's hand, managing to not grimace at the excessive force Lucas used. "Nice to meet you."

Lucas grunted.

Despite Lucas's feelings toward the man, Cal was grateful to have him aboard. Just when Cal thought they'd never find a new director for the show, Ian Kershaw's resume had come across his desk. Ian was overqualified for the job, and in accepting it took a pay cut. Cal had Lucas check out Kershaw, and he couldn't find any reason why the man would take a career step down to move from California to Dallas. He'd left his last job in L.A. with a glowing recommendation from a popular reality TV show's producer, sold his home in Malibu, and moved to Texas where—according to Lucas's report on the man—he had no friends or family.

"You're all settled in then?" Cal asked.

"We start taping the new shows with Elisa as the host next week. I've already been over the marketing plan, and the new products have arrived. Mr. Crosby's been invaluable in helping me get to know everyone and how things work. Everything's set."

"Glad to hear it."

"Hello, gentlemen." Elisa slid in between Cal and Ian. She nodded at her brother. "Lucas."

"Your brother's more of a gentleman than I am," Cal said, smiling despite Lucas's scowl. Cal gave Elisa a hug and a kiss on the cheek. "I guess this is my official chance to welcome you to *Pleasure at Home*."

Elisa had swept into the studio and delivered an audition that blew everyone away, including Crosby. And he wasn't easy to please. Lucas, on the other hand, had not been pleased. It was one thing for his wife to sell sex toys on TV, and quite another for his sister to do it.

After watching Elisa's tapes, there was no way Cal was

going to bend to his friend's wishes. Elisa was a natural. She glowed on camera the same way Mi and Lucy had, only Elisa had a little something more. Cal couldn't put his finger on what exactly that something was, but he heard the sound of cash being sorted while he watched Elisa, and he was sold.

"Thank you. I absolutely love it here. It's my dream job."

Lucas curled his lip at his sister. "Your dream job is touching fake cocks all day?"

"It was good enough for your wife." She gestured toward Cal. "And his wife. But it's not good enough for me? I'm not a virgin, you know, Lucas. I've had sex. I *have* sex. I've even tried out some of those fake cocks. They're pretty darn good. If they could earn a paycheck and rub my feet, I wouldn't need a man at all."

Lucas glanced up at the ceiling, exasperation with his sister in his body language and tone. "Jesus fucking Christ."

Cal noticed Ian sneaking a side glance at Elisa, an amused smirk on his face. Was he who Elisa was currently having sex with? Or working toward having sex with? That would be some fast work. For all of the ribbing he gave Lucas and how attractive Elisa was, Cal had only ever seen her as the sister of his best friend. Hell, she was almost a sister to him. He made a note to keep an eye on the situation. Not that Lucas wouldn't. But Cal had enough distance from Elisa to see things her brother might overlook. And if Elisa knew Cal intended to play honorary brother to her, she'd probably try to kick his ass.

"We can always count on you, Elisa, to tell it like it is." Cal clinked his beer bottle against hers.

Lucas let out a frustrated sigh and turned to walk away. "I'm going to go find Mi."

"He's seen stuff while in the Navy that the rest of us

can't begin to imagine, and yet Lucas gets all puritanical when it comes to sex." Elisa watched her brother put his arm around his wife. "If Mi wasn't pregnant, I'd wonder if he ever has sex at all."

"Give him a break," Ian said. "No man wants to imagine his sister having sex."

"Your sister has three kids," Elisa shot back.

"Immaculate conception." Ian took a sip from his cup.

Cal noticed that the man wasn't drinking alcohol, unless the clear liquid in his cup was straight vodka. He doubted it. Cal's daddy had taught him three things—never trust a woman who only talked about money, never trust a horse showing the whites of its eyes, and never trust a man with something to hide. And something told him that Ian Kershaw had something to hide. Something more than his affair or intended affair with Elisa.

"Welcome aboard, both of you. I'm looking forward to the new shows. If you'll excuse me, I'm going to find my wife."

Cal left the couple whispering to each other and trying—but failing miserably—at hiding their attraction. He looked around for Lucy, but she was nowhere in sight. He'd made sure that security was tighter than usual. As *Pleasure at Home* seemed to attract more than its fair share of negative attention—some of it threatening—there was always security on the premises. Especially since Mi had been the target of a stalker, and the original building the studio had been in had been blown up by a religious extremist group.

There was no reason for Cal to panic. Lucy was probably in the ladies' room and would be back shortly. In the meantime, he'd keep an eye on his assistant, Felicia. That business with Priscilla Barnes had revealed a leak in Cal's otherwise-tight ship. And that leak went by the name of Felicia. She'd been acting strange ever since Cal had gotten married. Her flirting, always easy to ignore, had become more brazen. She'd rub up against any part of Cal she could whenever she could. And her clothes bordered on breaking company policy. But she never did anything that would give him cause to let her go.

There had only been two people in his office when he had proposed the marriage deal to Lucy—him and Lucy. Cal hadn't given a thought to the fact that Felicia had been on the other side of the door. He certainly hadn't figured her for bugging his office, but when he had Lucas do a sweep after the magazine interview, they found one. Not only had Lucas found the listening device, but he was able to track it back to Felicia. Cal wasn't sure if she was working for someone else or if she was using the info she acquired for her own gain. Either way, Felicia was a problem that needed to be solved. He hadn't gotten where he was by acting too fast or in anger. So he was biding his time, watching Felicia, trying to figure out what her game was and making plans to move against her.

Felicia caught him looking at her, said something to the woman she'd been talking to, and headed over to where Cal was. She was attractive and—if he was honest—that had been part of the reason he'd hired her. She'd also come highly recommended and was a very experienced executive assistant.

"Hello, boss." Felicia fingered his tie, stroking her thumb along a nonexistent wrinkle. "Nice party."

He ran a hand down his tie, causing her to drop her hand. "Thanks. I'm glad you're having a good time." He looked out over the top of her head for Lucy. "Did you come here with anyone?"

"No." She angled closer, smashing her breast against his side. "I'm available."

He shifted away. "Have you seen my wife?"

"I think she went to the restroom. She looked a little

sick."

Cal made a move to go around her, but she stopped him with a hand on his arm. "I'm sure she's fine. Her friend went with her. Probably all of this rich food." She pulled at him so that he turned toward her. "I don't know about you, but I could use a drink."

The phrase *Keep your friends close and your enemies even closer* came to mind. "What are you having?"

"Whatever you are."

⋐⋑

Lucy splashed cold water on her face. She hadn't felt this sick this suddenly since…oh, God. She did some quick mental calculations and realized she should've gotten her period yesterday. She'd been so caught up in everything that had been going on she hadn't been paying attention to the little things. Like when her period was due. She was on birth control, so it should've come right on schedule. Even without birth control, her cycle was predictable practically to the minute.

She and Cal had talked briefly about having another baby. She'd gotten the impression Cal wanted to wait. Jinx them was right. Cal had joked about not talking about babies while he was still inside her, and that was probably the exact moment he'd gotten her pregnant. Damn it. She hadn't lost all of the weight from her first pregnancy, and here she was pregnant again.

Maybe she was overreacting.

She grabbed a handful of towels and blotted her face. Maybe she ate something that didn't agree with her. Maybe all of the stress had made her late. Maybe, maybe, maybe.

Placing a hand on her stomach, she closed her eyes. She was pregnant. She just knew it. That was the kind of luck she had. No sooner had she and Cal stopped doubling up on birth control, she got pregnant. Damn that man. Well, she guessed they'd make it work somehow. And if she dared to admit it, she was secretly glad. Poppy would have a brother or sister, and Cal would get to be there when his child came into the world—something he'd missed with Poppy.

Tears filled her eyes. She reached into her purse for a tissue. Behind her she heard someone come in and then the snick of the lock. She spun around to find Kevin standing just feet away from her.

"Hello, Lucy."

TWENTY-FIVE

⚥

"How did you get in here?" Lucy's heart pounded so hard she thought her ribs would crack.

Kevin leaned back against the door and ran his filthy gaze over her. He was dressed in the uniform of the catering company with a long-haired wig and a full fake beard. But she'd know him anywhere. He filled the corners of her mind, always lurking, always invading moments of her life where he didn't belong. Sometimes she even thought she saw him or heard him calling for her. She'd imagined a thousand times what she would say or do when she saw him.

Facing him now, she realized those moments hadn't prepared her. Everything she had thought to say or do fled her mind, leaving behind a frozen stillness and abject helplessness. She had no defense against him. He'd found her. She'd known he would. He would never give up until he got what he wanted. And what he wanted was her dead.

"Still fat," he sneered. "Dressed better though. A fancy pig in billionaire's clothing."

He came off the door and stalked toward her. She backed up against the sinks, the edge of the counter biting into her flesh.

"You can dress a pig up, but it's still a pig. Does he lift that fancy dress and pork you, pig?" He snorted at his own joke.

It was his laugh that Lucy had grown to fear most. He could do almost anything when he was amused. Like a bomb with a lit fuse Lucy never knew when he'd blow. It was the waiting that ate at her. He could explode at any minute, but until he did she kept a small hope that this would be the one time when he wouldn't.

"I'm...I'm not a pig."

His face that she'd thought so handsome once now creased into a frown. He wasn't used to her standing up to him. She'd never talked back when they were together.

He leaned closer. "What did you say, pig?"

"Get out, Kevin."

"Oh, you're giving me orders now?" He grabbed a fistful of her hair. Shaking her by it, he asked, "*You're* giving me orders, you rich, fat pig?"

Spittle dotting his chin, his face red, he crowded her, using his size and strength against her. She could see the explosion was near. He twisted her hair in his fist, and she grimaced in pain, biting back a cry.

"Just because you're fucking a billionaire doesn't give you the right to give me orders." He caught her under her chin with his other hand. "I could kill you. I could fuck you and kill you. You're *nothing*."

His fingers pressed into her neck on either side of her windpipe. He'd done this many times before—make her black out then wait for her to come back around so he could do it all over again. Sometimes she'd wake up with him on top of her, raping her. Sometimes she'd wake up locked in the closet or the bedroom. He'd torment her from the other room, making her feel small...*making* her nothing.

Her purse was trapped between their bodies, her hand

inside wrapped around a packet of tissues. She shoved her hand in deeper. Dots filled her vision as he lifted her. Blackness feathered the edges of her sight, narrowing in on his face so close to hers.

"Lu-cyyy," he chanted. "Lu-cyyy, Lu-cyyy—"

A muffled bang made them both freeze. Kevin's eyes widened as his grip on her loosened. He released her, putting the hand he'd had on her throat over the blood seeping out of his stomach. He stared at her in shock.

"Lucy?"

She pulled the trigger again. He pitched back, releasing her entirely. She gripped the edge of the counter and fired again. And again. And again until the gun clicked empty. She kept pulling the trigger until her knees gave way and she spiraled downward. The last image she saw was of Kevin lying on the floor, a pool of blood leaking out from under him onto the tile.

Then nothing.

ଔଇ

At the sound of shots, everyone in the room froze. And then pandemonium. Lucas gave Cal a look that said *stay back* as he pulled a gun from the small of his back. The hell he would. Lucas moved in the direction of where the gunshots had come from. Cal didn't hesitate. He raced after his friend. All he could think was Lucy...Lucy... *Where is Lucy?*

They hit the hall together. Cal cursed himself for not bringing his own gun. A couple of the security guys pounded on a closed door. The women's restroom.

"Lucy!" Cal shouted. "Lucy!"

Lucas rammed the metal door with his shoulder, but it didn't budge. "Somebody get a key!" He began to beat at the lock with the butt of his gun.

Cal spotted a fire extinguisher down the hall. He ran over, pushing partygoers out of the way, and grabbed the extinguisher. He took over smashing the lock until it bent and gave.

Lucas put a hand on Cal's chest, stopping him from rushing in. Gun drawn, Lucas eased the door open, going in low. "Somebody call an ambulance!"

Lucas ran in with Cal right on his heels. Lucy lay on the floor under the sinks, her gun in her hand. Next to her Walker lay still. Lucy must've put every single one of her bullets in him. Lucas went for Walker, and Cal went for Lucy. He dropped to his knees next to her and checked her pulse, nearly collapsing on top of her when he felt it strong and sure. Everything he ever wanted and didn't deserve was right there in front of him. If anything ever happened to her, he didn't know what he'd do.

He stroked her cheek. "Lucy. Lucy. Come on, darlin', wake up for me."

"Oh, my God!" Mi rushed over and knelt next to Cal. "Is she okay? Is she going to be okay?" She reached for Lucy's hand and rubbed it between both of hers. "Lucy. Wake up. Wake up, Lucy."

"He's dead," Lucas announced.

Cal could see the purple impressions of that bastard's hand on Lucy's neck. If he weren't already dead, Cal would've killed Walker himself.

"Darlin'—" His voice cracked. "Open your eyes."

Lucy moaned, and the whole room seemed to let out a collective breath.

"An ambulance is on the way," one of the security guards informed them.

"Oh, thank God," Mi whispered, tears streaking her face. "Thank God."

Lucy moaned again and turned her head toward Cal. Her lips moved, but she didn't make any sound. Her eyelids fluttered open, and Cal stared down into the most beautiful set of blue eyes he'd ever seen.

He swallowed back the emotion that had his chest in a vise grip. "Hey there, darlin'."

"Cal? Where—?" She tried to sit up.

"Stay down until the ambulance gets here," Lucas ordered. "Everyone else out of the room. This is a crime scene. That includes you, *querida*," he said to Mi.

"I'm staying," she told him.

"*Querida*..." Lucas seemed not to know what to do with his wife. "You're pregnant," he pleaded.

"I'm not leaving her." Mi slipped her sweater off and gently tucked it under Lucy's head. When she pulled her hand away, there was blood on it. She balled her hand and quickly hid it from Lucy's view.

Cal thought he might be sick, seeing Lucy's blood on Mi's hand. It could too easily have been Lucy lying in a pool of her own blood, her body riddled with bullets.

"Is he dead?" Lucy asked.

"He's dead all right," Mi answered before Cal could get a word in. "You filled him full of lead. Since when do you know how to shoot a gun?"

Lucy waved a hand toward her husband. "Cal got it for me."

Mi gave him a look that told him she was impressed with him. "I had my doubts about you. I thought you were going to break her heart. Thank you." She threw her arms around him and nearly made him hit his head on one of the sinks. "Thank you for taking care of Lucy and for getting her that gun."

He hugged her back and whispered in her ear, "I'd do anything for her."

When Mi pulled away, she had a whole new look on her face. "I think you'll do," she told him as she patted his cheek.

Police and paramedics came into the room. Lucas finally got Mi to leave Lucy's side and ushered her out with a gentle hand on the small of her back. To see his big, giant friend defer to his much smaller wife made Cal smile.

Lucy didn't want to go to the hospital, but Cal talked her into it. He didn't like the way her head wouldn't stop bleeding and how dizzy she was when they sat her up.

"I'm fine," she complained.

"Humor me. And while we're there, I think I'll have them check me out for signs of a heart attack. I'm pretty sure I had a massive one after seeing you on the floor, darlin'."

ೞ৪০

"Is he really dead?" Lucy must've asked that about twenty times from when she woke up until they released her from the hospital a few hours later.

The police had taken her statement at the hospital and confiscated her gun, which was fine with Cal as there was no more need for it now that Walker was dead. As soon as they walked in the front door of their home, Lucy demanded to see Poppy when she should've gone in and laid down. Cal had called Sam from the ambulance and had him put Poppy on screen so they could both see for themselves that their daughter was okay. Cal helped her up the stairs and kept her from running up them like she seemed to want to do. He waited for her to sit down before handing her Poppy to hold.

She looked Poppy over from her toes to the top of her head. Cal guessed she was checking to be sure there wasn't a mark on her. She folded Poppy into a fierce hug that made the child squeak before bursting into tears with her face pressed into Poppy's neck. Sam eased out of the room and shut the door behind him.

Cal knelt and embraced his wife and child.

They'd come so close to losing everything. Knowing they were now safe from Walker was overwhelming. He hadn't realized how much tension and anger he'd been holding in, but now it came rushing at him. He held on to his little family, buffeted by one wave of emotion after another.

"He can never hurt you again. He can never hurt any of us ever again. You stopped him, darlin'." He swept her hair back from her face and kissed her wet cheek. "You did it."

"I couldn't have done it without you. Thank you. Thank you for giving me the confidence to believe in something better for myself and for Poppy. And for giving me the strength to stand up to him. I looked him right in the eye, and I stood up for myself. I was never able to strike back before."

"You had it in you all along. If I did anything, it was to help you find the courage you already possessed."

"This isn't like you. The Cal I know isn't modest."

She had a teasing tone to her voice and the first real smile—one with no worry hovering in the background—that he'd seen on her since before he'd messed things up and caused their split. He hadn't noticed the difference until this moment. It was like looking at a picture and not knowing what was different about it until someone pointed it out and then it became painfully obvious.

"I've been brought to my knees and humbled. Everything you've been through can all be laid at my door. And don't think for a moment that I don't know it. Seeing you on the floor of that bathroom, I did drop to my knees. I'm just so grateful for you—" he kissed her, "—and for you." He kissed his daughter's head, which was nestled in the crook of her mother's shoulder.

"Stop." Lucy fanned her face, her eyes filling with tears. "I finally stopped crying, and now you're making me start up all over again."

"No more crying, darlin'. No more fear, no more worry. Nothing but good times ahead."

"And no more extra security. We can take Poppy out of the house. Oh! What about a vacation?"

"I think that's—"

Someone knocked on the door. Cal rose and opened it to find their housekeeper, Hazel, on the other side.

"You have a phone call, Mr. Sellers."

"Who is it?"

"Mr. Gleason. He's calling to confirm dinner tomorrow night."

Cal looked to Lucy and then back to Hazel. "Can you please tell Mr. Gleason that we'll have to reschedule—"

"No. Hazel, please tell Mr. Gleason we'll be there."

"But, darlin', you're hurt. We can reschedule. They'll understand."

"We're going back to life as usual. Besides we've rescheduled that dinner too many times already. Please relay the message, Hazel."

"Yes, ma'am."

Cal closed the door. "I don't know about you, but I'm not up to playing chase with the Gleasons on a good day, let alone the day after you were nearly killed." He knew his tone had an edge to it, but goddamn it. He'd almost lost her.

Poppy's head came off Lucy's shoulder, and she frowned up at Cal.

"I'm all right, Cal."

"Maybe *you* are."

"I don't know what happened with that article and Priscilla Barnes, but I have a feeling you somehow fixed it. I still have a job to do for you that includes schmoozing that pervy businessman into selling you his business. And I'm betting he called to confirm just so he and Anne can get all of the juicy details about what happened today straight from the horse's mouth. We're going to use that to your advantage."

"Darlin', I couldn't give three shits about what that asshole and his wife want right now. And I'm sure as hell not going to parade you around in front of them so that they can have the freshest, most accurate gossip to share with their friends."

"There's already been so much gossip about us. Wouldn't it be nice if some of it was accurate for a change?"

He let out a frustrated growl. "You're injured."

"I'm fine. Let me do this for you."

"No."

"Cal...please. I want to."

"Stop looking at me like that. Both you and Poppy give me that same look. I'm outnumbered here."

"What look?"

"*That* look. I can't resist you when you look at me like that."

"Then it's settled. Dinner tomorrow night at six with the Gleasons."

TWENTY-SIX

Lucy made Cal go into the office the next morning, wanting everything to go back to normal. Their new normal. The normal they should've had all along. She knew Cal didn't understand why she wanted to keep their dinner plans with the Gleasons, but she refused to let their lives be dictated by Kevin, even in his death. It would be back to the business of living *their* lives.

Besides, she had a pregnancy test to buy and take. She didn't want Cal around for that just in case it came back negative. There was no need to give him another reason to worry about her unless it was absolutely necessary. She thought she'd been nervous taking the pregnancy test when she got pregnant with Poppy, but this was a whole new level of nervousness. So much was riding on this test. A small part of her wished for a negative result. They'd been through so much and had barely started their lives together as a married couple. Did they really need the added stress of having another child so soon? Wouldn't it be better to wait until they decided they were ready?

She had Sam drive her to the store and wait in the car with Poppy. She really shouldn't have been out. The doctors had diagnosed her with a mild concussion, and she had a big bruise on her shoulder from when she had hit the edge of the sink. She was lucky considering what could've happened.

As soon as she got home, she went straight to their bathroom upstairs to take the pregnancy test. Locking the door behind her, she stared at the box in her hand. She read the directions twice to make she sure she didn't do it wrong. Pee on the stick. Wait three minutes. Seemed pretty simple, except there wasn't anything simple about whatever the results would be.

Three minutes was a long time.

She thought back to that first moment when she turned and saw Kevin in the bathroom… It was as though she'd been hurdled back in time to when she'd lived with him and the horrible things he'd done to her. Not just the physical damage. Bruises and cuts healed, pain faded. No, it was the way he got inside her head, the way he twisted everything so she didn't know which side was up. He'd thrown her into a mental pit of despair she didn't think she'd ever be able to climb out of let alone recover from.

The darkness of being so alone, so totally and completely wrong about Kevin when she'd first met him, crawled over her like a fungus, coating her from the inside out. It chewed away tiny bits of her until all that was left was the thin and holey fabric of the person she'd once been. Where she'd gotten the strength to leave, she'd never know. She couldn't even pinpoint the one thing he'd done that had drawn the line for her. One day she got up and got out. Walked right out of the house when she'd been so terrified to go anywhere without him or without his permission.

Maybe it was that something that had made her leave that had also made her stand up to him in that bathroom and fight back. She wished she could say she felt good about killing Kevin. Mostly she just felt sick. And sad. The sadness surprised her. Of all of the emotions she'd thought she'd feel when she was finally free of him, sorrow had to have been the very last, if it was even in the mix at all. Why should she grieve for him? He didn't deserve to be mourned.

She was furious with herself for wasting sorrow on a man who hadn't given her a thought unless it was how to torture her in new and continuously inventive ways. If he were here now, he'd laugh at her stupidity. She'd been *so* stupid where men were concerned. Cal included. She'd read that situation wrong. Twice.

The first time was in her thinking that she could be the one to change Cal. That somehow her love could change him from a billionaire playboy to a family man. The second time was in not recognizing that he *had* changed. He'd reinvented himself in the time they were apart. She guessed she could say that he'd grown up. Now he was every bit the family man she'd wanted him to be the first time around. But a small part of her still didn't trust that change. She had a feeling that the real test of their relationship was yet to come.

These were her thoughts as she waited for the timer to go off for the pregnancy test. She didn't know what to hope for—a negative result or a positive one. She closed her eyes and tried to imagine it coming back negative. Nothing would really change. But what if it was positive? So much would change. She'd get big and fat. Maybe Cal wouldn't like her pregnant. She hadn't lost all of the weight she'd gained from being pregnant with Poppy, and packing more weight on top of that would make it even harder for her to lose after a second pregnancy.

The stretch marks. And the gas, the bloating. The swelling. She'd felt like a giant bowling ball with arms and legs the first time around. What if Cal didn't want another baby? He'd seemed open to the prospect during the only discussion they'd ever had on the subject. There was a big difference between the possibility of a baby versus the reality of one.

At the sound of the ding, she hesitated. Her fate lay in the absence or presence of one tiny blue line. She crept over to where she'd left the test on the counter, took a deep breath, and looked down.

☙❧

Cal hung up the phone and stared off at nothing. Lucas had asked the question that had been hovering at the back of Cal's mind for months. How had Walker known when and where Lucy would be? He'd been ahead of them at every turn. The gun shop. The ball. The party. He knew where to be far enough in advance that he set that fire in the hotel. He'd dressed as one of catering staff at the party at the station. Someone had been tipping him off. There was only one person who knew exactly where Cal would be and when.

Felicia.

It wasn't enough that she'd bugged his office. She'd used her knowledge of his schedule to tip off Walker so he could get to Lucy. It was all he could do to stay in his seat and not go out to Felicia's desk and confront her. He could kill her for what she'd put Lucy through. She'd helped a potential murderer find his victim. Lucy could be dead right now because of what Felicia had done.

He got up and paced, trying to work off some of the murderous rage he felt. There was no way to prove any of it. He had nothing except the bug to hang on her. Unless he got her to confess to what she'd done, there was no way to confirm her involvement. The longer he paced, the more solid his plan became. He knew exactly how he'd trap her—by using her attraction to him. It was the only motivation she had for doing what she'd done. So he'd use it against her.

He went over to his desk and pressed the intercom. "Felicia?"

"Yes, Mr. Sellers?"

"Can you come into my office please?"

"Yes, sir."

He set the cameras in his office to record their conversation, then leaned back against his desk, placing his hands on either side of him, and tried to look casual. He could do this. He could make her believe he was into her to get her to confess. This was for Lucy.

Felicia came in with her tablet, prepared to take notes as she always did, and sat in one of the chairs. She pushed her arms together so that her breasts lifted, trying to get him to notice her. "What can I do for you, sir?"

"How long have we worked together, Felicia?"

"Almost two years."

"In that time have I ever told you how much I appreciate your hard work and dedication?"

"Well...no."

"I do. I want you to know that. I've recently realized some things about my life and the people in it."

She slid forward in her seat.

"You're one of the few people who I feel like I can really trust," he said. "You've become an important part of my business...and my life. Thank you."

She set her tablet on the chair and stood. "It's my pleasure, sir." She put a little extra sway in her hips as she closed the distance between them until they were mere inches apart. "I mean that. I'd do anything for you."

"I know you would. And I can't tell you how much that means to me."

Running a finger along his jaw, she leaned in so that she was between his thighs. He could smell her perfume—

something heavy and cloying. "You're one of the most handsome and powerful men I've ever known. So sexy."

"I'm glad you think so." He gripped her finger and held it between them. "You said you'd do anything for me. What exactly would you do?"

"Anything you want."

"I'm a married man. That doesn't bother you?"

"Why should it? You can't be happy. I mean, I get that she had your baby, but she's also brought you a lot of problems."

"And if I wanted to be rid of her...that's something you'd do for me?"

"In a minute. You don't even have to ask. In fact..." She wrapped her arms around his neck. "I've been working on that problem. I know how unhappy you've been. I see it on you every day. So I did a little digging."

"That's very perceptive of you." He put his hands on her waist and drew her in closer. Touching her made him sick. She didn't feel like Lucy or smell like Lucy. She didn't do anything for him except disgust him. "What did you find out?"

"I'm very disappointed in you."

"In what way?"

She moved away. He followed, hoping to get what he needed out of her.

Standing behind his desk, she ran a finger over one of the business awards he'd received. "I've always admired your business sense. You've always seemed so smart and capable. Except where she was concerned. What is it about her that makes you lose all perspective?" She whirled on him, her eyes narrowed. "What is she holding over your head? What is it she has that I don't?"

"We have a history together, a daughter." And so, so much more. He tamped all of that down to do what needed to be done. If she saw his true feelings for Lucy, she'd know this scene for the charade it was.

She wandered around the other side of the desk, her hips swaying. He stuck close to her. She glanced back at him, a sly smirk on her face. She liked him chasing her. If that's what it took to get her to confess, he'd follow her wherever she went until she told him what he needed to hear.

"Her husband stopped by here one day while you were out." She leaned back against the desk in a seductive pose. "He was very anxious to know where she was."

"You wicked, wicked girl, keeping secrets from me."

She grabbed his tie and pulled. He stumbled into her, catching himself on the desk so he didn't tumble her down across it. She wrapped his tie around her hand, and he could tell she liked pushing him around. It turned her on. He'd play her game.

"I was hoping he could convince her that they belonged together." She pulled him closer and whispered, "The way you and I belong together."

Just a few more minutes...

"Do you think we belong together, sir?"

"I want you to call me Cal."

"No. I like calling you sir."

He spoke next to her ear. "So damn sexy."

She pushed him away from her, still gripping his tie. "You didn't answer my question—do you think we belong together?"

"Without a doubt."

She yanked him close again. "I'm so glad to hear you say that."

Sliding her leg up his, she caught the back of his knees. He lost his balance, grabbing her to keep from taking them both down.

"I'd do anything for you, *sir*, anything to make you mine."

Closing his eyes, he pretended she was someone else—anyone else—and pitched his voice low, seductive. "Tell me what you'd do."

"I'll help you, but first tell me what you would do...for me...to me."

"Whatever you want. What is it you want, Felicia?"

"Call me honey the way you used to before *her*."

"What do you want, honey?"

"I want you all to myself."

"You said you didn't mind that I was married."

"I lied." She licked along his jaw, her breath hot in his ear. "I won't share you. I'm going to be the only one you fuck." She jerked on his tie. "Got it?"

"Yes, honey."

"It wasn't very smart of you to marry Lucy without a prenup. I'm very disappointed in you for that. A divorce would cost you a fortune."

"I wasn't thinking. My daughter—"

"Now it makes sense." She pushed him away again, his tie still in her grip.

She liked the power play, got off on it. He'd give her what she wanted to get what he wanted.

Licking her upper lip, she ran her gaze over him. "She has you by the balls." She moved fast, cupping his junk.

He grabbed her wrist and twisted, forcing her to let go of him, and brought her hand to his chest where he could control it. Son of a bitch, this woman was a piece of work.

"Something like that," he answered, trying real hard to remember he was supposed to be letting her seduce him.

"Hmm. I was hoping her ex-husband would take care of your little problem, but unfortunately she killed him, ruining all of my plans and hard work."

"You were willing to do that...for me?"

"I told you. I'd do anything for you."

He stroked the inside of her wrist. "What was your

plan?"

"It was rather clever really. I'd tell him where she'd be, gave him the security codes or whatever he needed, and he was supposed to convince her to go away with him. He was either too stupid or he overestimated Lucy's desire to be a rich man's wife. But I'm not like her. I don't care about your money. All I want is you."

She jerked on his tie, at the same time wrapping her legs around him, knocking him off balance. He landed on top of her on the desk, her mouth fastened to his.

"Oh, my God."

Lucy.

He shoved at Felicia and rolled off her to find Lucy standing in the doorway, one hand over mouth, the other fisted over her belly.

"It's not what it looks like," he said.

"It's exactly what it looks like." Felicia pressed herself against him and ran a hand up his chest, making a grab for his tie, but he caught it and flung it away.

He moved toward his wife. "Lucy, you've got to believe me."

Lucy shook her head. "I'm such an idiot. I can't believe I trusted you. Again." She spun on her heels and ran out of his office.

"Lucy!"

He started after her, but Felicia jumped into his path. "Let her go. We can finally be together."

"Shut the fuck up." He pushed past her and ran down the hall. The elevator doors closed before he could hit the button and call it back. "Goddamn it!"

He bolted for the stairs, running for his life. The look on her face—exactly the same expression she had the last time she caught him—shock, pain, and then hatred. He'd never forget that look, he'd never get out from under it. He would always be the man who broke her in two. She'd told him that if he ever cheated on her again, they'd be over. Really over. The fact that he hadn't cheated this time meant nothing up against the visual of him lying on top of Felicia on his desk.

He had to find her, had to somehow make her see that what she'd witnessed in his office wasn't the truth. He wasn't that man anymore. He hadn't betrayed her.

By the time he got to the lobby, Lucy was climbing into the car with Sam. They drove off before he could stop them. He raised his hand and flagged down a cab. Climbing in, he gave the driver directions to follow Sam's car. He called Lucy, but she didn't answer so he tried Sam.

"Hello?"

"Sam, it's Cal. Let me talk to Lucy."

There was some muffled mumbling and then Sam came back on the line. "She doesn't want to talk to you."

"Put me on speakerphone."

He could hear Sam asking Lucy if she wanted to hear what Cal had to say. And then Lucy's emphatic "No."

"Tell her that Felicia was the one who was helping Walker get to Lucy."

"I don't think that's going to help your case, man."

"I was getting Felicia's confession when Lucy walked in."

More mumbling.

"She says that's exactly what it looked like to her—taking down a confession."

"Damn it, Sam! I'm not having an affair with Felicia."

"She's crying," Sam whispered. "I'm sorry. I'm going to have to hang up now."

"Goddamn it!"

The driver glanced at him in the rearview mirror. "Lady troubles?"

"Yeah."

The driver pointed at his lips. "You got some lipstick... You should probably wipe that off before we catch up to that car."

Cal swiped a hand across his mouth. The pink of Felicia's lipstick streaked his skin, a damning reminder of what an idiot he was and how big a task he had ahead of him. "Shit."

ଔଓ

Lucy couldn't believe how stupid she was. Almost two years later and she was right back where she'd ended things with Cal the first time. She'd taken a chance on surprising him at his office to invite him out to lunch. Things with them had felt off kilter, and she thought maybe spending some time together might help. She'd planned for Sam to wait for her with Poppy just in case Cal wasn't available. It was a good thing. Otherwise she'd be having her breakdown in the back of a taxi.

"I'm sorry, Lucy." Sam patted her hand in her lap. "Men can be real assholes sometimes."

"I can't believe I trusted him again. I'm such an idiot. What am I supposed to do now?"

"Now you go home and have a good long cry and then you think about what you want to do."

"I can't. It's not my home, it's Cal's."

"I know you don't want to hear this right now, but is it possible you could've misinterpreted what happened back there?"

"Well, I don't know. If you walked into your wife's office and she had her secretary on his back on her desk and was on top of him, kissing him, what impression would you get?"

"It's just that I've seen the way he looks at you, and I can't see him looking at any other woman that way."

"He was doing a lot more than looking at another woman just now. This isn't the first time I caught him cheating on me, Sam." Putting her hands over her face, she collapsed forward. "What am I going to do?"

She had nowhere to go and no money that wasn't Cal's. She was homeless with a child to support. Things couldn't possibly get any worse.

"I don't even know where to tell you to take us." She swiped at the tears that wouldn't stop falling. "I don't have any money for a hotel room. There's no way I'd ever go back to my mother's house."

"I'm taking you home."

"I don't have a home anymore!" Her outburst woke up Poppy, who'd been asleep in the backseat. "I'm sorry, sweetie. Sshhh. It's all right." Lucy handed her daughter her favorite stuffed animal and noticed a taxi behind them with a familiar outline in the backseat. "How long has that taxi been following us?"

"Since we left Cal's building."

"That son of a bitch! Pull over."

"What?"

"Pull over."

"We're on the highway."

"Sam, if you don't pull this car over, I'm going to grab the wheel myself."

"All right, all right." Sam maneuvered the car to the side of the road and stopped.

Just as Lucy predicted, the taxi pulled up behind them. She opened her door and marched toward the other car.

Cal climbed out of the back and stood with the door open. "Darlin', you have to believe me. Nothing happened back there."

"I don't have to do shit where you're concerned, Cal Sellers. I told you that if you ever cheated on me, we were through. We're officially through, you lying, no good, dick-for-brains cheat!"

Cal slammed the car door and stalked toward her. "I didn't cheat!"

Lucy parked her hands on her hips. "Really? 'Cause where I'm from, crawling between the legs of your *honey* on top of your desk is cheating!"

They were feet apart now, yelling and gesturing at each other. Traffic slowed to watch.

"She attacked me. I swear to God, darlin'—"

"Don't call me darlin'! Don't call me anything ever again."

"There isn't another woman in this world I want more that you. I swear it. If you'll just listen to me—"

"Listening to you got me in this predicament in the first place. Listening to you is how I wound up in the exact same position as I was in two years ago. Listening to you is how I got my heart broken by you twice. I can't listen to you anymore, Cal. I can't afford your words. They cost me too much."

His voice softened to where she could barely hear it. "Dar—Lucy, I'm so sorry you're hurting because of me, but I swear to you—"

"You can swear out a formal statement in blood and I wouldn't believe a word of it." She threw her hands up. "I can't believe I've been such an idiot where you're concerned."

He started to take a step toward her, but she put a hand up to stop him. Seeing him now churned up every single emotion she had inside her. But the one that beat the others to the front was anger. She was so damned angry with him, with herself, and with the whole damn mess she was in. Before she knew what she meant to do, she hauled off and slapped him in the face. It was like something let loose inside her, and she went blind with rage, beating ineffectually at him until she was nearly out of breath and he caught her wrists.

He put his face close to hers, his eyes pleading every bit as much as his words. "Lucy, she's the one who was working with your ex. That's how he knew where you'd be and when. That's what I was doing with her before things got out of hand—getting her to admit it. On tape. I swear it. Please. You have to believe me."

She stopped trying to break free and stared at him, wondering how she'd gotten here. How had her life done a complete one-eighty, landing her right back where she'd last left off with him? And the thing of it was she *wanted* to believe him. She wanted him to prove to her that he hadn't betrayed her again, that she wasn't a fool to have trusted him a second time.

"Come back to the office with me. I'll show you. Please, Lucy."

Could this be true? Could he be telling the truth?

TWENTY-SEVEN

Cal was literally fighting for his family and his life with Lucy on the side of a highway with people slowing to take photos and video. She was furious with him. He could hardly blame her. He'd let things with Felicia get out of hand. He was only now realizing what a completely stupid idea it had been to try to seduce a confession out of her. Of course Lucy had walked in. That was his dumb luck. The look on her face...just like the last time she'd caught him with his assistant on top of his desk. Lucy was right. He did have a dick for brains.

"Come back to the office with me," he pleaded. "I recorded the whole thing. Come and watch the tape. You'll see I'm telling you the truth. I love you so much. I don't know what I'd do without you. Please. Please believe me."

"*She* told Kevin where I'd be?"

"Yes." He could tell his words were having some effect on her. She was starting to believe him. "She gave him the code to our security gate. That's how he got in with the flowers. She told him about the shooting range, the ball, and the party at the studio. She knew exactly where we'd be and when. I started to get suspicious of her after your interview with Priscilla Barnes. Felicia had to have been the one to feed her that info about our arrangement. She was in the outer office while you were in my office. She must've listened in. Don't you see?"

Lucy looked off past Cal. She was thinking now instead of reacting out of emotion. He could see it in the way her brow furrowed and her lips pressed together.

"I want to see this supposed tape you have," she said.

All the air left Cal's body, and he nearly dropped to his knees. She believed him. Or at the very least she was entertaining the idea of believing him. All he had to do was get her back to his office and show her the tape.

"Stay right there. Don't move. Let me pay my cab fare, and I'll ride back with you."

"No. I'll meet you there."

"Okay. That works too." He looked up at the news helicopter that circled above and around the traffic jam they were causing. Their scene would likely make the local news. For some reason he didn't care.

She started to walk back to the car.

"Lucy?"

She stopped but didn't turn.

"I love you, darlin', more than anything. Please know that."

She resumed walking to the car and climbed in. He ran back to the cab and jumped inside.

"We still following that car?" the cabbie asked.

"Yes. We're going back the way we came."

The driver glanced up at the circling helicopter through the windshield and then stuck his head and arm out of his window and waved. "I'm going to be on TV."

"Just go. Don't lose sight of that car."

It took them an extra fifteen minutes to get back to Cal's office building, and it cost him a fortune for the cab ride, but it was worth it. Lucy would see that he was telling the truth, and everything would go back to normal.

A new normal now that her asshole ex was lying in the morgue. A better normal.

"What are you smiling at?" Lucy asked as he held the front door of his building open for her.

"I'm looking forward to taking you home after this and celebrating our new normal without Walker, without extra security. That's all."

"You're awfully confident this tape will prove you're not lying, aren't you?"

"As confident as a man with one foot over the finish line."

Except he still wasn't all that confident where she was concerned. He'd fucked up before and she'd taken him back. Things might not turn out that way a second time. She'd trusted him enough on the side of that freeway to give him the opportunity to prove he wasn't the cheating bastard she thought he was. He wouldn't take a full breath until she saw the tape and believed him.

They rode the elevator in silence. He kept stealing glances at her. She was so damn beautiful with her hair fluffed out from the wind and her cheeks red from her anger. If she wasn't so boiling mad at him, he'd be thinking about putting more flush in her cheeks. To keep himself from touching her, he put his hands behind his back.

They exited the elevator, and he hurried ahead to open his office door for her. They both ignored the stares of the employees who had no doubt gotten quite a show with both of them tearing out of there, then coolly strolling back in.

He closed the door and went straight for the control panel behind his desk. The system was off. It should've still been on from when he'd set it up before confronting Felicia.

"Oh, shit. *No.*"

He flipped some switches and waited for the monitor to come to life. Gone. The whole scene was gone. Felicia must've seen that he'd had it on when she went behind his desk. That was why she'd jumped him. She must've planned to confront Lucy with the tape. But then Lucy had come in and he'd blown the whole thing by chasing after her. Felicia had to have known his plan then and deleted the tape because it incriminated *her*.

He sat down hard in his seat, fully aware that Lucy was standing a few feet away, waiting for him to prove something he had absolutely no proof of. He was totally fucked.

"It's gone." He turned to face her. "Felicia must've deleted it off the system after we left."

"Right."

"I swear..." He had no more fight in him. All he had to rely on was her trust, which he knew he hadn't fully earned back yet. "I swear to you I'm telling the truth."

There it was. All of it laid out before her for her to decide—their present and their future. If she didn't believe him, there was nothing left between them. The one thing she'd asked of him was to not cheat on her again, and in her eyes that was exactly what he'd done. He'd promised her, and he'd screwed it up.

"I told you that I could take anything, Cal, anything except you cheating on me. Then I walk in on you with your secretary *again*. And then you humiliate me by dragging me back in here to do what? Try to convince me that what I saw wasn't what I saw? You had your hands on her. You were kissing her."

"That's not what—"

"Don't tell me that's not what happened! I saw it with my own damn eyes. And the night you came home with lipstick on your face and you said it was Anne Gleason's, that was really Felicia's lipstick, wasn't it? How long have you and Felicia been sleeping together? From the beginning?"

"No. I've never done anything with Felicia. What I told you that night was the truth. It was Anne Gleason's lipstick." He could see it all through her eyes, all of the things that stacked up against him and chipped away at her trust.

"So you just go about your day and women throw themselves at you left and right. You're completely innocent."

"Yes."

She folded her arms across her chest. "How many?"

"What?"

"How many women have there been, Cal? All of those late nights at work, those last-minute out-of-town meetings. And I bought into it all, believing everything that came pouring out of your mouth."

"That *was* all business. There is only you. There's only ever been you. I swear it." He could tell she didn't believe him. The more he denied it the less she believed. He wanted to go to her and put his arms around her and tell her he didn't even look at other women, that she was it for him. If she left him, there would be no other.

She stood in front of his desk, her eyes dry, her back straight, staring at him like she couldn't believe what was happening.

"I'm pregnant." She laughed as though it was some kind of joke and she was the butt of it. "I'm pregnant and alone. Again."

Her words ripped through him, breaking open everything inside him. She was pregnant. His mind cataloged the information and spun its wheels trying to process it. He could only stare at her in disbelief. He'd worked like a damned dog to earn back her trust only to wind up where they'd left off the first time. He'd hurt her bad before, but this time there would be no second chance. There would be no reconciliation.

She'd have his child without him. He'd be there just outside the room, writing checks and making sure she got what she needed, but he wouldn't see his child come into the world. She'd go it alone, taking nothing from him, wanting nothing to do with him. He'd have to stand at the back of another church and watch her pledge herself to another man. And there wasn't a damn thing he could do about it.

Again.

She turned and walked out of his office. And his life.

It took everything inside of Lucy to stride out of Cal's office as though nothing was wrong when *everything* was wrong. He honestly thought she'd buy that crap about a tape. That he'd get her alone, do more of his swearing to the truth and double-talking, and she'd fall right back in line. Hell, if he'd kissed her in the elevator like she knew he'd wanted to do, she might've caved. She was that weak where he was concerned.

At least that bitch Felicia had the good sense to leave, or Lucy would've had to walk past the woman who'd destroyed her marriage. She made it just inside the elevator before breaking down. She'd told him she was pregnant and he'd sat there. No expression change at all. No elation. No disappointment. Nothing. She was carrying his child. And she was well and truly alone.

The past might've partially repeated itself, but she was going to make damn sure it didn't fully repeat. She wouldn't turn to the first man who would have her like she'd done with Kevin. She'd find a way to make it as a single mother of two children.

Goddamn Cal and his goddamned knack for making her believe in him then knocking her on her ass. The only way things could get worse was if she was carrying twins.

She laughed out loud at the possibility, knowing she looked like a lunatic crossing the lobby with tears streaming down her cheeks. It would be her luck to not only get knocked up by the same lowlife, cheating scum—twice—but to get knocked up the second time with twins. Twins.

Sam got out of the car when he saw her and came around to open the door for her. "No tape?"

"No tape."

"Ah, damn. I'm sorry, Lucy. Are you sure about this?"

Nodding, she climbed into the car and stared straight ahead. What was she going to do? Where was she going to go?

Sam's cell phone rang. He glanced at the display then answered it. "Sam here." He listened for a few moments. "All right. I'll tell her. Yeah. I'm sorry. Bye." He hit the End button. "Cal says to take you home. He'll stay somewhere else. He says the house is yours and Poppy's. The staff and I will stay on with you. That's what he wants."

"You know what I want, Sam? I want a husband who doesn't fuck his secretaries. That's what I want. When do I get what I want? Hmm?" She put up a hand. "Don't answer. It was a rhetorical question. I'm not accepting his home and his employees. Or his guilt. Please drop me and Poppy off at Mi and Lucas's."

"I'll stay with you."

"No offense, Sam, but you're fired. I can't afford to pay you. Besides, we don't need a ninja nanny anymore."

"But Cal—"

"Say his name one more time and I'll get me and Poppy out of this car, and we'll walk to their house."

"Yes, ma'am."

She had no plan other than to get through the next few hours. Sam insisted on going up to Mi and Lucas's apartment with her. She caught sight of herself in the mirrored elevator doors to their apartment and nearly gasped. Her hair practically stood on end, and her eyes were red and swollen. If they didn't take her in, she had no other options. How could they refuse her looking so pitiful with Poppy on her hip and nothing but what was in the diaper bag and her purse to call her own?

The front desk had announced them and sent them up in the elevator, so Mi and Lucas were waiting for them when it opened into their apartment.

"Lucy." Mi's voice was full of sympathy as she scooped her and Poppy into a hard hug.

Mi's big pregnant belly made it difficult to get very close. The thought that soon Lucy would be as big as Mi made her burst into tears all over again.

"Oh, sweetie. Come in and sit down." Mi guided Lucy into the living room and down onto the couch. "Here, let me take her." Mi held her hands out for Poppy.

Lucy handed her over and watched as Mi tried to settle the baby on what was left of her lap. "I'm sorry to barge in on you like this." Lucy swiped at the tears that wouldn't stop falling. "If I had somewhere else to go…"

"I'm glad you came here. What happened? Is Cal all right?"

"Oh, Cal's just *fine*."

Lucy filled Mi in on what had happened between her and Cal, right down to the humiliating scene in his office when he admitted there was no tape. The image of Cal on top of Felicia with his mouth on hers played over and over in a loop through Lucy's head. She couldn't get the picture of him standing next to his desk, his hair rumpled with lipstick on his lips, out of her mind either. What had made him think bringing her back to the scene of his crimes would help him convince her she'd imagined the whole thing?

"That son of a bitch," Mi breathed. "I can't believe he did that to you. Twice."

"I can't either. And I can't believe I fell for him and his lies all over again. And that's not even the worst part... I'm pregnant. Oh, my God, Mi, what am I going to do?"

"You're going to stay here as long as you need to. We'll help you get back on your feet."

"I can't put you out. You're about to have a baby of your own."

"You're not putting us out. We have plenty of room. Or if you'd rather have a place of your own, the tenants in my old house moved out last month. We've been working on getting it ready to rent out again. It's yours if you want it."

"You're way too good to me. Thank you for not saying I told you so. Because you did, the day we got married."

"I did?"

"You asked me if I was sure I wanted to marry him. At the time I didn't have any other choice. I had to protect Poppy, but now... I need to stop making decisions out of desperation where men are concerned. I need to be alone for a while to figure things out. Thank you for your generous offer."

"What about the baby and Poppy?"

"They'll be with me."

"What about their father? I've seen him with Poppy, and I can't imagine he'll give them up."

"I really don't care what he does or doesn't do right now. Right now I just want this day to end. I don't want to be in the day my life imploded anymore."

"Come with me." Mi took Lucy's hand and led her into one of their guestrooms. "This will be your room as long as you need it. Why don't you lie down and take a nap?"

"What about Poppy?"

Mi held Poppy to her. "She'll be good practice for Lucas

and me. Go on, get some rest. Things won't seem so bleak when you wake up, I promise."

"I doubt that. I'll still be a single mother with another child on the way when I wake up."

Mi helped her get into bed and pulled the covers over her. She held Poppy so Lucy could give her a kiss. "Now get some rest."

☙❧

Cal had received some good news on a night that was far from good. Gleason had finally agreed to sell him his company. Sellers Investments was saved. He wasn't sure what he'd said to Joel to get him to relent. He'd called to cancel dinner yet again. Joel had asked him if he needed anything, no doubt having heard all about his and Lucy's scene on the side of the freeway. Too far from caring what happened next, Cal had pathetically joked that he needed Joel to sell him Gleason Investments. There was silence and then by some miracle Joel had agreed. Just like that.

Closeted in his darkened office, he was now halfway to drunk. All evening long he'd sat with his phone in his hand, bringing up Lucy's number, then exiting the screen before placing the call. He knocked back the last swallow of whiskey and hurled the glass on an anguished roar. It hit the wall and shattered, raining shards across the carpet. That glass was fucking frustrating and deserved to die for being empty too goddamned soon. He'd clean it up in the morning. Right now he kind of liked the metaphor of the chunks of glass scattered across the floor like the pieces of his life—too sharp and painful to pick up and do anything with.

He'd been an idiot. Right from the start. Proposing marriage to her... He let out a merciless chuckle and took a swig straight from the whiskey bottle. What a fucking joke. He should've offered her a position in one of his other divisions. But he'd been selfish, wanting her back with everything in him, so he'd suggested marriage instead of what she'd really needed—a job and a loan to help her get back on her feet.

Then he'd gone about trying to bed her. What a clusterfuck that had been. Again he'd only thought of himself and what he wanted. She'd been broken and battered, but he was going to somehow fix her with orgasms and his magic cock. He'd helped her, all right, by taking the single greatest thing she'd given him besides their daughter—her trust—and shit all over it by using Felicia's attraction to him to get her to confess.

What a self-centered asshole he was.

Her words and hollow laugh looped through his head over and over. She was pregnant. He wouldn't get a second chance to experience any of the things he'd missed with Poppy like doctor appointments, ultrasounds, and seeing his child take its first steps.

And again he was only thinking of himself and how he was affected.

Because she was so proud and stubborn she'd made herself homeless, jobless, and penniless. She'd rather go through everything alone than take one single thing from him. He could hardly blame her. All he'd ever given her was pain, pain, and more pain. Anything he offered her would be a pale comparison to what she needed.

The whiskey wasn't working fast enough. He put the bottle to his lips and tilted his head back to take a good, long draw off it. He set it down with a thunk and blinked. At first he wasn't sure what he was seeing. The weak light from his desk lamp didn't quite make it to the doorway. He'd thought for a moment it might be Lucy, and his heart jackhammered.

The proportions were all wrong. Not Lucy. Hazel? No,

not Hazel.

"Hello, Cal."

Motherfucking Felicia.

How had she gotten in? Oh, fuck, that's right. He'd forgotten to change the gate code and tell Hazel he'd fired Felicia. Except he hadn't fired her. Yet.

"You tried to trick me." She closed the door and moved closer into the glow of the desk lamp.

She looked perfect just like she did every day she came to work. He'd hired her partly for her experience as an executive assistant and mainly for her looks. Not that he'd been interested in her. He'd built an image of himself that for some reason he'd felt the need to perpetuate. But now—staring at her past the barrel of her gun—those reasons seemed completely stupid and childish.

"Hands on the desk," she ordered.

The alcohol and the shock had made him slow to react, too slow to press the silent alarm before he had to follow her command.

"Did you think I didn't know what you were doing? I know you, Cal. I know you better than you know yourself. I know everything about you."

"Not everything."

"No?"

"No," he answered. "And by the way, you're fired."

She tilted her head to one side and considered him for a moment. "You're drunk."

"Not drunk enough. What's the gun for?"

"In case you do something stupid like you did in your office." She wagged a finger at him. "That was naughty of you to tape our...encounter. Too bad your hysterical wife came in and ruined everything." She took in the room. "Do you have cameras in here too?"

He couldn't wrap his head around what she wanted or why she was here. She stood there steady-handed and calm, wanting what?

"Yes."

"Are they on right now?" she asked.

"No."

"That's too bad."

"What do you want, Felicia?"

"I want you, but I don't think you want me, and that's a problem. I didn't like that game you tried to play with me in your office, pretending to be interested in me so you could get me to confess. Do you have any idea the things I've done for you? And that's the way you thank me." She shook her head and made a tsking sound. "You're lucky I didn't have my gun with me this afternoon."

"Why are you here?"

"I'm here to make sure *she's* gone. You see, with her out of the way it's just a matter of time before you love me as much as I love you. I love you so much. I don't think you really understand how much. Or the things I'd do to have you. So I'm going to tie you up and take care of her. Permanently. And then I'm going to come back here and see what fun we can have with you tied up and the cameras on."

"She's not here." And thank God for that. "She left me. Because of you."

"She is one dumb bitch to give you up just like that." She snapped her fingers. "What in the hell did you see in her?"

"Everything. I love her."

She reached into the duffle bag strapped across her chest and pulled out a pair of handcuffs. "Put these on." She tossed him the cuffs. He let them skid across the desk and onto the floor. "Pick them up!"

"No."

She rushed forward and pointed the gun inches from his face. "I *said* to pick them up and put them on."

He made his move, grabbing for the gun and pushing it left while twisting his body to the right. She landed on him, knocking him back in the chair. They hit the floor hard with her still on top. His head struck the floor with the brunt of both of their weight. The air rushed out of him, and light flashed at the back of his eyes. She used his momentary loss of control to her advantage, bringing her knee up to his groin. He shifted, and she caught him in the side of the thigh, barely missing his nuts.

She came at his face with her nails, raking them across his eyes and cheeks. He grasped her wrist. Grappling with her, he tried to get control of the gun. But she was too strong and he was too drunk.

BAM!

TWENTY-EIGHT

Lucy lay there in the big comfy bed, her head pounding, her eyes itchy and swollen, praying for sleep. But all she did was miss Cal and his big body lying next to hers. She thought about never being held by him, or kissed by him, or loved by him ever again. The pain spread through her, filling every inch to the point where she physically ached. This time was worse than the last. This time she'd invested more and loved him more. He'd been everything, and now she had to make him nothing.

After tossing and turning for what felt like forever, she got up and went to the window. It was dark outside. She hadn't thought it had been that long since she'd lain down. Poppy. She needed to go check on her baby girl. Creeping out into the hall, she wasn't sure which room Mi could've put Poppy in. Maybe the nursery? The door was ajar, so she quietly pushed it open.

Sam was asleep on the daybed next to the crib where Poppy slept. Damn that man. She had no way to pay him, and he knew it. She'd fired him, but there he was still caring for and guarding her daughter. If there was one hero in all this mess, it was Sam. God bless him. He was more reliable and trustworthy than her own damn husband. And that was a sad state of affairs, if she trusted her nanny more than her child's father.

She tiptoed back out of the room and headed toward the living room. The bluish light at the other end of the hall let her know that someone was up, watching TV. She hoped it was Mi, but as she came into the room those hopes were quickly dashed as she saw Lucas's large frame on the sofa, backlit by the television. She hadn't spent much time alone with the big man her friend had married and felt kind of awkward about disturbing him, so she turned to go back the way she'd come.

"Can't sleep, Lucy?" Lucas asked.

How'd he know it was her?

"These days Mi moans with practically every step she takes."

And psychic too? "Sorry. I didn't mean to disturb you."

He shifted to look at her. "You're not. I'm not much of a sleeper. Maybe we can find an old movie to watch or something."

"Sure." She made her way over and curled up in an overstuffed chair next to the couch. "What's on?"

"What do you like to watch?"

"I really don't care."

Lucas flicked through the channels slowly. "Let me know when something catches your eye."

"Thanks for letting me stay here. I know we sort of crashed in on you. And thanks for letting Sam stay. He should've left. I fired him."

"Why'd you fire him?"

"I can't afford him."

"But Cal—"

"I'm not taking anything from that man. So don't even say it."

"He takes care of what's his, so you're going to have a tough time making that stick."

She let out a frustrated breath. "I swear to God if one

more person tries to reason me into accepting so much as a stick of gum from that no good son of a bitch, I'm going to scream. He's taken care of things all right. He's taken great care to totally fuck up my life…again. Did Mi tell you that I'm pregnant?"

"She mentioned it. Congratulations? I'm sorry?"

"That pretty much covers it."

"I've known Cal a long time—"

"I don't need the sales pitch. I've already bought."

Lucas laughed. "I get it. I won't mention Cal again except to say that he's texted me about eighty times to check in on you and Poppy. And I know you're not going to like it, but you're stuck with Sam. He's been ordered not to leave you."

"Ordered. Of all the arrogant— Wait. Go back a couple of channels."

Lucas clicked back to a local news station.

"That's my house." She shook her head. "I mean Cal's house. What in the hell is going on? Turn it up."

"Local authorities were called to infamous Dallas businessman Cal Sellers's home just after nine o'clock this evening when the silent alarm was triggered by a bullet piercing a lower floor window. Apparently Mr. Sellers's former assistant, a Felicia McAdams who has been taken into police custody, broke into his home and shot at him. Along with the gun, McAdams brought a duffle bag in which she had rope, tape, handcuffs, and a taser—all of the tools required for a kidnapping. Mr. Sellers was home at the time of the break-in, and we're told he was treated on the scene and released with minor injuries.

"The police have been mum on what the motive might be for this crime, and Mr. Sellers was unavailable for comment." The picture changed to an aerial view of Cal and Lucy yelling at each other on the side of the freeway.

"Earlier this afternoon Mr. Sellers and his wife, Lucy Sellers, were filmed having what looks like an argument on the shoulder of the I-35 freeway. Could the two incidents be related? We'll have up-to-the-minute updates on this incident as information comes to us. Back to you in the studio."

Lucas got up and pulled his cell phone out, then went into the other room. Lucy grabbed the remote to try to find more coverage on another channel. Felicia broke into their house? The reporter said Cal had been treated and released, but what if he wasn't okay? What if "unavailable for comment" was code for lying bleeding in the hospital? If Felicia and Cal were having an affair, then why did she break in? Who had she planned on kidnapping? What in the hell was going on?

༺༻

The bullet smashed the window above Cal, setting off the security alarm. Glass rained down on them, lodging into his skin as he rolled Felicia and pinned her down. She fought hard, bucking underneath him. Security arrived and it took three of them to subdue her and cuff her hands behind her back with her own handcuffs. The rest was a blur of people coming in and out, poking at him with their questions. His head pounded from the fall to the floor, his face burned, and all he wanted was to see Lucy and Poppy to make sure they were okay. But the police wouldn't let him make any phone calls.

After giving his side of the story to the police, he had to recite it all again for Lucas, who had seen the report on TV. Cal finally got a report on Lucy and Poppy. He'd been terrified that Felicia had gotten to them first before she'd come after him. He was dying to talk to Lucy, but that might only make things worse.

Lucas had said Lucy was okay, but he knew she wasn't. None of them were.

He didn't deserve Lucy. He didn't deserve to have everything that came with being with her, including raising their children. He'd be the weekend dad, the Disneyland dad, always trying to make up for what he'd screwed up.

It didn't matter what Lucy said. He would take care of her. He'd promised her that she and Poppy—and now the baby—would always have a safe place to live, and he meant to keep that promise. She would have Sam as long as she needed him. He'd buy her a new home if she wouldn't take his. He'd be everything he could be to her from the outside. Always on the outside.

He'd never get to hold Lucy again. Never get to dance with her, make love to her, or just lie next to her. He'd never walk into a room and find her there or be greeted by her when he came home. He wouldn't be a part of her pregnancy, and she likely wouldn't want him there when she gave birth. He'd have to wait like a distant relative to find out if it was a boy or a girl. He wouldn't get to decide on a name or hold their child while he or she was still warm from Lucy's body.

He wouldn't get his family back.

He'd just started up the stairs when the doorbell rang again. "Goddamned cops," he mumbled. "Can't you come—" The rest of the sentence died in his throat when he opened the door to find Lucy standing on his doorstep. He blinked. This had to be part of the head injury.

"Oh," she breathed. "Your face."

He put a hand up to his cheek then regretted it when it burned.

"Lucas said you weren't hurt bad, but that looks very painful."

"It burns." He stared at her. Was she real?

"I wanted to see for myself that you were okay. They didn't give very many details on TV, and Lucas gave me even less." She glanced around at the doorway, the frame, the floor... "It's late. I should probably go."

"No!" He put a hand on her shoulder. She *was* real. He pulled his hand right back when she glared down at it. "I mean... Would you like to come in?"

She moved forward without comment. He backed up, giving her room. As soon as she was inside, he closed the door, afraid she'd flitter right back out like a butterfly.

She turned to him in the foyer, her hands clasped behind her back. He couldn't stop looking at her. She didn't have any makeup on, and her eyes were a little puffy, probably from crying, but to him she'd never been more beautiful.

"How's Poppy?" he asked.

"Fine. Sam's with her at Mi and Lucas's."

"That's where you're staying?"

"Lucas or Sam didn't tell you?"

"No. Lucas only gave me the barest details, and all Sam would say was that you and Poppy were safe."

"I'm surprised. I would've thought they'd report everything to you."

"I think they're almost as pissed at me as you are."

"Yeah, well..."

"I'm sorry," he blurted out.

"Me too."

"What are you sorry for?"

"I should've seen Felicia for what she was. But when I walked in on you with Felicia, all of those old feelings came back—the humiliation, the anger, the hurt. I couldn't see past that to what was real, and I'm sorry for it."

"You don't have a damn thing to be sorry for. When you laid everything out to me in my office, I knew how it must've looked to you. Add in our history and... I'm sorry. Honest to God, I'm so sorry I put you through all that."

She nodded. "We have some luck, don't we?"

"The worst. Look at you, knocked up by a no-account, dick for brains like me. And look at me—I can't stop fucking up the best thing that ever happened to me."

"Cal, what happened in your office and here tonight?"

"You want the short version or the long version?"

"I want your version."

"Will you come in and sit down?" He waited for her response with the same nervous stomach he'd had when he first started knocking on her bedroom door.

At her nod, he exhaled the breath he'd been holding and led her into their living room like she was a guest. He even offered her a beverage when she was seated. His head throbbed in time with his heart, which beat so hard he thought it might break a rib.

He sat on the sofa next to her, close enough to touch but not to crowd. The whole thing reminded him of the night she'd come to him wet from the rain to tell him that she'd marry him. Only this time around there was more at stake. So much more.

He began with the magazine interview, which was when he'd first had suspicions about Felicia and took Lucy through everything that had happened to him since he'd last seen her earlier that afternoon. She listened without comment and didn't ask any questions. When he ran out of words, he just stopped talking.

There was so much more to say, but he no longer trusted his verbal skills. *I want you* was too weak and easily misunderstood. *I love you* too trite and overused. *I need you* too small and ineffectual. He crossed his arms to keep from touching her and *showing* her all of the things that lived and burned deep inside him.

Lucy couldn't believe what he'd been through tonight.

She'd come so close to losing him. Too close. Since the beginning of their marriage she'd been the one in jeopardy. He'd been the one to protect her. And now when he'd needed her the most, she'd been curled up in a ball too afraid to look past what she'd seen to what she *knew*. Too scared to trust when all he'd given her was an open road to trust him. He'd *earned* her trust, and she'd refused to give it, holding on tight to it as though she needed for an escape hatch, a way out when things got too hard.

She was ashamed of herself. This man loved her and their daughter. He took care of them and cared for them. He was everything she wanted and needed. All she had to do was trust him.

"She could've killed you." Saying it out loud made the backs of her eyes sting.

"I thought for a moment she might," he said. "All the while I kept thanking God that you and Poppy weren't here."

"I wish I'd been here."

"No, darlin', you don't. I didn't have anything to lose when I grabbed for that gun. If you'd have been here, well, that would've complicated things considerably. I would've had *everything* to lose."

"I never really listened to you when you said things like that to me. I heard the words, but I didn't take them in. And you've backed up those words at every turn. I can't think of one time where your words didn't match your actions. If only I'd paid attention. If I'd only taken it all in. I *do* owe you an apology, Cal, for not believing you when you told me there was nothing between you and Felicia. Because I knew it. Deep inside I knew it."

"What are you saying?"

"I'm saying that I know you didn't cheat on me. That you've never cheated on me during our marriage and that you never will cheat. I'm hoping you can forgive me for not trusting you. And I'm really hoping that you're happy about this baby." She took his hand and laid it across her belly. "Because I can't have this baby without you, Cal Sellers. I just can't." She burst into tears, and before she knew it he had her wrapped up tight against him.

"Am I happy? Oh, darlin'. When you told me in my office about the baby, it was a kick to the gut after a beating. All I kept thinking was how I'd lost the right to be there with you, how I wouldn't get to see my children every day. I thought I'd lost you all forever. I'm happy. I'm so damn ecstatic I can hardly hold it in."

"Really?"

He cupped her face and grinned down at her. "Really, darlin'. *Really.*"

"Can I...? Can I stay here tonight?"

"You can stay wherever you like."

"I want to sleep in our bed. With you right next to me. I want to wake up wrapped in your arms, and I want to burn through a couple of options. If you're up to it."

"I'm up to all of that."

"Then what are you waiting for, cowboy?"

He scooped her up off the couch and took the stairs two at a time. "This, darlin', is going to be option number fifty-five."

CR&OCR&OCR&O

If you or someone you know is experiencing domestic violence, there is help through the National Domestic Abuse hotline. Trained advocates are available to take your calls toll free, 24/7 hotline at 1-800-799-SAFE (7233).

Donations to support the hotline can be made at: www.thehotline.org.

ACKNOWLEDGMENTS

I'm grateful for my family who supports my writing career and especially for my sons who get teased about the sexy books their mom writes. Sorry boys. Just try to remember that each book gets us that much closer to the pool you want. My thanks to my mom and my sister, who are the last set of eagle eyes to review all of my books before publication. Any mistakes are total theirs not mine. To the fine women of The Keeper Shelf—the mighty, mighty unicorns—you are truly my New York.

ABOUT THE AUTHOR

Best-selling author, **Beth Yarnall**, writes mysteries, romantic suspense, and the occasional hilarious tweet. A storyteller since her playground days, Beth remembers her friends asking her to make up stories of how the person 'died' in the slumber party game Light as a Feather, Stiff as a Board, so it's little wonder she prefers writing stories in which people meet unfortunate ends. In middle school she discovered romance novels, which inspired her to write a spoof of soap operas for the school's newspaper. She hasn't stopped writing since.

For a number of years, Beth made her living as a hairstylist and makeup artist and even owned a salon. Somehow hairstylists and salons seem to find their way into her stories. Beth lives in Southern California with her husband, two sons, and their rescue dog where she is hard at work on her next novel.

For more information about Beth and her novels, please visit her website. www.bethyarnall.com

Made in the USA
Charleston, SC
04 April 2016